BOUND IN VENICE

Alessandro Marzo Magno

BOUND IN VENICE
THE SERENE REPUBLIC
AND THE DAWN OF THE BOOK

*Translated from the Italian
by Gregory Conti*

Europa
editions

Europa Editions
214 West 29th Street
New York, N.Y. 10001
www.europaeditions.com
info@europaeditions.com

Copyright © 2013 by Alessandro Marzo Magno
First Publication 2013 by Europa Editions

Translation by Gregory Conti
Original title: *L'alba dei libri. Quando Venezia ha fatto leggere il mondo*
Translation copyright © 2013 by Europa Editions

Library of Congress Cataloging in Publication Data is available
ISBN 978-1-60945-139-4

Marzo Magno, Alessandro
Bound in Venice: the Serene Republic and the Dawn of the Book

Book design by Emanuele Ragnisco
www.mekkanografici.com

Cover photo © Eduard Andras / iStock

Prepress by Grafica Punto Print – Rome

Printed in the USA

To Marco and Peter
may books accompany them

"Outside of a dog, a book is man's best friend."
—GROUCHO MARX

CONTENTS

BOUND IN VENICE

1.

VENICE: BOOK CAPITAL OF THE WORLD

Today, if you want to go from the Rialto to Saint Mark's, you walk along a street called Mercerie (Haberdasheries). Peeping out from the shop windows are the goods Italy is famous for: shoes, clothing, purses, and jewelry. Gucci has a store there, and there's also a fire-engine-red Ferrari shop, proudly displaying an authentic Formula 1 racing car.

If we were to travel back in time and walk down this same street in 1520 we would have no difficulty recognizing it; in five centuries it hasn't changed much at all and, what's more, its vocation for commerce is identical. If today's Mercerie is a showcase for Made in Italy, back then it was a showcase for Made in Venice, a city that, relatively speaking, was much more important than Italy today. Although Italy is now the world's sixth or seventh industrial power, half a millennium ago Venice had a place on the podium. In the Europe of that time there were only three cities that we might call big; three cities with a population of more than one hundred fifty thousand: Paris, Naples, and Venice.

So, then, what would we have been able to find in the stores—which often were also workshops and homes—on the sixteenth century Mercerie? Cloth, for one thing, or rather the splendid red fabrics for which Venice was famous, dyed according to secret recipes inherited from the Byzantines. Or gilded leather; embossed leather panels decorated with gold leaf, used to embellish the interior walls of palaces, crafted using techniques imported from Moorish Spain, which in turn

had inherited them from the Arabs. Or weapons, lots and lots
of weapons: hankered over and vied for by plutocrats and sovereigns from all over Europe, who just couldn't go off to fight
unless expensively outfitted with the clanking iron weaponry
made in Venice. The names of a couple of nearby streets,
Spadaria (from *spada,* or sword) and Frezzaria (from *freccia,* or
arrow) still speak to us today of that ancient vocation.

But what struck foreign visitors most were the books: the
dozens and dozens of bookmaking workshops that were gathered here in a density unequaled anywhere else in Europe.
Word has come down to us of authentic book-shopping tours,
like the one described by the historian Marcantonio Sabellico
(the beneficiary of the earliest known form of copyright) when
two friends go from the *fontego dei Tedeschi* to the foot of the
Rialto bridge, on their way to Saint Mark's Square, and they're
unable to make it to their destination, overwhelmed by their
curiosity to read the lists of books appended outside the shops.
Fontego in Venetian means warehouse; the *fontego dei Tedeschi*—
which, like the *fontego dei Turchi* still exists—was a building
that functioned as a warehouse, market, business headquarters,
and lodging, primarily for German-speaking merchants from
central Europe).

Not even Gutenberg's Germany, where printing with movable type had been invented around sixty-five years earlier,
some time between 1452 and 1455, could challenge Venice's
predominance: in the early sixteenth century, half of all the
books published in Europe were printed in Venice. And
Venice was preeminent for quality as well as quantity, "for the
richness and beauty of the volumes her printers produced."[1]
Without the Venetian publishing industry of that era, the book
as we know it today wouldn't exist, nor would the Italian lan-

[1] Helen Barolini, *Aldus and His Dream Book*, Ithaca Press, New York,
1992.

guage as it is spoken today. Sure, Italian is based on the works of the Tuscan writers Dante and Petrarch, but it was the Venetian editions of their works, edited by the humanist Pietro Bembo and printed by the king of publishing, Aldus Manutius (whom we will hear more about in the next chapter) that accounted for their success.

Let's go into one of those shops. We're able to get an idea of what they were like thanks to Angela Nuovo, who describes them in her study of the book trade in Renaissance Italy. Part of the merchandise is on display outside the shop: arranged on some tables, we can admire the frontispieces (and that's all, to discourage thieves) of Latin and Greek classics (primarily the former); religious texts (the Bible and commentaries); and then prints, views of cities near and far, images of people that viewers would be unlikely ever to see first-hand; books in foreign or remote languages, but spoken by many visitors to the city, which as a melting pot is perhaps rivaled only by present-day New York. So here we have works in Armenian, a Bohemian bible, a text in the Glagolitic alphabet of medieval Croatia, another in Cyrillic, and, naturally, given that the Jewish ghetto in Venice, established in 1516, is the first in history, numerous volumes in Hebrew. Many of the shops are also workshops or printing houses, where most of the books for sale are the products of the printer-publisher. Lying on one of the outside tables or hanging from the door frame, there is almost always a catalogue of the books published or for sale, generally three of four pages, folded in half, one inside the other. Other bookshops are actually stationery stores or shops that sell works in manuscript and the instruments for making them: sheets of paper, bottles of ink, quills. With the onset of printing, stationers have simply replaced books written on desktops by an amanuensis with those produced on the printing press.

Now let's turn our gaze to the inside. The first thing we see is the shop window, shaded by an awning that protects the books from the sunlight and rain, but otherwise open because the technology for producing transparent window panes will not be developed until a few centuries later (sixteenth century windows are made out of small glass disks held together by strips of lead came). In the window, where the threat of nimble fingers is not quite so great, whole books are on display, some lying on their sides in loose sheets, some bound in volumes and sitting open on a lectern, so their pages are visible. Books are still an elite product, often very costly, and to make them more precious, miniaturists are called in to paint capital letters at the beginning of chapters, in spaces left empty by the printer, while rubricators draw the smaller capital letters at the beginning of paragraphs. Some books even contain woodcuts whose contents have raised more than a few religious eyebrows, like the phallic representations of Francesco Colonna's *Poliphilo* or the sixteen sexual positions that illustrate the *Sonetti Lussuriosi* (Salacious Sonnets) by Pietro Aretino, a work printed clandestinely in Venice in 1527 and, in the eyes of the readers of the time, bona fide pornography.

The interior of the shop-workshop looks very different than a bookshop today. Sixteenth century books are sold in loose sheets, and then the buyer has them bound (but also illuminated and rubricated) according to his own taste. Some bindings are works of art in their own right, made from precious fabrics and metals. If a book is destined for a monastery, the binding will be simpler, in smooth parchment, but even in this case the binding represents a considerable added cost compared to the unbound volume. The packets of loose sheets are wrapped in blue paper to be conserved, aligned, and piled up on wall shelves, each indentified by its own label with the author's name and title. Actually, there are also some already-bound second-hand books in the shop, kept in their own special section. They cost twice as much as the unbound edition, showing just how much the binding can add to the price of a book. These bound volumes are standing on the shelves but contrary to today's customary practice, they are not spine-out but fore-edge-out. Leaning against the wall, the books present a homogenous alignment of sheets of paper, some horizontal, some vertical, "with an overall look that is chromatically very compact."[2] Single books cannot be identified or found on the basis of their binding, evidently considered to be no help at all. Even contemporary editions of these ancient volumes often conserve the indication of their title and author impressed on the fore-edge. The role of the bookseller is not only essential in explaining the contents of the book but also for locating it and pulling it off the shelf. Nearly all of the illustrations of sixteenth century bookshops that have come down to us show the owner intent on explaining something to the customer.

The command post of the shop is the counter; that's where the lectern that holds the journal in which the owner makes a note of everything he needs is located. Sitting on the counter are various objects: an ink bottle, a quill, and anything else that might be useful in the day-to-day operation of the shop. The counter's numerous drawers and cubbyholes allow the owner to keep his accounts and receipts reserved, as well as to keep hidden bundles of sheets intended for a restricted readership (such as works originating in the countries of the Protestant Reformation).

Like a captain on the quarterdeck of his ship, the bookseller observes from the counter everything that happens in his shop, listens with discretion to the conversations, careful not to violate the rules of polite behavior. There are accounts of how Renaissance bookshops, meeting places for intellectuals, reverberated with discussions and debates, at times resembling the halls of academe.

---

[2] Angela Nuovo, *Il commercio librario nell'Italia del Rinascimento*, Franco Angeli (Milan 1998) p. 161.

The arrangement of the goods for sale is of the utmost importance. As much as customers might be attracted by lists of books hanging from the door or by the outside display tables, then as now potential buyers liked to look around the shop, eyeing the books on the shelves. We don't know exactly how the books were grouped together, but it is certain that law books were kept apart from the others and that their privileged position derived from their cost. "For their commercial value, prestige, and simple quantity, law books eclipsed all other fields of Venetian publishing."[3]

We too can enter a Renaissance-era Venetian book shop and have a look around, thanks to a daily journal that has come down to us. The *Zornale* (de Madi) of Francesco de'Madi opens with the date of May 17, 1484 (and it will close almost four years later, on January 23, 1488).[4] We don't know if that was the day that Francesco started his business, or if he simply started making notes in a new journal because the preceding one was full. We do know, however, that he had 1,361 books in his shop, subdivided into 380 editions (which means an average of 3.5 volumes per edition), that he had more than one edition for sale of some titles, for example the Bible and some prayer books. (Sixteen surviving bookstore inventories compiled between 1482 and 1596 show that a minimum of 104 and a maximum of 3,400 volumes were put on display and that the average number of volumes per edition went from a minimum of 1.8 to a maximum of 6.8; there were always few copies per edition so as not to immobilize too much capital.)[5]

A fourth of the books on Madi's shelves are Latin classics, flanked by a small group of Greeks and Medieval and humanistic authors elevated to the rank of the classics, such as Boc-

[3] Martin Lowry, *The World of Aldus Manutius: Business and Scholarship in Renaissance Venice*, Blackwell (London, 1979) p. 22.
[4] Nuovo, *Il commercio* . . . , cit. p. 116.
[5] Ibid., p. 158.

caccio and Dante. This section of the shop is meant primarily for schoolteachers in the humanities and it does not include any Latin grammars (reserved for students), though there are Greek grammars, a subject that is not taught in school. In second place for quantity (20 percent) are religious texts: Bibles and commentaries, writings of Church fathers and collections of sermons, theological and liturgical texts; this too, like, is in some way a professional section, reserved for the clergy. Next comes the section open to everyone, the section dedicated to reading for enjoyment, or books in the vulgate (16 percent); even though this section has a lot of titles, they occupy a smaller space. The section has a large variety of texts: devotional, cavalier romances, Petrarch and Boccaccio, translations of Latin classics (Livy, Cicero, Ovid) and especially the *Liber Abaci* or *The Book of the Abacus*. The book for learning how to make calculations is essential in a city of merchants, and it's written in the vulgate because there is no place in the humanistic school curriculum for the study of math in Latin. Now we come to the law section: not a lot of titles (7 percent) but vital for a Renaissance-era bookshop. Commentaries, repertories, and treatises are the most expensive books in the store and they occupy a much greater share of the shelf space than their percentage of titles. Our shopkeeper may not sell a single law book for months on end, but when a good customer shows up he buys a slew of them and pays in gold coins. During the slow month of September 1485, for example, total store receipts come to just thirty-nine and a half ducats, but a third of that figure comes from single sale of seven law books for twelve and a half ducats. Law books were off-limits for small printers because of the substantial investment of paper, time, and labor, but for established publishers they were a source of handsome and dependable profits.[6]

[6] Lowry, *The World* . . . op. cit. p. 34

The remaining books in Francesco's shop are trifles: scholastic texts and Latin grammars, university tracts on philosophy and medicine. Venice doesn't have a university, but if the shop were in Padua, the seat of the second-oldest university in Europe, after Bologna, this section would be predominant. A small percentage of the works for sale is made up of still unsorted volumes sitting on the shelves, as well as bound second-hand books. Even this last case is fundamentally different from our own time: the era of the used book as an old and therefore low-cost item is still a long way off. Its price is determined by the value of its binding and only secondarily by its condition. It won't be until the next to last decade of the sixteenth century that the market for used books will expand and begin the process of price depreciation that is still going on today. In the first half of the century, on the other hand, "the extraordinary abundance of new books meant that used books were not at all competitive as to price and useless in terms of assortment."[7]

In the four years of activity reported in his journal, our bookseller sells 12,934 volumes, for total receipts of 4,200 ducats (32.4 pounds of gold), but with remarkable ups and downs, from a low of 60 books in October 1485 to a high of 535 in May 1487, with monthly receipts ranging from 13 ducats to 210. Francesco de'Madi provides steady work to four binders. Some of the bound books in his inventory are reserved for the annual spring fair of the Sensa (the Ascension) in Saint Mark's Square, but this is the more popular and less costly part of his production. Since his regular clientele prefers to buy at the shop, Francesco's profits during the two weeks of the fair are not particularly generous, and if participation in the fair were not obligatory it's highly likely that he and the other Venetian booksellers would just as soon

[7] Nuovo, *Il commercio. . .*, op. cit. p. 170.

stay home.[8] In any event, the fair of the Sensa "allowed them to reach a different clientele composed of random passersby, who were often rather alien to the world of books."[9]

The publishing market in Venice is so important that the city is a sort of year-round book fair all year-round. Venetian printers and sellers are the dominant presence at Europe's two most important book fairs, Lyon and Frankfurt (the latter having conserved its international preeminence down to the present day), all the way through the early years of the seventeenth century, when they start to give way to their competitors from Antwerp (Anvers). In Italy there was no need to go to the fairs to stock up on books, as confirmed by numerous accounts of the perennial abundance of books of all kinds in Venice. Normally, anyone who was planning a large purchase of books sent his own personal emissary to that city charged with the task of calling on its leading booksellers.[10] The clientele of Venice's bookshops and stationers, therefore, is not composed only of Venetian intellectuals and visiting foreigners but also includes Italian booksellers who do their buying in the lagoon. Francesco de'Madi recorded the names of sixty-four of his customers, evidently his best ones, and most of them were colleagues.

Throughout the sixteenth century the number of works on display for sale grows steadily, but the growth is due primarily to an increase in the number of editions proposed rather than the number of copies of each single title, which instead tends to remain constant. Booksellers tried to outdo their competition by offering a wider assortment of books available in the shop and, as always, by offering quality accessory services, such as binding.[11]

[8] Ibid., p. 98.
[9] Ibid., p. 117.
[10] Ibid., p. 99.
[11] Ibid., p. 148.

They try to attract customers by offering the opportunity to find the titles they are looking for, but reading remains an elite activity until the nineteenth century. It is estimated that in eighteenth century Germany the regularly reading public was around 1.5 percent of the total population. Not until the following century would reading become a mass phenomenon. Nevertheless, sixteenth century Venice constitutes an exception even in this regard: a quarter of the male population between the ages of six and fifteen attends school,[12] a percentage undreamed of elsewhere, which accounts for the city's interest in books.

Unlike what we're used to seeing today, books from the sixteenth century don't have a cover price. "There was no precise rule for determining the price even for different copies of the same edition."[13] Everything is left up to negotiation, and it is very likely that booksellers and their customers engaged in intense bargaining; it's more like a Middle Eastern souk than a modern bookshop. Prices fluctuate from workshop to workshop, customer to customer, day to day. Important people are given bigger discounts, as was the case, for example, with the wealthy nobleman Federico Corner, who paid from twenty to thirty percent less than other buyers for the books he purchased from Francesco de' Madi. The oldest surviving insurance policies always include a price, the one charged to the bookseller by the printer, but this practice gradually died out, perhaps due to pressure from the booksellers who wanted to ensure themselves as much room to maneuver as possible. Prices could vary wildly, so much so that in 1502 a certain Johann Reuchlin wrote to the famous Manutius that he could buy one of his books in Pforzheim, Germany, for less than he was asked by the publisher himself in Venice.

[12] Giovanni Ragone, *Classici dietro le quinte. Storie di libri ed editori. Da Dante a Pasolini*, Laterza, (Rome-Bari, 2009) p. 43.
[13] Lowry, *Il mondo . . .* , op. cit. p. 188.

In any event, the passage from manuscripts to printed books ushered in an epoch-making collapse in prices. If, as we shall see, a compositor earns between three or four ducats per month and a proofreader between five and six, a 200-page luxury manuscript costs almost twenty-six ducats, while an economical one costs from four to fourteen. Notwithstanding its infinitely cheaper price (one ducat), a printed edition of Dante with commentary is still a luxury accessible only to the few, while popular books also sell for popular prices. Latin grammars used in schools can be had for as little as six soldi (a fraction of a lira, a ducat is worth six lira or, 120 soldi) and a vulgate work by Boccaccio costs only ten soldi.[14]

The fragmentation of Europe at the time into numerous small to midsized countries, each with its own currency, favors the high variability of prices and gives rise to commerce based on barter as a way of avoiding the price volatility caused by fluctuating exchange rates. Books are exchanged for books, but books are also exchanged for flour, wine, and olive oil. Stationers can buy on credit and the use of double-entry bookkeeping, an accounting technique introduced between the thirteenth and the first half of the fourteenth centuries in the Genoa-Florence-Venice triangle, becomes widespread. The first to theorize the double entry—practically speaking, its inventor—was a merchant from the city of Ragusa (now Dubrovnik) in Dalmatia, Benedetto Cotrugli (Benko Kotruljić) who served for many years as Consul of the Dalmatian Republic in Naples. He wrote his treatise in the second half of the fifteenth century and the first printed edition was produced in 1573, over a hundred years after the author's death, by the Elefante workshop in Venice. Entitled *Della mercatura e del mercante perfetto* (On Trade and the Perfect Merchant) this is the book that made his accounting technique, later cod-

---

[14] Ragone, *Classici . . .* , op. cit. p. 43.

ified by Luca Pacioli, well known, so that in Venice, in all like-lihood not by chance, double entry, trade, and printing reached their highest levels in all of Renaissance Europe.

In the meantime, little by little, book buyers begin to adopt the "Frankfurter Tax": the most important purchasers—first and foremost universities and libraries—arrange to be informed of the prices established at the Frankfurt book fair so they can better negotiate with their local retailers.[15] Prices of both for-mats—already bound and printed on looseleaf parchment—began to fluctuate less.[16] In the first case, the bookseller has to monetize in the best way possible a process whose costs he knows quite well; in the second, the value of the raw material takes precedence over all other considerations.

Paper accounts for as much as fifty percent of the cost of a Renaissance-era book, and it is consumed in vast quantities: three reams, or 1500 sheets, per day per press.[17] Smooth paper costs five times as much as paper of inferior quality and over time the price fluctuates wildly: from the beginning of the sixteenth century demand grows so much that competition becomes more intense and manufacturers are forced to lower their prices. Printers need to go into debt in order to buy paper and so it is fairly common for papermakers to become creditors, advancing a ream (500 sheets) at a time until the printing is finished, and taking control of the printing house when things go badly. Indeed, it is not infre-quent for suppliers of "white paper," who control the raw mate-rial, to start trading in "black paper" (printed paper), as in the case of Paganini, publishers of the first Koran.

As for equipment, the press is the least expensive. It is after all a known item, fairly similar to the press used in winemaking. Around 1480, a press with a movable undertable was intro-

[15] Nuovo, *Il commercio . . . ,* op. cit. p.
[16] Ibid.
[17] Jane A. Bernstein, *Print Culture and Music in Sixteenth Century Venice,* Oxford University Press (New York-Oxford 2001) p. 34.

duced, which made printing faster; an early-fifteenth-century press could print three hundred sheets per day and by the end of the century presses were printing four times that number.[18] What costs a lot, on the other hand, are the characters: the making of the punches is a highly specialized craft usually requiring a goldsmith (Gutenberg himself was a goldsmith), who naturally must be paid adequately. Few printers can claim to be self-sufficient and making punches from steel, matrices from copper, and characters from lead, tin, and antimony is generally performed externally. Little by little, a specialized industry develops until 1540, when the Frenchman Claude Garamond becomes the supplier of characters for nearly every printer in Europe.[19]

The press itself employs three people: the compositor, the inker, and the pressman; a small printing house might have six employees, while one that has from six to eight presses with thirty to forty workers is a firm of substantial dimensions. Only the compositor has to have specialized training and, judging from satirical comments of the time, there were a lot of unemployed servants and penniless students ready to fill any jobs that might open up.[20] In any case, it's a well-paid job; in Padova in 1475 a compositor earns three ducats a month, plus a ducat's worth of books that he can re-sell. Three ducats is also the monthly salary of a hydraulic engineer, an occupation certainly of no secondary importance in a city like Venice, whose survival depends on the proper regulation of water flow in its rivers and in keeping the sea from entering the lagoon. Apprentices are paid about one-tenth the salary of an expert compositor and are provided with free room and board for a period of three years.[21] The constant fluctuation of food prices is also a source of domestic quarrels between master and apprentice,

[18] Brian Richardson, *Printing, Writers and Readers in Renaissance Italy*, Cambridge University Press, Cambridge 1999, p. 23.

[19] Lowry, *Il mondo . . .* , op. cit. p. 19.

[20] Ibid., p. 20.

[21] Richardson, *Printing . . .* , op. cit., p. 19.

not unlike those between skinflint husbands and their neurotic wives. A proofreader could expect to be paid somewhere between four and six ducats per month.

These are the main items that contribute to the cost of a book but there is a long list of others, which are also important, such as the metals for casting characters—they wear out in a hurry and have to be remade frequently. A small printer could recompose already-printed texts or work for third parties, "but the more ambitious ones tried to obtain direct access to manuscripts, hire professional men of letters to edit them, and if possible to have proofreaders on staff to check the results. Manuscripts can be rented or purchased at a wide variety of prices.[22] Profits, however, are very high, ranging from 50 to 100 percent, and guarantee a good margin even with runs of only 300 to 400 copies. Nevertheless, returns on the investment are slow and uncertain, and booksellers take a commission of 10 percent, so a lot of printing houses close down after just one or two editions. The race to get into printing is probably due more to novelty than profitability, the business mortality rate is high: very few survive, and the great wealth envisioned by those who go into debt to purchase presses and characters exists only in their imaginations. When the publisher Nicolas Jenson dies, he wills his heirs 4,000 ducats: a tidy sum, but only a tenth of what a spice dealer earns in just one year.[23] The chronicler Marin Sanudo had written of Jenson: "*Vadagnò col stampar assai denari*" (He made lots of money in the print trade), but clearly the reality wasn't as rosy as it appeared.[24]

In the second half of the sixteenth century, the onset of the Inquisition brought with it a new risk, as books were seized and

[22] Lowry, *Il mondo* . . . , op. cit. p. 21.
[23] Ibid., p. 16.
[24] Lino Moretti, *Il libro veneziano nei secoli*, in *Venezia città del libro. Cinque secoli di editoria veneta e mostra dell'editoria italiana*, Venice, Isola di San Giorgio Maggiore, 2 September-7 October 1973, p. 15.

publishers put on trial. In 1568 a bookseller from Brescia enu-
merates a series of complaints: he has unpaid debts more than
eight years old, the book market is slow, every day so many new
books are banned that books published that year may be good
for nothing but wrapping fish the next. Between paper and
labor, the Bible printed in Venice in 1478 (281 sheets and 930
copies) costs the publisher 450-500 ducats. In 1580 a five-vol-
ume work for a total of 565 sheets in 1,250 copies costs the
printer 1,920 ducats.[25]

But none of these calculations seem to matter: what looks to
be an outright book fever induces a lot of people to jump into
the new business, so much so that in 1473, or just four years after
the introduction of printing in Venice, there is already a crisis of
overproduction. The warehouses are full of unsold classics and
production drops 65 percent (in the two previous years as many
as 134 editions had been printed). And this will not be the only
growth crisis: in 1563 Filippo and Jacopo Giunta will talk about
used books being used to package food.[26] From the outset there
is a constant trend toward lower prices, which becomes particularly acute with the introduction of books aimed at a more popular market, like the fair of the Sensa, and crises caused by outside events, such as wars or plague (Venice suffers a serious
military defeat on May 14, 1509, which deprives it of control
over the state from the mainland for several years, and it is struck
by the black plague in 1478 and 1576.

From 1469 to the end of the fifteenth century, 153 printers
printed 4,500 titles. If we estimate a run of 300 copies per title,
this means that Venetian presses produced 1,350,000 volumes,
equal to 15 percent of the European total (and this is a conservative estimate).[27] Keep in mind that that the number of

[25] Richardson, *Printing . . .* , op. cit., p. 25.
[26] Ibid., p. 27.
[27] Marino Zorzi, introduction to Scilla Abbiati (ed.), *Armeni, ebrei, greci
stampatori a Venezia,* Casa editrice armena, Venice 1989, p. 17.

Gutenberg Bibles is now estimated at around 200 copies, and the first book printed in Venice, Cicero's *Epistulae ad familiares*, had a run of 100 copies; but when they were all sold, in just three months, a second edition was printed in 300 copies. In the sixteenth century, at least 690 printers and publishers printed more than 15,000 titles, with an average run of around 1000 copies but with high points of between 2,000 and 3,000 for works that were expected to achieve massive sales, at a pace of 150 editions per year (we can't report the number of titles because some books, the Bible, for example, had more than one printer).[28] In any case, there are those who estimate that in the sixteenth century Venetian presses produced the handsome figure of over 35 million books.[29] It appears that printers worked from twelve to sixteen hours a day, printing from 2,500 to 3,500 sheets on just one side; they managed, that is, to print one sheet every twenty seconds, a level of productivity that is simply amazing.

The good fortune of the publishers was also the good fortune of their authors, and it can safely be said that the sixteenth century saw the birth of the best seller. Between 1542 and 1560, Gabriel Giolito de'Ferrari published some twenty-eight editions of Ludovico Ariosto's *Orlando Furioso*; practically one and a half editions per year.[30] In this case we're talking about a living author who had completed the work about ten years earlier. On the other hand, Petrarch had already been dead for quite a while (since 1374 to be exact) when he racked up "148 editions in Italy, maybe more than 100,000 copies, almost exclusively of his *Canzoniere*."[31] The man responsible for

[28] Ibid.

[29] Jane A. Bernstein, *Music Printing in Renaissance Venice. The Scotto Press (1539-1572)*, Oxford University Press, New York-Oxford 1998, p. 14.

[30] Guido Davico Bonino, *Lo scrittore, il potere, la maschera*, Liviana, Padua 1979, p. 72.

[31] Ragone, *Classici . . .*, op. cit. p. 35.

Petrarch's publishing success, and Dante's too, was the most important publisher of the sixteenth century, Aldus Manutius. Book ownership at that time was fairly widespread; it has been estimated that 15 percent of Venetian families had at least one book in the home (64 percent of the clergy, 40 percent of the bourgeoisie, 23 percent of the nobility, and 5 percent of the popular classes).[32]

The increase in the volume of printings also provokes an increase in demand for warehouse space. In 1491, when the bookseller Matteo Codecà makes his will, he has some 11,086 books in stock (and his is not one of the biggest houses); in 1562, when the Tramezzino brothers (one with a shop in Venice and the other in Rome) decide to divide up their warehouse, they record an inventory of 29,294 books, but these are only the books printed by them. One of the two brothers was an international merchant, and we can only assume that the total number of volumes, including those printed by other publishers, must have been much greater.

It isn't long before the cramped rooms of the workshops are no longer sufficient and the booksellers start looking for space wherever they can find it: in noble palaces and monasteries. By the turn of the sixteenth century, the Venetian patrician class is already well along in the process of conversion from a mercantile to a landholding nobility and is investing on the mainland; the warehouses previously used to hold cargo unloaded from ships arriving from the Levant are now empty. The request from publishers to rent them for book storage comes just at the right time. The religious orders, fully involved in the printing business, realize that ceding space to the printers can become a steady source of income. In 1564 the fathers of Saint Stephen rent out nine warehouses to booksellers. Thereby accumulating enormous numbers of books, though we are unable to determine just

[32] Ibid., p. 44.

how many. If a middling-size Milanese publisher, such as Nicolò Gorgonzola, possesses 80,000 volumes, how many must the large Venetian publishers have?

All this in a period in which private libraries rarely reach 2000 works, and public libraries do not go beyond a few tens of thousands. The imperial library of Vienna did not get up to 80,000 volumes until 1665 (today that same library—no longer imperial—holds over three million books, while the British Library has 14 million and the Library of Congress more than 33 million). Venice, yet again, is an exception. In 1523 the library of the noble and cultivated Cardinal Domenico Grimani contains some 15,000 volumes (but the number isn't certain) and the library of the historian Marin Sanudo, the largest private collection in Venice until the eighteenth century, contains more than 6,000.[33] 6,500 titles, a "true colossus in the Venetian and European panorama [. . .] the unsurpassed prototype of the library of the professional historian."[34] In any event, possession of a library is a mark of social prestige, worthy of an important person, and this may explain why it is such an elite phenomenon, much more so, contrary to our own time, than owning paintings. A survey of sixteenth century wills shows that "books were named in 146 of the 937 wills examined, around 15 percent, a modest showing when compared to the 90 percent presence of paintings."[35]

All that paper piled up in the same place increases the threat of fire, always looming in the wings in a city built primarily of wood. (The Doge's Palace burned down twice, in 1483 and 1577, and as early as 1290 the glass makers were obliged to move to Murano to keep their ovens from reducing the city to ashes.) The fires come one after another: on January 4, 1529 the monastery of Saint Stephen catches fire and in two hours the

[33] Marino Zorzi, *La circolazione del libro a Venezia nel Cinquecento: biblioteche private e pubbliche,* "Ateneo Veneto," n.s., 28 (1990), p. 135.
[34] Ibid.
[35] Zorzi, *La circolazione . . .* , op. cit., p. 129.

warehouses of several booksellers go up in smoke; in 1557 a fire nearly destroys the entire warehouse of the Giunta house, which risks going bankrupt. These accidental conflagrations are joined by fires commissioned by the Church to burn forbidden books: on March 18, 1559, from 10,000 to 12,000 volumes are incinerated in Saint Mark's Square.

Up to this point we have seen what the book capital of the world was like in the sixteenth century. Now let's try to understand how Venice got to be the capital. The German Johannes Gensfleisch, known as Gutenberg, printed his bible in Mainz between 1452 and 1455. The first dated book is from 1457. The first print shops outside of Mainz opened in 1465, in two other German cities and in Italy. In that same year, two German altar boys, Arnold Pannartz and Conrad Sweinheim, following the Benedictine Way from Mainz to Italy, bring with them all the equipment they need to print to the monastery of Saint Scholastica, in Subiaco (the place where Saint Benedict had founded the order) near Rome, and they publish Cicero's *De oratore*. This is the Italian debut of printing, which then spreads like wildfire. Of the 110 printing shops active in Europe in 1480, fifty are in Italy, thirty or so in Germany, nine in France, eight in Spain and the rest are scattered around the continent.[36]

It is another German who brings printing to Venice. Johann von Speyer (Giovanni da Spira) also publishes Cicero, the *Epistulae ad familiares*, in 1469, and he asks for and is granted a privilege by the Venetian Republic. A privilege is a fairly common institution in Europe at the time. Essentially, it is an authorized monopoly granted to someone who undertakes a new enterprise or who creates something new within the confines of an already established activity.[37] The privilege granted to Johann

[36] Lucien Febvre, Henri-Jean Martin, *La nascita del libro*, Laterza, Rome-Bari 1985, p. 229.
[37] Nuovo, *Il commercio* . . . , op. cit., p. 68.

has a duration of five years, but privileges can last as long as ten years, or even twenty-five. Privileges are tied, however, to the person to whom they are granted and since Johann dies just a few months after his is granted, Venice reverts to a free market and other printers, invariably Germans, immediately open their printing houses. Everywhere in Europe it is printers from Germany who spread the new techniques of typography. "Veritable nomads, they stop off in cities from where they have received orders and, rich only in their art and their often very limited equipment, they are all in search of a financier who will permit them to settle down and a city where they can find the conditions necessary to establish a stable printing house."[38]

There is no doubt that Venice owes its publishing preeminence to immigrant printers from central Europe; in the fifteenth century nearly half of the Venetian editions were produced by Germans and 80 percent of the 1600 Venetian incunabula conserved in the British Library "show signs of rubrication and ownership associated with the German-speaking world."[39] In short, the Germans invented printing, but in order to sell books they went to Venice; they discovered the technology, but in order to grow the business they had to emigrate, and wealthy and cultivated Italy was their preferred destination.

For printing books to become a successful enterprise, three conditions are necessary: a high concentration of literati, a ready availability of capital, and a solid capacity for business. Venice has all of these and then some. The nearby university of Padua provides the intellectual capital. Financial capital comes from the wealthy merchants who are converting to agriculture and want to diversify their investments. The business capacity and commercial network are those of the wealthiest and most

[38] Febvre, Martin, *La nascita del libro*, op. cit., p. 210.
[39] Ibid.

powerful European state of the fifteenth century. Indeed, the
books travel on board the same ships that for centuries have
carried the goods that have made the Serene Republic great.
Venice—at the height of its territorial expansion (to prevent it
from conquering Milan and to defeat it in the battle of 1509,
an alliance will be formed of almost all the European states of
the time)—has trading routes that connect it to central Europe
and the Middle East on a regular basis, and that stretch even
beyond. In 1432, after a fleet bound for Southampton was
shipwrecked, Pietro Querini ended up on the Lofoten Islands
and, sensing the potential of the cod trade, he succeeded in
establishing a long-lasting commercial trade with Norway.
Although the Silk Way traveled by the Venetian Marco Polo is
now interrupted, his fellow townsmen continue to frequent
Persia and Syria. Even William Shakespeare confirms Venice's
role as the heart of the commercial world when, in *The
Merchant of Venice*, Salerio says:

> Your mind is tossing on the ocean,
> There where your argosies with portly sail,
> Like signors and rich burghers on the flood,
> Or as it were the pageants of the sea,
> Do overpeer the petty traffickers
> That curtsy to them, do them reverence,
> As they fly by them with their woven wings. (Act 1, Scene i)[40]

Since naval transport is the most common and least costly
method of the time, the books are packed to protect them from
water: the unbound volumes in sacks or closed inside barrels
or in cases made waterproof by tarring. We know that in 1498
a case shipped by Aldus Manutius was recovered after the
wreck of the ship that was carrying it. The books were dam-

[40] William Shakespeare, *The Merchant of Venice*, Garzanti, Milan, p. 6.

aged but not irreparably and would later be put back on the market.[41]

But there is more: Venice, above all else, is free. Let me be clear, this is not to say that the Serene Republic is liberal in the modern sense, but compared to other contemporary states it offers an enviable climate of liberty and until 1553 there is no censorship. It is no coincidence that Venice is home to prosperous communities of foreigners and worshippers of various religions, something unthinkable elsewhere. Greeks and Armenians in exile from Ottoman domination, Jews escaped from persecution in Spain and other European countries, are offered asylum in the lagoon and will be, as we shall see, an extraordinary driving force in the development of print culture. And not only; the territory of the Venetian state, and particularly its overseas dominions, are inhabited by peoples who speak different languages—making them too an interesting market—and Venetian presses will print not the first but among the first books in the Glagolitic (old Croatian) and Cyrillic alphabets (Church Slavonic for the Russian Orthodox liturgy).

Furthermore, although in Germany printing was born under the auspices of the Catholic Church, in Venice it is financed by the patricians of the humanistic circles. While at the end of the fifteenth century 45 percent of European books are of a religious nature, this percentage shrinks to 32 percent in Italy and to 26 percent in Venice. The Roman Church remains unable to exercise its direct influence (for example, bishops must be Venetian subjects and their appointments must be approved by the government) and the Inquisition will arrive late and in attenuated form, so that in the first half of the sixteenth century freedom of the press will be nearly absolute.

[41] Nuovo, *Il commercio. . .* , op. cit., p. 168.

It's not at all strange, therefore, in a wealthy and free state, that entrepreneurs should come swarming like bees to flowers. There's more. Today, we tend to think of Venice as a city-state. Nothing could be more wrong. The borders of the Serene Republic of Venice were very extensive and compared with other states at the time, Venetia could be considered a large state that covered about one-third of present-day northern Italy, as well as ample portions of present-day Slovenia, Croatia. Montenegro, and Greece, including even the large Mediterranean islands of Crete and Cyprus. Moreover, the Venetian state was one of the most urban and industrialized states of the entire continent. Venice, as has been said, was one of the three big cities of the sixteenth century. Venetia also contained within its borders two of the twenty European cities with more than 50,000 inhabitants (Verona and Brescia), and its medium-sized cities were incommensurably larger than analogous medium-sized cities in other European countries (the city of Arzignano near Vicenza had 7,000 inhabitants, while the English city of Manchester had only 4,000). Venetia and Flanders alone accounted for 16 percent of the urban European population (additionally, in Venetia 20 percent of the population lives in cities of more than 10,000 inhabitants)[42] and only Venetia and Lombardy (most of which belonged to the Serene Republic) enjoyed enormous quantities of water power supplied by the streams and rivers of the Alpine foothills.

This stable supply of water power makes the Republic the leader in paper production, which is concentrated along the Brenta and Piave rivers and on the western shore of Lake Garda (it is estimated that, at the time, to produce a kilogram of paper you needed 2,000 liters of water and it had to be

[42] Filippo De Vivo, *Information and Communication in Venice, Rethinking Early Modern Politics*, Oxford University Press, Oxford-New York 2007, p. 5.

limpid and transparent, otherwise the paper turned out badly), and that's why "Venice soon dominates the printing industry in Italy and, for a period, also in Europe."[43] Venice produces 5,000 of the 12,000 incunabula printed in Italy, 45 percent of European production (the incunabula are books published prior to 1500). For this same reason, the leading Italian printer in 1470 is a Venetian subject: Clemente da Padova. The boom peaks between 1526 and 1550, when Venice publishes almost three-fourths of the editions printed in Italy and half of all those produced on the continent. In the ensuing twenty-five years this percentage would decline to a still-respectable 61 percent. Books published in Venice are also distinguished by their particular characteristics, or for "the specifically Venetian attention to all that which facilitates reading: tables of contents, indexes, and marginal notes."[44]

Amid this tumult of successes, there is also room for a legend to bloom: in the nineteenth century, thanks to some unidentified documents, later to be lost, Gutenberg's invention of the printing press was contested and attributed instead to Panfilo Castaldi, physician and humanist, born in Feltre, a splendid sixteenth century town in the Alpine foothills of Venetia, and a longtime resident of Capodistria (Koper) and Zara (Zadar) that on the shores of the Adriatic (places, were then part of the Venetian Republic). For a time, Castaldi gives up medicine and devotes himself to printing. After looking around and noticing that there is still nobody in Milan involved in managing presses, punches, and characters, he arranges to have himself granted a privilege by Duke Galeazzo Maria Sforza, and in 1471 he publishes the first book printed in the Lombard city. The local market is so appetizing that a certain Filippo da

[43] Richardson, *Printing . . .* , op. cit., p. 5.
[44] John R. Hale, *Industria del libro e cultura militare a Venezia nel Rinascimento,* in *Storia della cultura veneta,* vol. III, t. II, Neri Pozza, Vicenza 1980, p. 247.

Lavagna challenges his monopoly and sets up a new printing house in Milan. In 1472 Castaldi is forced to concede, sells his equipment, and goes back to practicing medicine on the seashore. These are the historical facts. During a good part of the nineteenth century, however, the claim is made in Italy that Castaldi was the real inventor of movable type and that Gutenberg had copied him and managed to get credit for the invention, rather like Alexander Graham Bell later did with Antonio Meucci. Only in Castaldi's case it wasn't true. Nevertheless, even today, on the pedestal of the monument erected in his honor in his hometown, he is credited with the paternity of an invention not of his own making.

Venice is the birthplace of the book but also the birthplace of the book business. It is here that the term "publisher" is first used to refer to those who invest in printing, and their ranks include stationers, merchants, printers, literati, and sometimes the authors and editors of the works themselves.[45] The first big publishing houses and trade associations are formed, some of them multinational. The most important publishers of the sixteenth century, first among them the Giunta (later Giunti) family from Florence, begin their activity in the Republic of St. Mark. Specializing in religious and devotional books, under the table they sell and even publish books that are targeted by church censorship and preside over a sales network that covers all of Europe.[46] The two most important cultural and commercial centers of Renaissance Italy, Venice and Florence, are direct close ties. Almost immediately, in fact, the Florentine Girolamo Strozzi sets up shop on the lagoon, where he organizes the sale of books to Florence, Siena, Pisa, Rome, Naples, and to the branch of the Banco Medici in Bruges and to Marco Strozzi in

---

[45] Ragone, *Classici* . . . , op. cit., p. 44.
[46] Moretti, *Il libro . . . ,* op. cit., p. 28.

London, availing himself of Venice's commercial shipping lines. His potential customers are Florentine merchants residing in the two foreign cities. Every two weeks one of Strozzi's agents makes the rounds of local stationers to make sure that the books are actually on the shelves and haven't been lent out to friends rather than sold. The agent also checks all the books before delivery to ensure that there are no missing pages, so the booksellers will not be able to claim a new copy to replace the supposedly defective one. Finally, before supplying the sellers with replacements for sold books, the agent has to collect the money from the sale, not a simple task because the shopkeepers tend to buy on credit and delay payment for as long as possible.[47]

Just ten years after the first presses were brought to Venice by Johann von Speyer (his brother Windelin takes over the business and in 1477 publishes the first edition with commentary of Dante's *Divine Comedy*), some of the bigger publishing houses join together to form large groups. In 1479 the Compagnia di Venezia is established, a publishing house formed primarily by non-Venetians, which in just one year publishes twenty editions. The Frenchman Nicolas Jenson, the founder of the royal mint in Paris, dies almost immediately, leaving the reins to Peter Ugelheimer, a renowned merchant from Frankfurt and the owner of a hotel for German pilgrims passing through Venice en route to the Holy Land. Ugelheimer devotes his life to the "international and interregional development and distribution of the Venetian book."[48] He also owns a collection of exquisitely illuminated and bound books (two of these, published by Jenson, have been called "the most extraordinary of all fifteenth century Italian bindings").[49]

The activity of the Compagnia gives rise to a cartel of mer-

[47] Edler De Roover, *Per la storia dell'arte della stampa in Italia,* "La Bibliofilia," LV (1953), p. 114.

[48] Nuovo, *Il commercio . . .* , op. cit., p. 76.

[49] Ibid., p. 76

chants with its headquarters in Venice, capable of organizing a large-scale trade in books, produced both by themselves and others, especially between north-central Italy and Germany.[50] The Compagnia hires stationers, on salary, in the cities where it sells its books. They are free to carry on their traditional activity, selling manuscripts, but with the addition—at no risk, since they receive a monthly salary—, of the new product. In 1485 Ungelheimer moves to Milan and sets up a network of branch offices in the most important university towns of Tuscany, which then become major outlets for Venetian production.

Reinforcing the Venice-Florence connection, the Giunta family establishes one of the most important multinationals of the era (a Giunti publishing house still exists, but it was founded in Florence in 1840 and is not a direct descendant of its Renaissance namesake). Lucantonio the Elder is born in Florence and moves to Venice in 1477, at the age of twenty, to devote himself to the paper trade. His transition in grand style from white paper to black paper comes about in 1491 and it is estimated that from then until his death in 1538 he published some 410 titles. The business will be carried on by his children. The Giuntas directly operate book shops in Spain and Palermo. In 1520 they open a branch in Lyon, and each of their foreign locations is managed by a member of the family. The hottest sector of the market at the time is prayer books for use during Mass, and Lucantonio plunges right in: he publishes one in every language requested and ships them to Spain, Germany, Austria, and Croatia. He becomes the world's most important printer of religious books. He is very intent on marketing and reserves a certain number of complimentary copies to be presented to well-known and powerful figures (and he always enhances his list of books with a range of other products: silk, sugar, pepper, olive oil, and spices).

[50] Ibid., p. 79.

His distribution network has two channels, one professionally operated and the other entrusted to religious orders. The friars, who distribute his volumes to the various monasteries of the order, sell 40 percent of Giunta's production, and their sales bring in huge profits because half of the books sold by the friars are religious books, but the remaining 50 percent are books of other genres, such as the *Iliad*. It is possible that the friars had access to distribution channels from which lay booksellers were excluded—for example, hospices for pilgrims en route to the Holy Land. In 1560 Venice was still the hub of the Giuntas' trade, followed by Lyon, at a ratio of two to one. Surprisingly, although they are a Florentine family, sales in Florence are very low. But Lucantonio and his heirs don't pay much attention to the local market. They are international merchants who specialize in books in Latin and who brilliantly resolve the problem of supplying a certain number of products, at a low unitary cost, to buyers located throughout the continent. Their primary objectives, therefore, are the development of a powerful commercial network, also used for other goods, and the establishment of solid commercial relationships. Thanks to their wholesale business, they succeed in dominating the entire book sector in Europe.[51]

Industrialization, globalization, and marketing: Renaissance Venice already has it all. We may be talking about an enterprise dating back half a millennium, but the productive and commercial capacities expressed by the book capital of the world in the first half of the sixteenth century easily rival those of today's tycoons of the information age.

[51] Ibid., p. 184.

2.
ALDUS MANUTIUS, THE MICHELANGELO OF BOOKS

P ainting has Raphael, sculpture Michelangelo, architecture Brunelleschi, and printing Aldus Manutius. Though he may not be as well known to the general public as the creator of the *David*, Manutius is a genius, an innovator, a revolutionary—a turning point in history. After him, publishing will be irreversibly different from what it was before. His intuitions led to changes that are still part of our lives today. It will be up to the e-book, maybe, to finally make him obsolete. Something that the paperback, for example, was not able to do. Why not? Because Manutius invented it. And how about cursive characters, which, not coincidentally, in English are called italics? Another invention of Manutius. The best seller? Manutius was the first to print one. As we have already recalled, he made it possible for Petrarch, dead and buried for a century and a half, to sell the astronomical figure of 100,000 copies (not only in the Manutius edition, obviously). Selling 100,000 copies is a huge success even today, so just imagine what that meant in the sixteenth century. And while he's at it, Manutius even revolutionizes punctuation, becoming the father of the semicolon. He is the first to use it, at the suggestion of the humanist scholar Pietro Bembo, transporting it from Greek to Latin and then to the vernacular, along with the apostrophe and accent marks.

Aldus Romanus (as he was fond of signing his name to honor his Roman origins) is the first to conceive of the book as entertainment. He is the inventor of reading for pleasure, and this invention brings about a bona fide intellectual revolution that transforms what was an instrument used for praying or learning into a pleasant pastime. Aldus is the first publisher in the modern sense. Before he came on the scene, printers were rude pressmen. Often uneducated, they were interested in the book only as a commercial object. Proof of this is the quantity of errors that typically marred editions prior to those published by Manutius. Printers could even be unsavory characters. In 1493 Matteo da Pavia is tried for having murdered a deaf-mute in the Fontego dei Tedeschi, and in 1499 a printer named Morgante is accused of murdering a common prostitute.[1]

Aldus, on the other hand, is a refined intellectual, one who chooses which works to print on the basis of their content, rather than only on their potential sales. He is the first to bring together cultural heritage, technical skills, and an intuition for market demand, so much so that the history of publishing is divided into before Manutius and after. He is also adept at choosing collaborators, the best and the brightest in the various fields of knowledge that interest him.

His move to Venice seems to have been dictated primarily by a cultural mission: to print, and thus to distribute among intellectuals like himself, the Greek and Latin manuscripts that Cardinal Giovanni Bessarione had donated to the Republic of Venice in 1468, and which constituted the initial nucleus of the Biblioteca Marciana (even if recent studies indicate that the Bessarione collection was not easily accessible and that Aldus may not even have consulted it).[2]

But there's more: the presses owned and operated by Manutius produced what many consider to be the most beautiful book ever printed, the *Hypnerotomachia Poliphili*, a work that in

---

[1] Martin Lowry, *The world of Aldus Manutius: Business and Culture in Renaissance Venice*, p. 29.

[2] Mario Infelise, *Manuzio, Aldo, il Vecchio*, in *Dizionario biografico degli italiani*, vol. LXIX, IEI, Rome 2007, p. 237.

many ways is still a mystery today. It is lascivious and pagan, despite being written by a Dominican monk, with erotic, sometimes almost pornographic illustrations (the edition conserved in the Vatican Library has been carefully censored). George Painter, the former assistant keeper in charge of the incunabula held by the British Museum (and also the biographer of Marcel Proust), considered this book a milestone in the history of publishing:

> Gutenberg's 42-line Bible of 1455, and the *Hypnerotomachia Poliphili* of 1499, confront one another from opposite ends of the incunabula period with equal and contrasting pre-eminence. The Gutenberg Bible is somberly and sternly German, Christian, and Medieval; the *Hypnerotomachia* is radiantly and graciously Italian, classic, pagan, and renascent. These are the two supreme masterpieces of the art of printing, and stand at the two poles of human endeavor and desire.[3]

Among the buyers of Aldine editions were the most famous names of the Italian Renaissance: Federico Gonzaga, Isabella d'Este, Lucrezia Borgia, and Pope Leo X (Giovanni de' Medici). Among Manutius's students were Ercole Strozzi, a future poet, and Prince Alberto Pio, a refined diplomat. His friends included Pico della Mirandola, Erasmus of Rotterdam, the humanist poets Pietro Bembo (Venetian) and Angelo Poliziano (Tuscan), the bibliophile Jean Grolier de Servières (the treasurer of France), the Venetian patrician and chronicler Marin Sanudo, the English humanist William Latimer, who taught at Cambridge and Oxford, and the English humanist and physician Thomas Lynaker of Canterbury, a professor of Greek at Oxford.[4]

As is so often the case with figures of that era, we know very

---

[3] As quoted in Helen Barolini, *Aldus and His Dream Book*, Italica Press, New York, 1992, p. 6.
[4] Ibid., p. 4.

little of Aldus Manutius before he began his career as a publisher. He was born, probably around 1450, in Bassiano, a small village in the Duchy of Sermoneta, fifty miles or so southeast of Rome. Obviously, the pole of attraction for anyone from that area who is interested in humanistic studies is the papal city, where, between 1467 and 1475, Manutius frequents circles patronized by Cardinal Bessarione. He attends the lessons of the Professor of Rhetoric Gaspare da Verona, and probably comes into contact with German Benedictine monks who had imported the art of printing into Italy. In 1475 he moves to Ferrara, where he improves his knowledge of Greek. His students there include Giovanni Pico della Mirandola, uncle of the young princes Alberto and Lionello Pio; it is Mirandola who advises his sister, the widow of the Lord of Carpi, to hire Aldus as the tutor for her children. In 1480 Manutius moves to Carpi, where he lives for nine years. A concrete sign of his presence there is found in the fresco in the city's castle, where a portrait of the by-now mature Manutius is still visible today next to his young and robust student, Alberto Pio. Witness to the profound influence that his sojourn in Carpi exercised over the future prince of publishers is the fact that his full signature will be Aldus Pius Manutius Romanus, where Pius is intended as a tribute to Prince Alberto. It seems that in that same period Aldus wrote a Latin grammar, the manuscript of which has been identified in the Querini Stampalia Library in Venice, and that he had printed by the Venetian typographer Battista Torti an anthology of Latin elegies.[5]

Sometime between 1489 and 1490 Aldus moves to Venice. We don't know why. There is another illustrious Roman living in the city, Marcantonio Sabellico, official historiographer of the Republic and, as the librarian of the Biblioteca Marciana, custodian of the enormous treasure of Greek manuscripts that

[5] Infelise, *Manuzio* . . . , op. cit., p. 237.

are conserved there. There is only one eyewitness account, however, of a direct contact between the two, and it actually seems that Aldus became friends with Sabellico's major rival, Giambattista Egnazio.[6] In a letter to Poliziano he is rumored to have written that Venice is "a place that resembles an entire world more than a city," but it is a second-hand source and there is no guarantee of its truthfulness.

Nor do we know why only three years later he decides to print his first edition. In Martin Lowry's *The World of Aldus Manutius*, he is described thus:

> He was approaching forty, an age at which men of the time began to be bothered by aching joints and dwindling eyesight. His career had been absolutely respectable if not quite brilliant [. . .]. He had won protections, which constituted the best form of security to which a second-class man of letters could aspire.[7]

Some observers have conjectured that he decided to make books because he had grown tired of reading Greek and Latin classics that were full of errors and desired works that were more cleanly printed. The editions "were prepared at breakneck speed, generally taken from an extremely limited selection of manuscripts, often from a single copy, or from a previously printed edition."[8] The volumes ended up in the hands of students, who wrote their teachers' comments in the margins, perhaps adding a comment or two of their own, and they were quite content to pass it all on for just a few ducats to the printer, who was thus able to turn out a new "annotated" edition. Angelo Poliziano, Marcantonio Sabellico, and Giorgio

[6] Lowry, *The World* . . . , op. cit., p. 72.
[7] Ibid., p. 81.
[8] Ibid., p. 45.

Valla all complain that their ideas are plagiarized with this system.

We know, however, that the Aldine library (donated by Aldine's nephew to the Vatican Library in 1597) contains nothing that could support the finding of a vast publishing program, either in Greek or Latin. "The manuscript collection was nothing more than a banal assortment of Latin classics, local chronicles, devotional works, anthologies and commentaries."[9] The first book he publishes his Greek grammar, although he doesn't print it on his own but rather in the workshop of Andrea Torresani, known as Andrea d'Asola (Asola, near Mantua, is one of Venice's most distant possessions in Lombardy). Manutius will marry the daughter of Torresani and move to the family home in Campo San Paterniàn (now Campo Manin). The first book that he prints in his own print shop is also a Greek grammar, the *Erotemata* by Costantino Lascaris, the maestro of Pietro Bembo.[10] We are in February, 1495, and this is the beginning of the activity of not only the most important print shop of the Italian Renaissance but probably in the entire history of publishing. Nowhere else is there such a high concentration of inventions and innovations as there are among these work benches and character cases.

We also know that Manutius is fascinated by language, by the "structure of its sounds with musical rhythms and rich nuances. [He demonstrates] an almost morbid sense of grammatical accuracy and correctness of pronunciation."[11] It's no coincidence that he publishes so many grammars. In 1501 he publishes a Hebrew grammar, for which he uses the same characters that had been used by the Jewish printer Gershon Soncino in 1492 (in all probability, it is Soncino himself who

[9] Ibid., p. 84.
[10] Infelise, *Manuzio* . . . op. cit., p. 238.
[11] Lowry, *The World* . . . op. cit., p. 85.

composes it), and which is printed as an appendix to Greek and Latin grammars.[12] In his *In Praise of Folly*, written right after his departure from Italy, Erasmus of Rotterdam pictures the goddess who sustains the grammarians in their furious disputes over the dubious distinctions between parts of speech. In all likelihood, Erasmus had observed such arguments in person in Aldus's workshop. "Whereas if another but do slip a word and one more quick-sighted than the rest discover it by accident, O Hercules!, what uproars, what bickerings, what taunts, what invectives!,"[13] he writes of the madness of the grammarians and the erudite, adding, "we have as many grammars as grammarians, nay more, forasmuch as my friend Aldus has given us above five."[14]

In any event, in the early years of his career what most absorbs Manutius is printing in Greek. He begins to publish the works of Aristotle, collaborating with intellectuals like Zaccaria Calliergi and Marco Musuro, whom we will get to know better in the chapter dedicated to books in Greek. Sales, at any rate, are slow. The catalogue for 1513 (three of Manutius's catalogues have been preserved) still includes incunabula, many of them offered at reduced prices. In 1498 Aldus comes down with the plague. Fortunately he recovers, but he evidently regretted having vowed to take holy orders if he were to be healed, and on December 6th of that year is granted, a dispensation from his vow by the Senate.

In his earliest editions Aldus introduces an important innovation: printing in two columns per page, recreating the look of the ancient handwritten codices. Before this, the standard lay-

[12] Giuliano Tamani, *Edizioni ebraiche veneziane dei secoli XVI-XVII,* in Simonetta Pelusi (ed.), *Le cicilità del libro e la stampa a Venezia,* Il Poligrafo, Padua 2000, p. 33)
[13] Erasmus of Rotterdam, *In Praise of Folly*, Dover Publications, Mineola, New York 2003, p. 41.
[14] Ibid., p. 41.

out consisted of a single column. To print his first editions Aldus uses an elegant round character (Roman, in English) prepared by Nicolas Jenson, but it will later be redesigned by Francesco Griffo, the Bolognese goldsmith who will design the first italic characters. The definitive version of the Aldine round character appears in his printing of the *Hypnerotomachia Poliphili* (1499). This will be the model chosen by Garamond for the design of his own characters, and it is also the base character for all the antique-looking rounded characters, that we continue to use today, including the one that you are reading in this book, which is set in Garamond Simoncini.

The *Hypnerotomachia Poliphili*, commonly known as the *Poliphilo,* is widely considered the most beautiful book ever printed (in July, 2010, the auction house Christie's of London sold a copy for 313,250 pounds, over 500,000 dollars). All of its 234 *folio* pages have images, including 172 woodcuts by an artist whose identity remains unknown but whom recent studies place in the school of the Paduan miniaturist Benedetto Bordon[15] (whom we will meet in the chapter on geography books as the author of the first *isolario* (atlas of islands) in history). The woodcuts are so extraordinary that in the past they have been attributed to Andrea Mantegna or Giovanni Bellini. Even the text itself is composed in an artistic layout which lends the pages an unusual and attractive look.

"The most glorious book of the Renaissance, profusely illustrated and beautifully ornamented, which to this day remains a mystery, a text of symbols and bizarre jargon in various languages and dialects."[16] Specifically, a mixture of Italian, Venetian, Latin, and Greek, with elements of Hebrew, Chaldean, Arabic, and inventions of the author:

[15] Infelise, *Manuzio. . .* , op. cit., p. 239.
[16] Barolini, *Aldus and His Dream Book*, op. cit., p. 91.

A monstrous book [. . .], a marvel of graphic beauty and variegated composition, the most beautiful of all books containing wood-cut illustrations, and the undoubted masterpiece of the school of Venetian wood engraving.[17]

It was written thirty-two years earlier by a Dominican monk from Treviso named Francesco Colonna. This man had taken holy orders in 1455 and when he is writing, in 1467, he is well aware that he is devoting himself to a work that has little to do with the precepts that he has been called to observe. In 1471 Friar Francesco enters the Venetian monastery of San Zanipolo (Saints John and Paul) where he will die in 1527, at the venerable age of ninety-four; the *Poliphilo* is published when the author is sixty-six. The edition is financed by Leonardo Crasso, a wealthy lawyer from Verona, and it is dedicated to Guidobaldo di Montefeltro, Duke of Urbino. The name of Aldus Manutius appears only in small print on the *errata* page.

The storyline consists of an amorous journey in search of an elusive lover: Polia, part real woman, part abstract, and spiritual ideal. It is likely that the model for Polia is Lucrezia Lelli, a niece of the bishop who at the time was the friar's superior, and of whom the friar was probably enamored. The book is autobiographical—that's why it remains unsigned—but the author's name can be reconstructed by way of an acrostic composed of the initial letters of each chapter.[18] *Hypnerotomachia* is a combination of three Greek words meaning dream, love, and strife. Poliphilo, the book's protagonist, dreams of the lovely Polia, and in order to reach her he has to overcome several initiation trials. The woman hides in a wood where she finds a number of plaques from the classical age. The man wakes from his love dream in Treviso on May

[17] Ibid.
[18] Ibid., p. 93.

1, 1467,[19] the traditional day of sweethearts before the theme was taken over by Saint Valentine's Day and moved to February 14th.

For a long time after its publication, the tale's arcane and artificial language, though pleasant and not particularly complicated, left the book rather forlorn, and in search of an appreciative readership. A few years after its publication, Baldesar Castiglione cites it with disdain in *Courtier* (1528), asserting that an hour of such conversation seems to last a thousand years. James Joyce, who evidently knew the *Poliphilo*, wrote of it in his *Finnegan's Wake*: "A jetsam litterage of convolvuli of times lost or strayed, of lands derelict and of tongues laggin too." Carl Jung, whose profession was based on the interpretation of dreams, read the *Poliphilo* in the French translation in 1925.[20]

We don't know what Aldus Manutius thought of this work. In all likelihood he saw it mostly as a typographical challenge. But he must have realized how unorthodox it was if just one year later, in 1500, he published at his own expense the *Epistole* (Letters) of Saint Catherine of Siena, written in the more accessible Italian vernacular, a volume whose historical importance lies in the fact that it contains the first phrase, albeit very short, printed in italics: *Jesu dolce Jesu amore* (Jesus sweet Jesus love). On March 23, 1501, Manutius asks the Venetian Senate for a privilege to protect his new cursive character which according to Italian scholar, Mario Infelise, "was inspired by the manuscript forms in use in Italian chanceries in the second half of the fifteenth century and which he proposed as a way of ensuring for printed works the elegance and beauty of humanistic manuscripts."[21] But there is also another aspect

[19] Ibid., p. 94.
[20] Ibid., p. 103.
[21] Infleise, *Manuzio . . .* , op. cit., p. 241.

to this choice in an era when the raw material—paper—costs an enormous amount: oblique characters take up less space, the lines are more compressed compared to lines of round characters, and so they make it possible to save paper. It almost seems as if there are no disadvantages to the new character. When it comes right down to it, italics are less legible than round characters, but the concept in vogue in the sixteenth century is that printing should try to imitate writing and the new character designed for Manutius by Francesco Griffo is as close as you can get. Italics are one of the most successful innovations of typographical history,[22] and as Frédéric Barbier writes in his history of the book, they are "especially appreciated by sixteenth century printers for their elegance, as well as because they are the very prototype of the Italian Renaissance, and thus of modernity."[23]

On November 14, 1502, Aldus obtains the privilege to print in Greek and Latin with italics throughout the territory of the Venetian Republic. The partnership between Manutius and Griffo lasts ten or twelve years at most, and the printing house is active for seven of them—that period is of fundamental importance because during it Griffo creates twelve series of characters in three different languages (Latin, Greek, Hebrew).[24] The costs involved in obtaining the new characters are enormous, not hundreds but thousands of ducats.[25]

Francesco Griffo is destined to meet an ugly end. In 1516, having returned to his hometown of Bologna, he undertakes a publishing enterprise of his own, printing Petrarch's *Canzoniere*, but shortly afterward, for reasons we can only guess at, he splits open the head of his son-in-law with a metal

[22] Barolini, *Aldus and His Dream Book*, op. cit., p. 146
[23] Frédéric Barbier, *Storia del libro. Dall'antichità al XX secolo*, Dedalo, Bari 2004; p. 182.
[24] Lowry, *The World . . .* op. cit., p. 121.
[25] Ibid., p. 125.

bar that may well have been an unfinished typographical punch.[26] Tried for murder (the verdict is unknown) he disappears, swallowed up by the waves of history, and nothing more will ever be known of him.

The diffusion of italics proceeds apace with another great innovation introduced by Aldus, the pocket book, the *libelli portatiles*, as he called these small-format editions, with no commentary on the text, and therefore affordable to all. It was inexpensive enough for students and scholars who traveled between Europe's great universities.[27] Aldus is not the first to use the small format (in octavo); it is already authorized for religious texts, to allow clerics to carry their books with them, something that would have been very complicated with large volumes in *folio,* which had to sit open on a lectern. But Manutius is the first to print the classics in octavo. He starts with Virgil, in April of 1501, and then a year later the volume with the Latin poets Catullus, Tibullus, and Propertius sells more than 3,000 copies, a best seller for those times. Also in 1501 he publishes Petrarch in octavo and this is his first book in the vernacular.

Manutius was fully aware of the revolution that he was fomenting. He writes to Marin Sanudo that his portable book makes it possible to read in moments free from political commitments or study obligations, while to the soldier of fortune Bartolomeo d'Alviano (who a few years later will be responsible for Venice's defeat at Agnadello) he suggests carrying small-format books with him during his military campaigns.[28] The concept of reading as a pastime, and not only as study, comes to life; reading for pleasure, a concept five hundred years old, and still in fashion today.

For Aldus, creating new inventions is like eating cherries;

---

[26] Ibid., p. 120.
[27] Barolini, *Aldus and His Dream Book,* op. cit., p. 83.
[28] Infelise, *Manuzio . . . ,* op. cit., p. 241.

one leads to another. And when he prints a geography book by Pietro Bembo, *De Aetna*, in which the cardinal and Venetian humanist describes the impression made on him by the eruption of the Sicilian volcano, he accepts the author's suggestions and uses for the first time the hooked comma along with apostrophes, accents, and semicolons. In 1502 he starts branding his books with the anchor and the dolphin, a symbol he used for the first time (horizontally) in an illustration in the *Poliphilo*, and he even gets involved in binding, adopting the Greek-style binding, olive green Moroccan leather with stylized flowers and geometric figures embossed in gold, which will soon spread across all of northern Italy.

Manutius founds an academy of Greek studies, the Neaccademia, or Aldine Academy, a clever and intelligent way to gain free access to the opinions and judgments of the humanists of the time. This literary circle was active in Venice in 1502. Its by-laws were accidentally brought to light by the undoing of a book binding in the Apostolic Library in the Vatican (it was quite normal to use old sheets of paper for book bindings). The members vowed to speak Greek among themselves and, in case of errors, to pay a fine which went to finance convivial gatherings.[29] Inspired by the confraternity of Cardinal Bessarione in Rome, where Greek was the language of choice, the Aldine circle becomes the fifth academy of the Italian Renaissance, after two in Rome, one in Florence, and another in Naples.[30]

At about that same time Aldus also went through some great changes in his personal life. In 1505, Aldus, at this point in his fifties, marries Maria, a twenty-year-old, the daughter of Andrea Torresani. They will have five children. Prince Alberto Pio invites the couple to Carpi for their honeymoon, but instead of departing with his young wife, Aldus throws himself

[29] Ibid., p. 42.
[30] Barolini, *Aldus and His Dream Book,* op. cit., p. 243.

into his work. He prints Aesop's *Fables* and the *Asolani*, by Pietro Bembo, in two versions: with and without the dedication to Lucrezia Borgia. One year after his wedding Aldus leaves Calle del Pastor and moves to San Paterniàn, sharing a printing shop and a house with his father-in-law.

At this point Aldus takes a break and goes to Milan, Cremona, and Asola in search of manuscripts. But some Mantuan soldiers arrest him by mistake, and he is thrown "into a dark and malodorous prison," and then released thanks to the personal intervention of the president of the Milan Senate, to whom he will dedicate Horatio's *Odes*.[31]

In 1507 he returns to work in the printing shop but not without first forming a new partnership with his father-in-law Torresani and Pierfrancesco Barbarigo, son and grandson of doges (Marco elected in 1485 and Agostino, who succeeded him, in 1486). Pierfrancesco himself becomes a Senator and the Barbarigos, a powerful patrician family, provide the partners with capital and protection at the highest levels.

On October 28th of that same year, Erasmus arrives in Venice to oversee the edition of his *Adagia* (Adages). The Dutch visitor portrays daily life in Aldus's workshop in his *Opulentia sordida,* with Torresani described as a super rich skinflint who "economizes on food by serving delicacies such as mollusks taken from the public latrines, soups made from old crusts of cheese or rotten tripe, and watered-down vinegary wine."[32] Erasmus had contacted Manutius to ask him to print his translation of Euripides because the beauty of the Aldine characters would guarantee him immortality. When the Dutch philosopher comes to Venice, he energetically dedicates himself to the publication of the first edition of the *Adagia*, working every day in Aldus's workshop, checking the

[31] Infelise, *Manuzio* . . . , op. cit., p. 243.
[32] Cited in Lowry, *The World* . . . , op. cit., p. 105.

proofs and correcting the text. It appears that the composition
was done at a rate of three pages a day, and so it took nine
months to complete the job. The volume came out in 1508.[33]

By now we are on the eve of the war between Venice and
the League of Cambrai, and in the darkest years of the conflict
Manutius takes refuge in Ferrara, a guest of Duchess Lucrezia
Borgia. He goes back into business in 1512, and in this period
he devotes considerable energy to printing in Hebrew. He
publishes Pindar and Plato, and with the appearance of the
folio edition of the philosopher's work he completes the task
that he had set for himself: printing all of the most important
Greek classics.[34] The business's recovery is sealed by Greek
editions of the highest quality and the continuation of a line of
Latin classics in octavo. Furthermore, because of the war,
many literati leave Padua (occupied by the imperial army) and
seek refuge in Venice, where they are more than happy to earn
their living by collaborating with Aldus's workshop. One of
these refugees is Marco Musuro, who edits Aldus's editions of
Plato and the Greek rhetoricians.[35]

Proof of Aldus's great success are the many counterfeit versions of his characters. There are some Italians among the coun-
terfeiters, but most are French. Printers in Lyon become rapidly
expert in reproducing the italic types and exact texts of their
models, even down to Aldus's prefaces.[36] Manutius spends time
and money to obtain privileges in Venice and abroad to protect
his own editions, but nothing will be truly effective. "The Lyons
printers," writes Martin Davies in *Aldus Manutius, Printer and
Publisher of Renaissance Venice*, "who never precisely claimed
to be producing Aldines, went on printing in 'Aldine' italic for

[33] Barolini, *Aldus and His Dream* Book, op. cit., p. 141.
[34] Ibid., p. 143.
[35] Infelise, *Manuzio . . .* , op. cit., p. 243.
[36] Martin Davies, *Aldus Manutius, Printer and Publisher of Renaissance Venice*, The British Library, London 1995, p. 46.

the rest of his life, cheerfully aware of the ineffectiveness of privileges, bulls, and warnings coming from the south."[37] Aldus scores his most clamorous own-goal by printing a list of the errors made in the counterfeit editions. His objective it to make the counterfeits easily identifiable, but he doesn't realize that in so doing he is providing his forgers a perfect and authentic manual for correcting their mistakes.

In any event, Manutius has become a star: the prince of printers is now a sought-after celebrity, and he laments his status. In 1514, one year prior to his death, he writes a letter to a friend:

> I am hampered in my work by a thousand interruptions [. . .] Nearly every hour comes a letter from some scholar and if I undertook to reply to them all I should be obliged to devote day and night to scribbling. Then through the day come calls from all kinds of visitors. Some desire merely to give a word of greeting, others want to know what there is new, while the greater number come to my office because they happen to have nothing else to do. "Let us look in upon Aldus," they say to each other. Then they loaf in and chatter to no purpose. But even these people who have no business are not so bad as those who have a poem to offer or something (usually very prosy indeed) which they want to have printed with the name of Aldus. These interruptions are now becoming serious for me; I must take steps to lessen them. Many letters I simply leave unanswered, while to others I send very brief replies; [. . .] I have now put a big notice on the door of my office to the following effect "Whoever you are, you are earnestly requested by Aldus to state the business briefly and to take the departure promptly."[38]

---

[37] Ibid., p. 47.

In January, 1515, Manutius prints his last edition, the *De rerum natura*, by Lucretius. He dies on February 6th, and his coffin his put on view in the church of San Paterniàn, surrounded by piles of books which the deceased had printed. The funeral oration is given by Raffaele Regio, a professor from the University of Padua.

There is no doubt that Manutius changed the European way of learning. "When the protagonist of Thomas More's *Utopia* (1516) wants to teach the Utopians how to print," notes Davies, "it is naturally the Greek books of Aldus that he shows them, symbols of the best that European literature and technology could offer."[39]

In twenty years Aldus Manutius the Elder published 132 books, including seventy-three classics (thirty-four in Latin), eight in the Italian vernacular, twenty contemporary works in Latin, and eighteen scholastic manuals (twelve in Greek). Of the forty-nine first editions in Greek published by all publishers, Aldus alone printed thirty. Apart from the war years 1506-1512, in which he published only eleven books, he managed to publish an average of ten books a year, or almost one a month, at a time when composing was done by plucking characters out of their cases with tweezers (exactly as it was done up until a few decades ago).[40]

Aldus's father-in-law Andrea Torrsani stayed on as head of the print shop until November, 1517, and his son Giovanni Torresani took over from him until 1528. On the death of his father, disagreements among the heirs led to the closing of the print shop. The business was started up again in 1533, by

[38] David Amram, *The Makers of Hebrew Books in Italy,* The Holland Press, London 1963, p. 177.
[39] Davies, *Aldus Manutius,* op. cit. p. 62.
[40] Barolini, *Aldus and His Dream Book,* op. cit. *p. 148.*

Paolo Manutius, who died in 1574, and then it passed into the hands of Aldus Manutius the Younger who died in 1597, bringing an end to the dynasty of printers that changed the history of the book the world over.

3.
THE FIRST TALMUD

Take a Fleming, a German, and a Tunisian, bring each of them to Venice, put them together, and you'll have assembled the greatest concentration of Hebrew book-trade expertise in the first half of the sixteenth century. The encounter of these three minds, so different with respect to geographic and religious origins (a Christian, a converted Jew, and a practicing Jew), made the Serene Republic not only the capital of publishing in general but also the indisputable capital of Hebrew publishing. But in order to understand how it came about that the first printed rabbinical Bible and the first printed Talmud were produced in Venice, it is necessary to understand the long relationship—complicated and discordant, but nonetheless productive—between the Venetian Republic and the Jews.

The world's first Jewish ghetto was "seraglio of the Judeans" instituted on March 29, 1516, in Venice, in the parish of Saint Jerome, in the Cannaregio district. But the Jewish presence in the lagoons dates back to long before that. It seems—though it has not been proved—that Giudecca, an island to the south of Venice, owes its name to the presence of at least one synagogue there in the thirteenth century. It is certain, on the other hand, that the necessity of using a boat to move around the city gave rise to a rabbinical dispute that couldn't be more Venetian: whether or not it is licit to take a gondola on the Sabbath. The seventeenth century dispute made reference to a precedent from 1244, when Rabbi Isaia da Trani had navigated through the canals of Venice on the day when labor of any kind is not permitted. Four centuries later, Rabbi Simone Luzzatto submits that it is licit to use a gondola on the Sabbath, basing his position on the case of Isaia da Trani, but the council of the community rejects his argument on grounds that it is too modernist and venturesome.[1]

In any event, Jews were not allowed to live in the Dominant (as the city was called by Venetians back in the days when it was a capital), but only on the mainland. After 1492, when Ferdinand and Isabelle expel the Jews from the Iberian Peninsula, many of them find refuge in the Venetian state, a relatively tranquil land of asylum. The turning point comes after the Venetians' defeat at Agnadello, in Lombardy (May 14, 1509), when the Serene Republic risks being erased from the map by a coalition of all the major powers of the age untied against it. The Jews flee from the mainland occupied by the imperial and French forces, and large numbers of them take refuge in the Dominant, protected by the safe waters of the lagoon. They take up residence just about everywhere in the city, but fear that their ever more visible presence might provoke resentment, and they ask to be put all together in a safe place. In her study of Venice's relations with the Middle East, Maria Pia Pedani writes, "The model of a separate neighborhood for people of a different nationality and religion had been developed in some Islamic areas and was not considered in a negative way but rather as an element of greater safety for those who lived there."[2] In Constantinople, for example, Genoese Christians live isolated—and under surveillance—in the Galata quarter. Even the Venetian *fondacos*, like the one created in the sixteenth century for the Germanic nation, were modeled on structures where Christian merchants customarily

---

[1] Riccardo Calimani, *Storia del ghetto di Venezia*, Rusconi, Milan 1985, p. 16.
[2] Maria Pia Pedani, *Venezia tra mori, turchi e persiani,* Vicenza 2005, p. 28.

lived in Islamic territories.³ Actually, the *Fondaco dei Tedeschi* existed as early as the thirteenth century; it was the *Fondaco dei Turchi* (for Turkish merchants) that was instituted in the sixteenth century.

The idea of the ghetto, therefore, is an additional refinement to a system that was already well known. The difference—and it's certainly not secondary—is that while the Jews ask to be isolated, they are in fact segregated. In the spring of 1516 the Serene Signory sends the Jews to live in an area completely surrounded by canals and thus easily closed at night, an area previously occupied by foundries for cannons, where the metal for the cannons was *gettata* (cast). Pronounced by German Jews (the first settlers were Ashkenazy) with a hard "g," the Italian *getto*, pronounced jetto, becomes *ghetto*. This is the most accredited etymology of the word destined to become so sadly famous.

As often happens, negative events also have positive outcomes: the Venetian Jews are granted permission to build themselves a place of worship. And in order to pray they need books, and so it is that an event as dire as the birth of history's first ghetto has as an immediate consequence: the flowering of a clamorously successful Hebrew publishing business, which spreads from Venice throughout Europe and the Mediterranean.

> Venice keeps its Jews locked up [. . .] But "the seraglio of the Judeans," symbol of discrimination and segregation [. . .] managed to keep alive and transmit to future generations the entire ethical and cultural heritage which has always distinguished Judaism down through the centuries [. . .] The book [. . .] became, from the earliest tormented years, an essential element of survival for every community.⁴

³ *Ibidem.*
⁴ Umberto Fortis, *Editoria in ebraico a Venezia*, Arsenale, Venice 1991, p . 6.

Among all the large communities of foreigners present in Venice—Greeks, Armenians, Dalmatians, and Jews—visible traces of which remain in the urban fabric of the city today, only the Jewish community has profoundly influenced and modified Venetian society. To be sure, there have been highs and lows in the centuries-old relationship between Venice and its Jews. The periodic reiteration of the requirement to wear a yellow cap indicates that in some periods this imposition was not respected. During the wars against the Turks, the Jews were subjected to harsh crackdowns because they were considered (wrongly) fifth columnists of the Ottoman Empire. This happened particularly during the war over Cyprus, which started during the Battle of Lepanto (October 7, 1571), and ended with Venice losing that large Mediterranean island. That war had been supported, promoted, and fomented by a singular figure, Joseph Nasi, a wealthy Portuguese Jew who, after having passed through Venice and then establishing himself in Constantinople, became an advisor to Sultan Selim II, and vented his hatred for Venice by helping to unleash the full force of the Ottoman Empire against it.

But there are also times when relations between Jews and Christians are good. In the first half of the seventeenth century, Leone da Modena, perhaps the most important Rabbi of Venetian Judaism, attracts many non-Jews to listen to his sermons. A man of his time, he loves gambling and the pleasures of Venus, and so he suffers from no lack of occasions for spending time with Christians. His student Sara Copio Sullam, the "poetess of the ghetto," starts one of the most famous salons in Venice, frequented by Jews and Gentiles, clerics included. The Jews are the first to celebrate the exhilarating victories of Francesco Morosini in Morea (the Peloponnesus) during the war against the Turks in 1684-1699, with enormous demonstrations held in the campo of the Ghetto Nuovo. It is customary for erudite Jews to be called on to compose verses

for weddings between members of illustrious patrician families. Social and cultural interactions of this kind are unknown
elsewhere, except perhaps in Vienna at the beginning of the
twentieth century.

This rarefied atmosphere of sixteenth century Venice is the
setting for William Shakespeare's *The Merchant of Venice*. The
drama of Shylock and Bassanio could not have taken place anywhere else, since Jews were not usually so well woven into the
social fabric. As Riccardo Calimani points out in his study of the
ghetto, "Shylock, the most celebrated Venetian Jew, never
existed. Nevertheless, in his play William Shakespeare transformed him into an elusively symbolic figure portrayed in tragic,
painful, even ruthless hues [. . .]. Shylock, an imaginary but
plausible figure of flesh and blood, hate and vengeance, is
extraordinarily modern."[5] He is a symbol.

Inside the ghetto, there is a differentiation among the various components of Venetian Judaism, with "pledge loans
being the domain of the German 'nation,' and the prosperous
maritime trade run by a nucleus of Sephardic families."[6] Moreover, it is the "Germans" who reactivate religious practice, creating an "incentive toward a cultural and scientific development within the confines of tradition."[7]

This is the context that gives rise to the Hebrew publishing
business, which—contrary to what happened elsewhere—is
not run by Jewish publishers because the Serene Republic prohibited Jews from publishing books. In the exhilarating years
of the boom in Venetian publishing, which soon brings the city
"to the apex of European Hebrew publishing,"[8] there is only
one important Jewish publisher, Meir Parenzo. Despite
repeated attempts, the man who has been called "the greatest

[5] Calimani, *Storia* . . . , op. cit., p. 9.
[6] Fortis, *Editoria* . . . , op. cit., p. 8.
[7] Ibid., p. 30.
[8] Ibid.

Jewish printer of all time,"[9] Gershon Soncino, will never make it to Venice. He will, however, settle for some time inside the Venetian state, in Brescia, where in 1494 he will print a Bible destined to have an enormous role in history, the so-called Berlin Bible, the one used by Martin Luther to create his German translation that will pave the way for the Reformation.

The first to print Hebrew texts in Venice is a Christian from Antwerp, Daniel Bomberg, who will also be the first in the world to publish the Rabbinical Bible and the Talmud. Not that he is welcomed with open arms; he has to struggle to obtain government permission to print in Hebrew and his applications, accompanied by growing offers of money, are rejected again and again. Only on his fifth attempt, and after shelling out some 500 ducats, is he granted a ten-year privilege. Obviously, there is a golden barrier beyond which the religious scruples of the patricians are unable to go and, just as obviously, if Bomberg can afford to spend such a large amount, it means that he expects a considerable return on his investment.[10] In 1515 he sets up a print shop, availing himself of the collaboration of a Jew-turned-friar, Felice da Prato, who makes a request to the Venetian government "to take on as assistants 'four well-instructed Jewish men,' perhaps of foreign provenance, who might enjoy the privilege of donning a black cap."[11] The Fleming's arrival in the lagoon is part of the great migratory flow of printers descending from the German-speaking world to Italy, and another German immigrant, Cornelius Adelkind—before his conversion,[12] Israel ben Baruk—will edit the debut edition of the Talmud.

[9] Ibid.
[10] Horatio Brown, *The Venetian Printing Press 1469-1800*, John C. Nimmo, London 1891, p. 105.
[11] Riccardo Calimani, *Gli editori di libri ebraici a Venezia*, in Abbiati (ed.), *Armeni . . .* , op. cit., p. 57.
[12] Ibid., p. 58.

The first works printed by Bomberg have been lost; they probably did not survive the book burnings of the Inquisition. In 1517 he releases the first edition of the Rabbinical Bible, which also contains the Aramaic tradition and commentary by celebrated Medieval Hebrew exegetes:[13]

> It was edited by the Jewish convert Felice da Prato and dedicated to Pope Leo X. Because of the identity of the editor and the dedication, the Jews refused to recognize the edition and began numbering the Rabbinical Bibles [. . .] from the next one to appear, again in four volumes and again *in folio*, in 1524-25, completely renewed and edited by Yaaqov ben Chayyim, a Jew originally from Tunis.[14]

It is fairly evident that these first examples of printing in Hebrew were not intended primarily for Jews but for Hebrew scholars, whether Jews or Christians. The dedication to Leo X indicates that the readers of Hebrew books were not exclusively Jews, and that interest in Jewish culture was widespread in humanist and religious circles.[15] There is no doubt that the boom in Hebrew publishing is also the result of genuine literary interest on the part of figures extraneous to Judaism[16] who wished to know in their original forms that were fundamental to the development Western culture.

In any event, Chayyim, an expert philologist, takes a different route from that traveled by his convert predecessor, one well grounded in tradition, and undertakes a thorough study of manuscripts. His edition of the Rabbinical Bible is destined to

---

[13] Ibid., p. 57.
[14] Giuliano Tamani, *Edizioni ebraiche veneziane nei secoli XVI-XVII*, in Simonetta Pelusi (ed.), *Le civiltà del libro e la stampa a Venezia*, Il Poligrafo, Padua 2000, p. 30.
[15] Calimani, *Gli editori . . .* , op. cit., p. 57.
[16] Fortis, *Editoria . . .* , op. cit., p. 34.

remain the key reference point for four centuries, at least until the Hebrew Bible is printed in Leipzig in 1913, it is the most widely distributed in the European theological faculties, especially the Protestant ones:[17]

> Whether for the composition of their texts or for the financial investment in their production, the Rabbinical Bibles must be considered among the most important editions printed by Bomberg.[18]

While working on the Rabbinical Bibles, the publisher also has the Talmud in mind. Its publication is supervised by Cornelius Adelkind, who edits the edition of the Babylonian Talmud, which is printed in twelve volumes between 1520 and 1523, while the four volumes of the Jerusalem Talmud roll off the presses between 1522 and 1523. In this case too, Bomberg's edition is memorable "not only for its philological accuracy and the beauty of its characters, but for the layout of its pages";[19] it is destined to serve as a model for subsequent editions.[20] In this brief span of years, the Flemish printer in Venice puts out the first editions of some of Judaism's most fundamental works. But his business is much broader—he works on commission for "numerous communities of the Diaspora of the time: in Rome, Spain, Germany, and Greece, and as far away as Aleppo in Syria."[21] A perfectly conserved copy of the twelve volumes of Bomber's Talmud has been put up for sale by Sotheby's, along with another thirteen thousand rare Hebrew books, at an asking price of 40 million dollars. They

[17] Tamani, *Edizioni. . .* , op. cit., p. 30.
[18] Ibid.
[19] Fortis, *Editoria . . .* , op. cit., p. 39.
[20] Anna Campos, *La cultura ebraica nei libri a Venezia,* in Abbiati (ed.), *Armeni . . .* op. cit., p. 63.
[21] Ibid.

are the volumes of the Valmadonna Trust Library, an unmatch-
able collection assembled over a period of sixty years by Jack
Lunzer, Count of Valmadonna. This gentleman, who was born
in Antwerp to an English father in 1924 and moved to London
as a child, became one of the most important international
traders of industrial diamonds. In the 1950s he begins collecting Hebrew books. In 1956 he learns that Westminster Abbey
conserves, substantially forgotten, the Babylonian Talmud
printed by Bomberg. It is a copy commissioned by Henry VIII
to assist him in evaluating whether he should convert to
Judaism to obtain a divorce. But when the twelve volumes
arrive in London, years later, the sovereign has already founded
the Church of England and no longer has any use for them. He
has already paid for them, however, and so he sends them to the
Abbey where they sleep for several centuries. Lunzer enters
into possession of them twenty-five years later, in the 1970s,
thanks to a trade: he "donates" a nine-centuries-old copy of the
charter of Westminster Abbey in exchange for the Venetian
Talmud. His nephew recounts that the curator of the Abbey's
library, having heard that the charter had been put on the market, greeted the collector saying, "Mr. Lunzer, we've been
expecting you."[22]

But let's return to the sixteenth century, when another important figure makes his entrance into Bomberg's shop, he too is a
German, Eliyyah ben Asher ha-Levi Askenazi, better known
as Elia Levita, who from 1528 to 1549 (with an interruption of
four years) works in the printing shop as "advisor, editor, and
proofreader."[23] Levita flees Rome in 1527, when, during the
sack of the Eternal City carried out by the Lansquenets, he loses
"all of his properties, books and manuscripts, and escapes death

[22] Michael Orbach, *My uncle, the Count of Valmadonna*, "The Jewish
Star," 27 February 2009.
[23] Tamani, *Edizioni* . . . , cit., p. 33.

with his family by seeking refuge in Venice where he will earn a living as a proofreader in Bomberg's printing shop and as a Hebrew teacher for several highly placed Christians."[24] Elia Levita will lend his name to the first published comprehensive grammar of the Hebrew language. Actually, there had already been several previous attempts, even illustrious ones, to print Hebrew grammars, such as the *Introductio per brevis Hebraicum linguam*, almost certainly composed by Gershon Soncino, printed by Aldus Manutius starting in 1501-02 as an appendix to Greek and Latin grammars.[25] The *Massoret ha-Massoret*, "a true and proper classic of Hebrew culture,"[26] is put into print by Elia Levita in 1538. The scholar is the first to establish that the dots used to indicate vowels are not as ancient as the Hebrew alphabet, as was then commonly believed, but an innovation introduced only in the fifth century of the Christian era. For this reason, he has Bomberg print on the inside of the grammar a little hand with a pointing index finger which, as explained in the introduction, is a way of saying, "Look, this is something new."[27] Levita is enthusiastic in describing his employer, calling him "a master printer, an artist without equal in Israel,"[28] and he remains indissolubly tied to him, notwithstanding his own success in becoming the Hebrew teacher for two cardinals: first Egidio da Viterbo and then Domenico Grimani. The second, a Venetian patrician, plays a fundamental role in the history of the book: he has handed down to us what can be considered to the publishing field what the Sistine Chapel is to frescoes: the *Grimani Breviary*. The Breviary is a codex of 832 pages, all decorated, and fifty full-

[24] David Amram, *The Makers of Hebrew Books in Italy*, Holland Press, London 1963, p. 184.
[25] Tamani, *Edizioni . . .* , op. cit., p. 33.
[26] Calimani, *Gli editori . . .* , op. cit., p. 58.
[27] Amram, *the Makers . . .* , op. cit., p. 194.
[28] Ibid., p. 196.

page miniatures painted by Flemish artists. It is certain that the cardinal was its owner in 1520, now the codex of wonders is conserved in the Biblioteca Marciana in Venice.

"The Aldus of Hebrew Books"—as Bomberg came to be called with a clear reference to Manutius, who was already recognized as the greatest of the great—prints more than 180 works in his thirty-two years of activity between 1516 and 1548. He uses excellent-quality paper, with a filigree of an anchor inscribed in a circle crowned by a star, paper yellowed by time but still robust and substantial. David Amran in his study of Hebrew book printing in Italy attests to the quality of the paper when he writes:

> The censors of the Church inked pages in thousands of volumes, but the paper showed itself to be more durable than the ink because the ink has faded while the printed words once cancelled out are now legible again; proof that Domenico Gerosolimitano, Fra' Luigi da Bologna, and Giovanni Domenico Carretto (three of the most zealous censors) lived and inked in vain.[29]

In reality, things don't always work out that way: in the *Mishne Torà* printed by Bomberg in 1525 and conserved in the Renato Maestro Library of the Jewish Community in Venice, numerous pages have lines blacked out by the censors. In some cases, the canceled words are indeed newly legible beneath the time-faded ink, but in others the ink has ruined the paper, putting holes in the pages (the volume has a dedication in Spanish, calling it a precious book all over the world and the most precious in all of Italy: "*Este es un precioso libro que aj en el mundo [. . .] mas precioso libro en toda Italia*").

It is not known exactly why the Flemish publisher retired

[29] Ibid., p. 193.

from the business. His son David keeps publishing for some time but then the characters are sold to other printers. The next figure to follow in his footsteps is Marco Antonio Giustiniani, a Venetian patrician who establishes a printing house at the Rialto, in Calle dei Cinque. He stays in business for seven years, from 1545 to 1552, and, using the Temple of Jerusalem, as his emblem publishes eighty-six editions. The quality is first-rate thanks to his hiring of some of Bomberg's collaborators and his use of characters engraved for him by the most celebrated punch-maker of the time, the Frenchman Guillaume Le Bé, who arrived in Venice in 1545.[30] Le Bé also supplies characters to the only Jewish printer working in those years, Meir Parenzo. Formerly one of Bomberg's proofreaders, Parenzo, using the menorah as his symbol, publishes books on various subjects between 1545 and 1549.

By now we are at the beginning of the end, which arrives on the heels of a dispute—first commercial but then doctrinal—between Giustiniani and another publisher, he too a Christian patrician, Alvise Bragadin (like Bomberg, Bragadin works for the international market and he prints pocket-size prayer books for the Sephardic communities).[31]

The Bragadin printing house makes its debut with an edition of the *Mishne Torà*, by Mosé Maimonide, with commentary by Meir Katzenellenbogen, a German Rabbi who had studied in Prague, and a representative of the Paduan anti-cabalists. At almost the same time and in competition with Bragadin, Giustiniani prints the same codex, obviously without Rabbi Katzenellenbogen's commentary. At this point, Bragadin and Giustiniani lock horns in a furious squabble that soon degenerates into an all out war.[32] The former accuses the latter of unfair

[30] Fortis, *Editori . . .* , op. cit., p. 39.
[31] Tamani, *Edizioni . . .* , op. cit., p. 32.
[32] Calimani, *Gli editori . . .* , op. cit., p. 59.

trade practices in the printing of the Talmud. The rabbi from Prague gets involved in the dispute and calls for help from the highest authorities of the time. Rabbi Moses Isserless from Krakow, after a careful investigation, threatens to ex-communicate all those who had purchased the edition printed by Giustiniani. The first round goes to Bragadin, but his opponent won't take it lying down and appeals to the papal authorities to condemn Bragadin's edition, hoping to get rid of the competition once and for all. If he'd had any idea of the consequences that this move would provoke—shutting down the presses, suspending Hebrew publishing in Venice for the next ten years, and the end of Venice's hegemony in this sector—he almost certainly would have thought better of it.

Things in Rome were changing. The Florentine Pope, Leo X, a member of the Medici family, son of Lorenzo the Magnificent, student of Poliziano, refined and cultivated humanist, protector of Michelangelo, Raffaello, Ariosto, and Machiavelli, with his thoroughly Renaissance interest in Jewish culture, dies in 1521. The Inquisition is now headed by the doctrinaire cardinal from southern Italy, Gian Pietro Carafa, who will go on to sit on the papal throne with the name of Paul IV. He is a rigid and inflexible custodian of orthodoxy, imbued with hatred for the Jews, who makes the struggle against heresy his sole reason for living. In all likelihood, he sees the chance to intervene in the dispute between the two Venetian publishers as a golden opportunity. Giustiniani and Bragadin do their best to provide Carafa with enough rope to hang them. According to Calimani, "Each of the two printers, in his attempt to damage the other, claimed that the work of the other contained elements of blasphemy and propositions that were contrary to the Christian religion,"[33] aided in this effort by the slanderous advice and council of converted Jews. Things go as they were

---

[33] *Ibidem.*

destined to go. In August of 1553 Pope Julius III issues a bull ordering the seizure and burning of Hebrew books; the Vatican's ire is directed particularly at the Talmud and its collection of norms with their relative interpretations, so much so that ten years later, when the tempest had died down, the ostracism of this work will remain and it will be allowed to be printed only on condition that the word "Talmud" not appear on the frontispiece. Meanwhile, in Rome, the enforcers of the Inquisition enter the homes of the Jews, seize and throw into the street everything they can find that's printed. The first burning of the Talmud and Hebrew books takes place in Rome, in the Campo dei Fiori on September 9, 1553, the day of Rosh Hashanah. This time, Venice, which on other occasions had resisted the papal authorities to the point of being issued an interdict (the writ of excommunication for governments), gives in. The Papal Nuncio, Ludovico Beccadelli, from Bologna, does everything he can to sustain the requests of the papal secretariat, and in October the Council of Ten orders that a burning also be held in Venice for the works under indictment. A month after the events in Campo dei Fiori, the fires burn in the lagoon. The Nuncio himself communicates the news on October 21st, practically in real time: "Without prior notice they seized all of the remaining Talmuds of the gentleman's edition, which were then publicly burned at the Rialto, and the copies belonging to Jews were set apart so that this morning a lovely burning was held in St. Mark's Square."[34] By the time of the burning in Venice, Giustiniani, overwhelmed by the unbearable damage inflicted, had already ceased printing for over a year, and in 1553 Bragadin's printing shop closes too, both victims of themselves.

Not until 1563 does the printing of Hebrew books in Venice resume, and in the meantime several smaller cities take

[34] Ibid., p. 60.

advantage of the inactivity in the Serene Republic: Ferrara, Cremona, Mantua, and nearby Sabbioneta, where Cornelius Adelkind moves, and also Riva del Garda, where it is actually the bishop-prince, Cardinal Cristoforo Madruzzo, who supports the Hebrew printing house. But no publisher, despite their appreciable production, ever succeeded in equaling the quality achieved in the lagoon.[35]

When Hebrew publishing finally reappears in Venice, the Counter-Reformation is in full swing and all published volumes—Hebrew and otherwise—are subjected to preventive censorship. Starting in 1564 Pius IV allows the printing of the Talmud, as long as it is censored and as long as the word "Talmud" does not appear on the frontispiece.[36] The government of the Venetian Republic establishes strict controls on the importation of books, and an officer from the Holy Office of the Inquisition works alongside the customs officials to check arriving shipments. The situation becomes even worse during the years of the Ottoman–Venetian War for Cyprus and the Battle of Lepanto (1571). The return of peace and the reactivation of trade with the Ottomans restore an atmosphere of serenity to the lagoon, but the boom years are definitely a thing of the past: "At the end of the sixteenth century the Jews of Venice adopted a sort of self-censorship. Every volume had to contain the approval of the Rabbinate which attested to the absence of any kind of offense with respect to both Judaism and Catholicism."[37]

The seventeenth century is a bleak period for several sectors of Venetian publishing, but the Hebrew sector is an exception. It will remain remarkably lively, thanks largely to Rabbi Leone da Modena, perhaps the most prominent figure

[35] Fortis, *Editoria* . . . , op. cit., p. 42.
[36] Calimani, *Gli editori* . . . , op. cit., p. 61.
[37] Ibid., p. 62.

in the history of Venetian Judaism. The *Haggadot* (liturgical books for Passover) are not a Venetian invention, but it is here that they reach the peak of their sophistication. In 1609 three copiously illustrated linguistically important editions are published: "One for the Spanish rite with the first translation in Ladino in Hebrew characters; one for the German rite with the first translation in Yiddish; and finally one for the Italian rite with the first Italian translation in Hebrew characters."[38] This last *Haggadà* is truly an original because it written in a vernacular Italian crammed with Venetian words, so that it could well be described as Venetian in Hebrew characters, a strange Venetian—Hebrew that will continue to be published throughout the century. The *Haggadot* printed in Serene Republic will be the model for the Livorno *Haggadà* of 1892. The 1640 edition—forty-eight pages and a hundred or so illustrations—has an introduction by Leone da Modena, and the texts are at least partially attributable to him as well. He is also the author of the *Historia de riti hebraici* (History of Hebrew Rites), addressed first and foremost to gentiles, and of the *Novo dittionario hebraico e italiano*, meant primarily for Jews. The genesis of Rabbi Modena's dictionary is interesting. He realizes that translating the entire Bible from Hebrew into Italian would be an arduous and costly enterprise, it would have a difficult time obtaining authorization to be published, and the Church would not look upon it kindly. At the same time, a working knowledge of Hebrew is becoming more and more limited to a small circle of scholars and therefore knowledge of the scriptures in Hebrew is gradually dying out. So the rabbi compiles a dictionary to make the Hebrew Bible more accessible to those whose knowledge of Hebrew is limited. The dictionary is printed in 1612 in an edition that today

---

[38] Tobia Ravà, *L'immagine proibita. L'interdetto visivo nell'arte ebraica*, degree thesis, University of Bologna, 1985-86, p. 177.

would be termed "mass market,"[39] and reaches a sizable readership.

For the entire seventeenth century, however, Hebrew publishing in Venice will remain under surveillance, and this will mean Venice, losing its role as the point of reference for the Diaspora. In the eighteenth century this role will be taken over by Livorno, Amsterdam, and London. The last Hebrew book to be produced by a Venetian press will be printed in 1810.[40]

[39] Giuliano Tamani, *Il Novo dittionario hebraico e italiano di Leon Modena*, in *Studi in onore di Marino Zorzi*, Bertoncello arti grafiche, Cittadella 2008, p. 444.

[40] Giovannina Reinish Sullam, *Il libro ebraico a Venezia*, in *Venezia città del libro*, Venice Isola di San Giorgio Maggiore, 2 September – 7 October 1973, p. 125.

4.
THE LOST KORAN

Venice can be infernally hot in the summer and Thursday, July 2, 1987, happened to be one of those days when the tropical heat makes the air almost unbreathable. Yet even on a scorching hot day like that you can break into a cold sweat. For example, if you put your hands on a copy of the Koran that has been lost for over half a millennium; the first sacred book of Islam printed in Arabic, a work that nobody had set eyes on since the first half of the sixteenth century, and whose very existence had come to be doubted. Less than six months earlier, at a conference of the international association of Arabic studies, it had been labeled "a legend without any documented basis."

But that book exists and it is now in the hands of a young Italian scholar, Angela Nuovo. At the time she is thirty years old, tall, slender, chestnut hair, and hazel eyes. She works in one of Italy's oldest and most prestigious libraries, the Braidense, in Milan, and she is following the tracks left by Alessandro Paganini, the Renaissance printer who is the subject of her research. An interesting figure Paganini. A printer son of a printer father—his father, Paganino, moved to Venice from Tuscolano, on the western shore of Lake Garda, where the family owns a paper mill—he distinguishes himself as a publisher who is "enterprising, innovative, the inventor of the 'twenty-fourmo' format, exceptionally skilled in the composition of characters," says Angela Nuovo, today a professor of the History of the Book at the University of

Udine. Featuring the elegant characters of Alessandro Paganini, one of the most celebrated books of the Italian Renaissance was printed in Venice, the *De divina proportione*, by Luca Pacioli, with figures of solids conceived by Leonardo da Vinci and his Vitruvian man destined to become an icon (immortalized on the Italian one-euro coin). Paganini is also the publisher of the *Baldus*, by Teofilo Folengo, an extremely amusing satirical poem in broken Latin, published in seventeen cantos in 1517, and today unjustly forgotten.

The young scholar Nuovo knows that a rare book made by this printer is conserved in the library of the monastery on the cemetery island of San Michele, in Venice. A few words about this place are in order. Founded in the Napoleonic period with the unification of two islands—San Michele and San Cristoforo della Pace—it is the resting place of the American poet Ezra Pound and the Russian composer Igor Stravinski. But the Benedictine monastery of San Michele is much older. The church, built entirely of Istrian stone and thus completely white, is one of the most beautiful creations of the Renaissance architect Mauro Codussi.

Before the monastery was suppressed under Napoleon, its library contained more than 40,000 volumes and 2,300 manuscripts. Some of the works were enormously valuable, for example those of Fra' Mauro da Venezia, the celebrated cartographer who worked in the monastery and died there in 1459. A large part of the library's holdings were transferred to the national Marciana library in Saint Mark's Square. In 1829, after the Napoleonic tempest had passed, custody of the monastery, by now empty, was assigned to the Franciscans so they could keep watch over the cemetery, and the friars instituted a new library. The suppressions of 1866, when Venetia became part of the unified Kingdom of Italy, left the monastery and library unscathed because it was believed that everything of value conserved there had already been taken, and that all that remained were the "books for priests" that were disdained by the new, liberal, anti-clerical Italy.

Today the church and the monastery are empty once again. The friars have gone, as have the books, which, since the summer of 2008, are conserved far away, in the brand new Franciscan library of San Francesco della Vigna, on the other side of the branch of the lagoon that separates San Michele from Venice. In 1987, when Angela Nuovo went there, the library had for decades been under the direction of Vittorio Meneghin (1908-1993) a little old dried-up friar who had become a sort of institutional figure in the monastery. Cultivated, a profound cognoscente of the books in his custody, Meneghin, and he is originally from Fener, a town in the hinterlands, at the bottom of the Alpine foothills, on the shores of the Piave, the river where the Italians held out against the Austrians in the First World War (a curious coincidence that the same town is the birthplace of another Meneghin, Dino, who became the greatest Italian basketball player of all time, winner of the silver medal at the Moscow Olympics of 1980). It was Fra Vittorio, half a century before, who completed and updated the library catalogue.

He is also the one who keeps the library rigorously closed; he doesn't want anyone to pass its threshold. Giorgio Montecchi, professor of Bibliography and Library Science then in Venice now in Milan, recalls, "It was a library completely unknown to scholars. And those of us who knew it existed were absolutely convinced that there was nothing of interest there because most of the old holdings had been transferred to the Marciana. Meanwhile, however, the Ministry of Cultural Heritage produced a catalogue of sixteenth century books according to which right there within those walls was conserved one of the two extant copies in the world of a spiritual exercise by Antonio da Atri, published by Alessandro

Paganini in 1514. The other copy is in Spain, in Seville, but Montecchi has not been able to see it because whenever he goes there he finds the Columbine library closed. Montecchi wants to examine that volume and so does his student Angela Nuovo, because she is doing her research on Paganini. But they have to overcome a seemingly insurmountable obstacle: Father Vittorio Meneghin, who doesn't want any intruders among his books. As often happens, pure chance intervenes to resolve the situation. The director of the main library of the University of Venice, Anna Ravalli Modoni, is one of Fra Vittorio's penitents, and so she becomes the intermediary, arranging an appointment between the two scholars and the librarian-priest.

The Franciscan doesn't want to admit anyone to the library because he's afraid that the city administration will take his books away from him. As will later come to light, not all of the monastery's ancient collection had been delivered to the new library; there are still numerous manuscripts that had been hidden and had never left the island. Moreover, one room in the library hosts several thousand volumes, maybe as many as 5,000, some of them ancient, most from the first half of the ninth century, all marked with the stamp "Commune of Venice." In all likelihood this is an old collection that the municipality had deposited at San Michele and then completely forgotten. The man of faith will be somewhat consoled when the man of science explains to him that the city wouldn't have any idea where to put those books and that, in any case, after all that time, their ownership had long ago passed to the Franciscans by virtue of adverse possession.

On that dog-day morning of July 2nd, Professor Montecchi has to preside over exams at the university so he and Anna Nuovo don't board the *vaporetto* (a sort of water bus, for those who don't know Venice) until early afternoon, and they get off at the San Michele stop together with a considerable number of elderly women on their way to visit the graves of their dead husbands. As the Venetian widows proceed through the cloister to the various burial grounds of the cemetery, Angela and the professor slip into a door on the left side and come out on the other side in the cool air guaranteed by the thick walls of the monastery. The volume they had requested is there waiting for them.

After examining the book printed by Paganini, the young scholar asks the librarian if she can take a look at the catalogue that he wrote at the typewriter some fifty years earlier. This is before the Internet, and the only way to find out what is kept on the shelves, particularly in small libraries like this one, is to consult the on-site list of book conserved there. Something that Angela Nuovo does with great care as Professor Montecchi chats with the friar, partly to distract him from his jealousy for this intrusion among his books, and partly because he is a real expert from whom they can learn some interesting things. Angela Nuovo's glance happens to fall on a *Alcoranus arabicus sine anno*, and she asks to examine it. But it has to be located and brought out, and because she's a woman she's not allowed to enter the cloister. Father Vittorino goes, accompanied by Professor Montecchi. The library stacks are one floor up. One room conserves the books belonging to the city and the books that Fra Vittorio fears will be taken from him; the other room houses the older and more precious volumes. An old photo shows that it's not a particularly large room, with its walls partly covered with volumes and paintings, with two windows on one side. At the center sits a large lectern. It's from one of the shelves in this second room that the Koran emerges. The professor knows a book from the sixteenth century when he sees one, and this book definitely dates from that century. "I recall that from the window you could see the cemetery, and I was being given a book that was coming back to life," Montecchi observes. Then he goes downstairs, following the priest, and when he sees his student in the parlor he gives her a sign of triumph.

Now the book passes into the hands of Angela Nuovo. She opens it, looks at it, reads the note of possession, and recognizes it immediately. "Even though it was ninety degrees that day, I felt a chill," she recalls. She turns to face the professor and confirms: "This is it." He maintains a bit of academic incredulity. "Are you sure?" But she has no doubt. "Yes."

Among the few things that were known about this lost Koran is that it was owned by a Renaissance-era expert of Eastern languages, Teseo Ambrogio degli Albonesi (1469-1540), from Pavia. And the copy of *Alcoranus arabicus* conserved on the island of San Michele bore the signature of Teseo Albonesi. "I knew other works from his library in Pavia, dispersed after the death of the owner," Nuovo says, "and the handwriting was the same. Besides, the note of possession dated the book, because the man died in 1540." Those were the years during which the presumed Koran could have been printed (not after 1538, because in that year the publishing business of Alessandro Paganini was interrupted).

"She's the one who found it, I just did a lot of talking; she found it in the catalogue. Every rediscovery of a book is a question of recognition, and she recognized it," Giorgio Montecchi still concedes today. Meanwhile, the woman, radiant with joy, announces her discovery to Father Meneghin (happy, yes, but also amazed, poor man, which is understandable; he had been the custodian of that book for over fifty years without ever realizing what it was), and he calls his confreres, who crowd around to look at the volume. "This Koran has many fathers and one mother," Angela Nuovo recalls having commented at the time (the monks were none too happy that a young woman had arrived from outside and the day she set foot in their house she had discovered a treasure that they had never realized they had). That evening, to celebrate the find, Professor Montecchi takes his student to dinner at a restaurant in Venice. "It was really a lovely evening," he affirms, and recalls having run into a colleague that night who sometime later would say to him, "But what were you so happy about walking down the street that night with that young woman?"

The next note of possession in the lost Koran, after the one by Albonesi, is by Father Mancasula de Asula, vicar of the Holy Office of the Inquisition in Cremona (Angela Nuovo was born in Cremona, just to add one more coincidence) and later the Inquisitor General in Como. In all probability the *nihil obstat* of the Inquisition was issued because the Koran was not considered a dangerous book. Nobody would have been able to read it unless they knew Arabic. Besides that, in the early period of the Counter-Reformation the Inquisition was not as strict as it became later on.

After that: nothing. The volume is swallowed up by the shadowy recesses of history until it shows up again in the hands of the young Angela Nuovo. "A book that for centuries was believed to have been lost, about whose fate the most complex hypotheses were fabricated, haunted by an aura of mysterious—and not always benevolent—legend: the Koran printed in Venice for the first time in Arabic, one of the most fascinating unanswered questions in Renaissance bibliography, as well as a fundamental moment in East-West relations, reappears today, in an excellent state of conservation in the very city where it was printed exactly 450 years ago," she writes in her article announcing the rediscovery of the lost volume.[1]

"There couldn't have been very many publishers capable of printing the Koran," Professor Nuovo observes, "and after it was rediscovered all of the testimony of those who had seen it converged in support of its authenticity. The most important

[1] Angela Nuovo, *Il Corano arabo ritrovato*, "La Bibliofilia," LXXXIX (1987), disp. III, September-December, p. 237.

was that of Albonesi who spoke of "an Arabic Koran printed in Venice." In that period there was a growing interest in Middle Eastern languages. Albonesi knew Hebrew, Syriac, Arabic, Armenian, and Ethiopian, and he had published an *Introductio* to various oriental idioms, some real, others much less so, such as the "language of the devil," about which one wonders if he had ever heard it spoken. It is therefore possible that he happened to be in Venice (at that time an Eastern port and thus an essential location for anyone interested in such studies) when the Koran was printed and that he procured a copy to take back to Pavia. Probably the only copy present in Italy and perhaps even in Europe, seeing as no other Orientalist will ever mention it.

So the book went to Cremona and then disappeared. What is thought to have happened to it we will see in a moment. For now, we will limit ourselves to reconstructing the events leading to its rediscovery. The Koran, by way of an itinerary absolutely unknown to us, arrives in Cèneda—a town north of Venice and known today as Vittorio Veneto—the birthplace of Mozart's librettist, the Jew Emanuele Conegliano, better known as Lorenzo Da Ponte, his baptismal name—as well as the place of origin of the wooden interior synagogue walls on exhibition today in the Museum of Jerusalem. Here the book remains, for how much time we do not know, in a monastery that is also a victim of the Napoleonic suppressions. Nevertheless, here too the friars try to save the most precious volumes; they leave them on the shelves to "take some air," as they say, or they move the books to places where they know the functionaries of the state won't go (the functionaries announced their visits, so it was well known when and where they would show up.) In this case, the library's collection ends up in the bishop's seminary, not subject to expropriation by the state, on the condition that it would be given to the first Franciscan monastery to reopen. When the Franciscans are called to take care of the cemetery in Venice, the group of books that includes the Koran makes its way to San Michele Island.

The reason nobody ever realized how important the book was, despite its being regularly catalogued and conserved in a library, is quite simple: nobody knew how to read it. "In the span of five centuries, whoever saw it did not realize what it was and the many who held it in hand did not destroy it," Nuovo observes, recalling a period of history in which book burnings were not unusual.

Paganini's Koran is completely in Arabic. There is no date or place given for the printing; there is no text in Latin except a few translation notes written by Albonesi, which perhaps made it possible to catalogue it as the Koran. In all of Europe at that time scholars, with a knowledge of Arabic may have numbered ten; as far as its various owners knew, the book could have been a copy of *A Thousand and One Nights*. Ignorance often destroys, but in certain cases it saves. In order to identify the book you had to know where to look. Angela Nuovo knew where to look; the others didn't. That's all there is too it. But discoveries always come about a little by chance, and a little by luck, and that's exactly what happened here. They were looking for A, what they found was B, and B turned out to be of inestimable value.

By rediscovering the world's first printed Koran, Angela Nuovo became for bibliography what Howard Carter and Lord Carnarvon, the discoverers of the tomb of Tutankhamen, were for Egyptology. "I realized that the discovery was going to change my life. I was a librarian but I had chosen to do research, and the event was decisive for my career. It is rare today for such clamorous discoveries to be made in this field." And thanks to what happened in that torrid early afternoon in July, the young researcher would become a university professor and her fame would reverberate far beyond Italy's frontiers.

But Angela Nuovo doesn't let her newfound fame go to her head, and she does what a scholar would be expected to do. "I carefully examined the Koran and took notes; everything pointed to the first half of the sixteenth century, even without the deciding factor, the name of Albonesi. An article had to be written immediately." Discoveries have to be claimed in order for their maternity to be recognized.

The young researcher goes back to Milan, but then she returns to Venice to conduct a meticulous examination of "her" Koran. She photographs it because writing about it is not enough; the proof has to be displayed. There is a real danger, if the news leaks somebody may try to steal the merit from those who actually made the discovery. "I immediately phoned Luigi Balsamo, editor of the professional journal *La Bibliophilia*, so he would keep some pages free in the September issue to publish the results of the discovery right away," Montecchi recalls.

At this point, however, they had to think of how to safeguard the volume. "As long as nobody knew what it was it had no value, but once it was known, it would become precious," Montecchi notes.

The publication of the news of the discovery immediately provokes the inevitable explosion of academic envy. Angela Nuovo becomes the object of snubs and slights that she doesn't like to recall; it's Giorgio Montecchi who comments, hissing, "the academic world is sexist." Professor Nuovo prefers to highlight those who congratulated her, for example the most important Italian Arabist of the time, Francesco Gabrieli, president of the Lyncean Academy in Rome, who writes her a letter. Or Giorgio Vercellin, now deceased, professor of Afghan language and literature in Venice, who had been searching for that Koran for years and had been the first to intuit that its discovery would depend on a combined effort of Arabists and library scientists. At that time Vercellin had no students because

Afghanistan had been occupied by the Soviet Union, and nobody ventured to study its language and literature, so he could devote himself to studies of a different nature; finding the lost Koran had become almost an obsession for him.

News of the discovery echos throughout the academic world of bibliography and Arab Studies but more so abroad than in Italy. Angela Nuovo goes to Paris, to the *Institut du monde arabe*, then recently inaugurated by President François Mitterrand. Within a few months she is invited by all the institutes of Arab Studies and all their publications cite her. The Italian media, on the other hand, devote very little space to the discovery, even though the episode could be claimed as a source of national pride: the first printed Koran was published in Italy, conserved in Italy, and rediscovered in Italy by an Italian. If the episode had happened in any other country the news would have been blasted on the airwaves, but in Italy it's already something that the discovery is the subject of an article in a Catholic weekly, *Famiglia Cristiana*, always attentive to an inter-religious dialogue, with a short sidebar published in June of 1988, and by a daily, *il Giornale*, with an article by a professor of Arab Studies, Sergio Noja, on March 3, 1989, almost two years after the discovery. "The first Koran in Arabic, an enterprise that, frankly speaking, must be considered superb," he comments.[2]

"In the West there hasn't been a whole lot of interest," confirms Giorgio Montecchi, "the printing and rediscovery of the Koran has always interested a niche audience. It has not, like the printing of the Gutenberg Bible or the editions of Aldus Manutius. That the first Koran was printed in Venice is something almost nobody knows. Yet it is the highest achievement of Venetian printing."

From that moment on, however, the first edition of the

---

[2] Sergio Noja, *Il Corano che riappare*, "il Giornale," 3 March 1989, p. 3.

Koran becomes a sort of star among scholars, exhibited in shows, the object of lectures at conferences, and in 2008 a team from the BBC arrives in Venice to shoot a documentary. In the Islamic world the news echoes widely. An Arabic translation of the article by Angela Nuovo is published in Tunisia; there are contacts with the Aga Khan Foundation and with a university in Saudi Arabia. Sometimes, however, these contacts don't lead to anything. "In the Arab world, the fact that the discovery was made by a woman doesn't go down easily, Professor Nuovo observes. Every now and again someone makes the journey from some Arab country to see the book. In the registry of visitors to the library of San Francesco della Vigna there is a recent signature by a Sheik from Oman, and a while ago a member of the Saudi royal family came to see it.

Today the task of keeping watch over the first printed Koran has fallen to Father Rino Sgarbossa. In 2008, the book has left the old monastery on San Michele Island to rest on a shelf of the brand new library of San Francesco della Vigna, which also houses another remarkable book: the third edition (1525) of the Hebrew Bible in manual form, or without commentary. A Christian monastery that conserves a treasure of Islam and a treasure of Judaism at a distance of thirty feet or so, in the only city where in past centuries the three religions were able to come together without it leading to a bloodbath: Venice.

Father Rino is a modern Franciscan. Sure, he wears the standard-issue sandals, but they are anatomically designed shoes with a Velcro latch; he's dressed in black, but with a polo shirt and shorts with hip pockets. He's the one who pulls the Koran off the shelf and brings it to visitors. The book is kept inside a cardboard box that protects it from sunlight and dust (at San Michele, when it was an unknown book, it was kept standing on the shelves in between some other volumes. It's not very big; its format is about the size of a regular sheet of letter paper. Its binding, in simple smooth parchment, looks eighteenth century, and its pages have probably been trimmed to make them exactly the same size as the binding, thus reducing the borders that Alessandro Paganini may have meant to host richly decorative illuminations. *"Alcoranus arabicus sine anno"* is written in Latin on the spine; its collocation number is "Rari—A V. 22." On the inside someone has noted, in pencil, the number of pages: 464. "It's a very beautiful book," says Angela Nuovo, and looking at it one cannot help but agree. The paper is very thick, the characters sharp and precise, with no smudges, the lines are straight. Its state of conservation is also excellent. There are some traces of humidity on the outermost pages but the inside is perfect: no marks, no dirt, it looks like it came off the presses just a few days ago. Every now and again, in sepia-colored ink, there are some handwritten annotations made by Teseo degli Albonesi, the man to whom we owe this treasure—a son of the Renaissance who unknowingly saved for future generations a book that is also a symbol of how religions can engage in dialogue, if they want to.

When all is said and done, the story of the Islamic holy book printed in Venice is the tale of an attempt—unsuccessful—to pull off a business proposition that seemed absurd and potentially colossal. Whether the book conserved in San Francesco della Vigna is the only surviving copy of a lost edition, as Angela Nuovo maintains, or the trial edition of a book that was never published, as submitted by Mahmoud Salem Elsheikh, the Egyptian former professor of Arabic Studies in Florence, makes little difference. A Venetian publisher had come up with the idea of printing the Koran and distributing it in the territories of the Ottoman Empire. If his project had succeeded he would have become fabulously wealthy, but instead it went badly and he went bankrupt. In 1538, the year his Koran was published, Alessandro Paganini went out of business. As Angela Nuovo elegantly puts it: "The story of this

Arabic Koran is the thoroughly Venetian story of a sector, the printing business, that was productive, ingenious, intensely dynamic, inasmuch as it was driven by unbridled competition [. . .]. Imagine the huge business potential represented by such a numerous and profoundly religious readership. And that explains how, with its geographical position and its history, Venice was the only place where such an enterprise could have been undertaken."[3] In any event, Paganini's crash makes so much noise that none of his contemporaries or their immediate successors in Venice or anywhere else will ever again think about publishing the Koran. The whole adventure is never mentioned in the correspondence of printers that has been handed down to us, and only many decades later, at the end of the sixteenth century, will the Medici printing houses in Florence again print in Arabic. But in this case it's a totally different operation, financed by the Church. The Medici presses will print the Gospels aimed at a readership of Arabic-speaking Christians.

The idea that the peoples of the East constituted a potentially vast virgin market must have occurred to someone else in Venice, because as early as 1498 a man named Democrito Terracina asks for a twenty-five-year privilege to print "works in the Arab, Syrian, Armenian, Indian, and Barbary languages."[4] But he doesn't put his idea into practice and doesn't print anything. His children will renew the privilege but they won't make use of it either. The expiry date is fixed as 1538, not coincidentally the same year that our Koran was published.

Anyway, Venetian printers are accustomed to dealing with alphabets that are decidedly exotic. In 1515 Giorgio Rusconi publishes a missal in Cyrillic characters addressed to the

[3] Nuovo, *Il Corano* . . . , op. cit., p. 253.
[4] Ibid.

Orthodox faithful in the area around Ragusa (now Dubrovnik), which is actually a Catholic city. His daughter Daria marries Alessandro Paganini, probably including in her dowry the technical expertise necessary to help him carry out such difficult tasks. But publishing books in Cyrillic—or in Armenian, Glagolitic, or Greek—is probably child's play compared with the effort necessary to print in Arabic. "Printing in Arabic characters presented problems much more challenging than printing in Cyrillic [. . .] There exist great difficulties in the joining of letters in as much as they have different forms depending on their position and ligature."[5]

The first Arabic words to appear in a printed book are the ones inserted by Bernhard von Breydenbach in his *Peregrinatio in Terram Sanctam*, printed in Mainz in 1486, and by Aldus Manutius in his *Polifilus* in 1499. But in both cases the words appear in woodcuts and not in movable type. The first typographical text in Arabic comes off the presses fifteen years later, in 1514, and it is the *Kitab salat al-sawa'i* or *Horologium breve*, a holy book addressed to Christian populations in the Middle East. The printing is done in Fano, in the Marches, better the territory of the Papal State, probably to get around the privilege granted to Terracina and heirs, which impedes using this type of character inside the borders of the Serene Republic. The typographer from the Marches who prints the *Horologium*, Gregorio de' Gregori, has a Venetian partner who is none other than Paganino Paganini.

It is quite evident, therefore, that the Paganinis' printing house had already developed the basic skills and knowledge necessary to undertake the enterprise of printing the Koran, "whose audacity is striking even today, so much so that it appears to have been conceived by a mind so thoroughly entre-

[5] Ibid., p. 256.

preneurial and with such a high propensity for risk as to bor-
der on the bizarre."[6] Additionally, the Paganinis have at their
disposal the raw material, in so far as they produced and sold
paper, the prestigious paper of Toscolano on Lake Garda, in
high demand in the Arab-Turkish market, and they were thus
able to trade in printed paper together for white paper without
additional costs.[7]

The capital invested must have been remarkable. The
engraving of the characters probably took years and no doubt
required at least one Arab compositor and an Arab proofreader, which there was no shortage of in Venice. Besides, this
was a book of remarkable quality, printed on quality paper and
from characters executed with refined engraving. The size of
the necessary investment convinces Elsheikh that there must
have been a customer, still unknown, who commissioned the
work. In any case, Alessandro's printing shop rolled out 232
sheets of paper printed in Arabic, which ended up in the hands
of the first owner of the volume, Albonesi. It is highly likely
that the Koran served him for his studies and he presumably
bought it during a visit to Venice—or had it sent to him—once
he had learned that a printer was in the process of printing it.
It is certain that the copy once owned by him is the only extant
copy in Europe. It is nevertheless possible that there are some
surviving copies dispersed in libraries in the Islamic world,
though searches have not turned up anything yet. Anyway,
thanks to Albonesi we are able to identify and date this copy of
the Koran. It is he who makes it possible to attribute its publication to Alessandro Paganini by explaining that, sometime
later, on behalf of the Parisian printer Guillaume Postel, he
intended to buy the characters that had been used to print the
book but could not conclude the deal because the characters

[6] Ibid., p. 258.
[7] Nuovo, *Il commercio* . . . , op. cit., p. 49.

had been lost. And it is Postel who indicates the place and year of the edition, by writing in a letter to the Flemish Orientalist Andrea Meas, dated March 4, 1568, that the Koran had been published thirty years earlier in Venice. Angela Nuovo has established that the publication took place between August 9, 1537, and August 9, 1538. The year 1538 is also the year of the death of Paganino Paganini and of the end of his son Alessandro's printing business.

What happened to that Koran remains a mystery about which all we have are hypotheses. "The edition was already lost as early as the seventeenth, century, and no catalogue, ancient or modern, conserves any memory of it," writes scholar Aleramo Hermet.[8] A German font from the second half of the seventeenth century, and so not verifiable, confirms that the printed copies and characters had been sent by ship to Constantinople. In fact, it was common practice for printers to open printing shops in cities that didn't have one and to ingratiate themselves with the local sovereign by making him presents of rich volumes, showing him already published books, and demonstrating their capacity to produce large numbers of copies. In exchange for their willingness to establish themselves in the chosen place, the printers asked for a privilege that the sovereigns were happy to grant because the production of books was a prestigious activity that could benefit their image as well as the finances of the territory under their rule. It is possible, therefore, that the Paganinis had decided to replicate on a grand scale what their colleagues had done in the various states into which Italy was divided. But their calculations were egregiously wrong. Their attempt is a total flop. The Sultan, according to the same late German source, considers their book the work of the devil, a blasphemy of the infidels,

[8] Nuovo, *Il Corano* . . . , op. cit., p. 240.

and so he orders that the ship, with the printed copies of the book and the characters used to print them, be accompanied out of the port and scuttled in deep waters.

Whether this version is true or not, or alternatively that the copy conserved in San Francesco della Vigna is only the trial run of an enterprise that was later abandoned, the fact remains that with Alessandro Paganini's exit from Venetian publishing there is no further trace of this book. In 1620, in his work *Rudimenta linguae arabicae*, Thomas van Erpe (Thomas Erpinius, a Dutch Orientalist) writes about an Arabic Koran published in Venice around 1530, all the copies of which had been burned.[9] There's certainly nothing out of the ordinary about a Protestant attributing the disappearance of the Koran to the papal fires at the height of the Counter-Reformation, when book burning was in full force. But that's not how things went. The vicar's stamp of approval clearly disproves this hypothesis; moreover, the Church had no reason to fear a book that nobody could read. It is Hermet who points out that "any modern historian cannot fail to see the absurdity of the thesis regarding the pontifical destruction of the book, considering that in 1547 a vernacular version of the Koran was printed in Venice by Andrea Arrivabene and no pope ever ordered its destruction (despite the much more serious threat represented by a vernacular text that everyone would be able to read) and numerous copies of it are still conserved today."[10] This vernacular Koran was "a work whose distribution was not insignificant since copies of it have been found just about everywhere in Europe and the Levant."[11] Finally, in 1543 a Latin edition of the Koran was published in Basel.

[9] Ibid., p. 244.
[10] Ibid., p. 52.
[11] Giorgio Vercellin, *Venezia e le origini della stampa a caratteri arabi*, in Simonetta Pelusi (ed.) *Le civiltà del libro e la stampa a Venezia*, Ill Poligrafo, Padua 2000, p. 58.

Nevertheless, the legend persisted, and in 1692 the German historian Wilhelm Ernst Tentzel espouses the thesis of the pontifical book burning, asserting that God does not permit printing the Koran in Arabic and anyone who dares to do it will meet with a premature death (supported by the fact that Paganini the elder, though he didn't die on the spot, passed away after publishing the work). Repeated lies often become the accepted truth. The Protestants insist so strongly on the story of the papal burning of the Arabic Koran that Catholics end up sustaining the same argument. At the beginning of the nineteenth century, a scholar from Parma, Giovanni Bernardo De Rossi, repeats the myth, which is presented again at the end of the century by the Scottish historian, Horatio Brown ("an Arabic Koran published by Paganini in 1530")[12], but then silence reigns until 1941, when the Orientalist archaeologist Ugo Monneret de Villard is the first to declare "its destruction by order of the pope is totally void of supporting documentation and therefore unreliable."[13] Just three years before its fortunate and fortuitous rediscovery, a specialist in Arabic printing, Geoffrey Roper, speaks of "the mysterious Venetian Koran of which not even one copy survives,"[14] and there were also those who denied that the Venetian Koran ever existed.

Now let's return to the Paganinis and the Koran. It seems fairly clear that theirs was a commercial rather than a cultural enterprise, that they were thinking only of export directed to "the peoples of Islamic religion who still did not have typographical printing."[15] If they had been interested in the narrow market of European Orientalists, they would have produced a polyglot edition, as was then the custom. Instead their book

[12] Horatio Brown, *The Venetian Printing Press 1469-1800*, John C. Nimmo, London 1891, p. 107.
[13] Nuovo, *Il Corano . . .* , op. cit., p. 249.
[14] Ibid., p. 250.
[15] Ibid., p. 253.

has not a single printed word that is not in Arabic and thus sharply distinguishes itself from other books in this period printed with Arabic characters whose purchasers "remained absolutely within the Christian and European market. Moreover, there was no intention of exporting them in lands where Arabic was widely used. Nor, obviously, could they have been directed to Islamic customers living in Europe."[16]

In short, the Koran did not disappear, it simply was not circulated in Europe.[17] Alternatively, according to the thesis of Elsheikh, it was not printed and never got beyond proofs. Giorgio Vercellin, an Islamic expert who died in 2007, seems to favor the thesis of the lost book, calling it "a splendid *in folio*, having miraculously survived an as of yet uncertain fate, which led to the disappearance of all the other printed copies."[18] In any event, what the Paganinis fail to grasp is that their commercial enterprise could never be successful because it is woefully premature. At that time the binomial Koran-copyist is still indissoluble. The holy book of Islam must be written by hand by an expert Islamic scribe, who is held accountable for any errors that may occur during the copying, "one error was enough to risk being decapitated," Elsheikh confirms. It's true that the pages of the Paganini edition of the Koran have ample white margins, meant in all likelihood to be decorated by hand, but it is also true that "Muslims demonstrated then, and later—until the eighteenth century—a great aversion to printing [. . .] For the Arabs the handwritten word was a vehicle of cultural unity, as well as an artistic and spiritual aesthetic sense."[19] Therefore, printing with movable characters standardized "in an unacceptable manner the harmonious fluidity of handwriting,"[20] which is

---

[16] Vercellin, *Venezia* . . . , op.cit., p. 57.
[17] Nuovo, *Il Corano* . . . , op. cit. p. 253.
[18] Vercellin, *Venezia* . . . , op. cit., p. 57.
[19] Nuovo, *Ill Corano* . . . , op.cit., p. 261.
[20] Ibid.

a form of religious art: for Muslims classical Arabic is the language of God.

Arabic characters are printed in the Islamic world for the first time in 1706. But yet again this technical innovation is the work of a non-Muslim who wishes to publish non-Islamic texts. In fact, in those years the Melchite patriarch of Aleppo, Athanasios III al-Dabbas, uses Arabic characters in the Syrian city to print Christian devotional works.[21] It will take another couple of decades, until 1727, before the Ottoman sultan Ahmed III authorizes printing in Arabic (explicitly excluding sacred texts). The presses produce grammars and history and geography texts. In Constantinople, Ibrahim Müteferriqa publishes a two-volume Arabic-Turkish dictionary.

The other factor that makes the Koran printed by Paganini intolerable is the huge number of errors. We have seen that a single imprecision could cost the scribe his head, yet here we have a volume with scarcely a single page printed correctly. "There is not a word without errors," Elsheikh emphasizes, "the distinction between the similar forms of the Arabic language is completely ignored. The compositor does not recognize the letters of the alphabet." A compositor who must have copied the words from an unknown original,which must necessarily have been error-free.

Angela Nuovo points out that the elevated technical investment was not matched by a careful checking of the text, and she reports the opinions of some Arabists, that the text is riddled with errors typically made by Jews who speak Arabic. The Paganinis, therefore, evidently looked for compositors and proofreaders among the flourishing world of Hebrew publishing at the time rather than in the long-established Muslim community in Venice. Elsheik does not agree. "That hypothesis just doesn't hold up. In Venice there were all the Arabs you could

---

[21] Vercellin, *Venezia . . .,* op. cit., p. 58.

want. The city is full of beautiful manuscript versions of the Koran." And so? The 1538 Koran doesn't only contain errors that we might call orthographical (for example, a letter that should be written with three dots is written with two),—there are also errors that amount to outright blasphemy, such as the omission of the name of God. "Certainly, there was a lack of copyists and writers," Angela Nuovo declares, "unlike what happened for the Greeks close to Aldus Manutius; in this case they had to make do with what they had."

What makes Mahmoud Salem Elsheikh believe that the Koran conserved in Venice is a proof and not a surviving copy of a print run is the presence of an error in only one of two repeated pages. This requires a brief explanation. Every edition of the Koran begins in the same way: the first page is a frontispiece and the second begins the text with the four verses of the so-called Sura of the Cow. This is followed by the other Sure, for a total of 114, but in this case Albonesi counts 115. It's not that there is an extra Sura; rather, the last page of the book printed by Paganini simply repeats the second page, the Sura of the Cow. In the first Sura of the Cow there is an error that has been corrected in the second, but in the second there is another error which is not present in the first. In Elsheikh's opinion, this proves that there was another printing form for the corrected version of the same page. "It's clear that somebody tried, but the rest of the picture is totally obscure," observes the Egyptian professor, "we don't know if the operation was blocked by the customer who financed it, by a consultant, by a lack of money; anyway, the printing of the book was stopped because the proof is full of errors." Even the characters are wrapped in mystery: who engraved them, who cast them, what became of them, whether they were the same characters used in 1516 by Agostino Giustiniani in Genoa to print the *Salterio*, a polyglot Bible in five different languages (Arabic, Hebrew, Latin, Greek, and Aramaic). The only sure thing is that nobody in Venice will use Arabic characters again for decades. "The 1538 Koran is important from a philological point of view. As for the rest, it was a commercial operation, pure and simple, like so many others. From a religious point of view it has no value whatsoever," Elsheikh concludes.

Exactly. Regardless of who's right—the discoverer of the Arabic Koran or the Egyptian professor—what's important is that the Paganinis dreamed the impossible dream. The failure of their enterprise marks the outer limit of the commercial expansion of Venetian publishing. The books printed in Venice that had triumphed in Germany and Great Britain and had penetrated the Balkans, were stopped on the threshold of the Sublime Port and the world of Islam. Aleramo Hermet writes, "The negative outcome of the enterprise marks the limit *non plus ultra* of the Serene Republic's typographical expansion in the Middle East, in the very same years that it definitively lost its preeminence in the international high-culture book market."[22]

---

[22] Nuovo, *Il commercio* . . . , op. cit., p. 49.

5.
ARMENIANS AND GREEKS

All we know for certain is that his name was Hakob and that he printed the world's first book in Armenian in 1512. No small feat, considering that another 126 years would pass before an Armenian book would be published in the Middle East (in New Julfa, a suburb of Isfahan, in Persia), and another 260 years before the appearance of an Armenian book in present-day Armenia, produced by the printing house of Edjmiatzin, the seat of the Catholicos of All Armenians (at the time the Catholicos was Simeone Yerevantzi).

The rest is unknown. Not even Hakob's surname is definite. "Meghapart", which appears in his books, could indeed be indicative of a family, but it could also be an adjective, given that it means "sinner." Something along the lines of: "I, Jacob, sinner, hereby publish this book." When he arrived in Venice and what he did there remains a mystery, along with where he lived, where his press was, where he got the characters he used. A further mystery surrounds the meaning of the obscure logo with which his books are signed—DIZA—at least as far as the first letter is concerned, since it's likely that the other three letters as representing "the initials of the famous engraver and printer Zuan Andrea"[1] and the "I" for "Iacobus," or Hakob in Latin.

[1] Baykar Sivazliyan, *Venezia per l'Oriente: la nascita del libro armeno*, in Scilla Abbiati (ed.) *Armeni, ebrei, greci stampatori a Venezia*, Casa editrice armena, Venice 1989, p. 23.

The mystery of what happened to this man, who, after printing five books, "mysteriously disappeared into the void"[2] remains to be solved, and it would be interesting to understand what happened between Hakob's last book, printed in 1514, and the next Armenian book, the perpetual calendar that Abgar Dpir sent to press in 1565. Is it possible that in a period of fifty years not even one Armenian book was published in a city where the Armenians were such a significant presence? Well, possible, perhaps, but it seems highly unlikely "especially because it coincided with a highly fertile period for Venetian printing."[3] It is more likely that the editions presumably published in those years have been lost or that they are waiting to be rediscovered in some library. After all, even Hakob's first book, *The Friday Book (Urbat'agirk')* was not rediscovered until 1889, when an Armeno-Venetian scholar, the Mechitarist priest Ghevond Ališan, one of the most important figures in modern Armenian cultural history, mistakenly identifies it as the firs Armenian book ever published; it will later be revealed that two books in Armenian pre-date it.

What is certain, on the other hand, is that Hakob's volume must have achieved great popularity in its time. If that were not the case, it wouldn't have been possible for a legend to have grown up around this book. It is not a religious book but a sort of propitiatory commonplace book in which the publisher gathers together "a collection of prayers and magic texts to protect oneself against illness and all kinds of accidents."[4] This made it highly useful to a flotilla of Armenian merchants who

---

[2] Baykar Sivazliyan, *La nascita dei primi libri a stampa armeni nel cuore della Serenissima*, in Boghos Levon Zekiyan (ed.), *Gli armeni in Italia*, De Luca edizoni d'arte, Rome 1990, p. 94.

[3] Ibid.

[4] *Le livre arménien à travers les âges*, Catalogue de l'exposition tenue au Musée de la Marine, Marseilles 2-21 octobre 1985, Maison arméenienne de la jeunesse et de la culture, Marseille 1985, p. 74.

were sailing to Venice via the usual route along the Dalmatian coast. The eastern shores of the Adriatic, rife with inlets and dotted with over a thousand islands, offer safe havens in case of storms, as well as convenient hiding places for pirates. And indeed the good Armenian merchants who had left Smyrna (Izmir) with a precious cargo of bales of raw silk and dyes, spy a flotilla of twenty fast pirate vessels closing in on them at full speed. It's a Friday, an ill-omened day, certainly not a day that offers any protection from bad luck, and the sun is shining brightly in the pellucid blue sky. The merchants are already imagining themselves at best robbed and driven into poverty, and at worst transfixed by the swords of the Dalmatian pirates (in the Adriatic at that time there were two important hideouts for seafaring marauders, both in present-day Croatia: at the mouth of the River Naretva and in the city of Senj, where the Uskoks were based). What to do? Three of the merchants believe that the ill omens of Friday can be effectively confronted by using the *Friday Book*, so they open it and start to read from it out loud. Their intuition couldn't have been more on target. Their salvation soon arrives in the form of a thick blanket of fog that envelops everything and makes the merchant ships invisible to the pirates. The commander of the flotilla, named Gaspar, immediately takes advantage of the fog to tack toward the Italian coast, where the marauders would never follow. All's well that ends well, so honor and glory to the *Friday Book*,[5] a one-of-a-kind volume that is apparently capable even of staving off attacks from Dalmatian pirates.

The Armenians had been at home in Venice for centuries (and they still are). In fact, there was even an Armenian Dogaressa—the First Lady of Venice—Maria Argyra, a Byzantine princess and niece of Basil II the Bulgaroctonus. In 1003

[5] Aleramo Hermet, POL Cogni Ratti de Desio, *La Venezia degli armeni. Sedici secoli tra storia e leggenda*, Mursia, Milan 1993, p. 78.

Maria married Giovanni Orseolo, who the following year became co-Doge.[6] Two and half centuries later, in 1253, Marco Ziani Sebastiano, Doge of Venice grandson of Doge Sebastiano Ziani, leaves in his will a sum to be used for the foundation of an Armenian House in one of the palaces owned by his family. Doge Sebastiano himself had lived for many years in the Kingdom of Armenia (which does not correspond to the territory of present-day former Soviet republic of Armenia but to Cilicia, for a long time part of Syria and now in Turkey.)[7]

The Armenian House—*Hay Dun*—is a stone's throw from St. Mark's Square, at the foot of the Ferali Bridge (*ferali* means "lanterns" in Venetian), on the corner of the Calle degli Armeni. Nearby is the little church of Santa Croce degli Armeni. The present-day church was built between 1682 and 1688, but its foundation dates back to at least the thirteenth century. It is the oldest church of the Diaspora and since the eighteenth century it has been entrusted to the Mechitarist Catholic priests. The entire neighborhood must have been awash with the Armenians, given that the documents mention a certain Petros whose shop sold *mezé*, bite-size tidbits to stimulate the appetite—tiny fried fish, pumpkin seeds, boiled shellfish[8]—which may well be the original version of what Venetians today call *cicheti*, the appetizers that accompany the *ombra*, or glass of wine. In any event, the Middle Eastern presence was not limited to this neighborhood. In 1348 (the year of the black plague which exterminated at least half of the European population) a testamentary legacy assigns five ducats to the Armenian monks of the church of San Giovanni Elemosinario, at Rialto.

The turning point comes in 1375; with the fall of the

[6] Ibid., p. 45.
[7] Sivazliyan, *Venezia. . . ,* op. cit., p. 26.
[8] Hermet, Cogni Ratti di Desio, *La Venezia degli armeni,* op. cit., p. 40.

Kingdom of Cilicia and its sovereign Leon V, many Armenians take refuge in Venice, land of asylum and freedom.[9] Even the title of King of Armenia, though by now a mere honorific, passes to Venice by way of Caterina Corner (better known as Cornaro), Queen of Cyprus and Armenia from 1473 to 1489, that is, from the death of her husband James II Lusignano until she abdicated in favor of the Serene Republic. These titles now belong to the Savoy family, who ruled Italy from 1861 to 1946, cousins of the Lusignano line, but in any event the titles are carved into the white marble of the tomb of Queen Caterina Corner in the Church of San Salvador, between the Rialto and St. Mark's Square.

An overview of the Armenian presence in Venice would not be complete without mentioning a figure who has nothing to do with books but a lot to do with the history of the Republic and, especially, with the relationships between Christian Europe and the Islamic Levant. It rarely happens that the outcome of a battle is tied to the intuition and capacity of a single individual, especially when he is not a great leader like Caesar or Napoleon. But without the contribution of Antonio Suriàn, known as the Armenian, the Battle of Lepanto could have had a different outcome. He comes to Venice in the middle of the sixteenth century from Syria (hence the surname Suriàn). At the time Venice has some 3,400 merchant ships at sea, built in private shipyards, while its warships are produced at the Arsenal, the largest industrial complex in the world. The ships are galleys, or vessels powered by both sails and oars, and there were smaller (fustas or galliots) and larger (galleasses) variations. The "arzanà de' viniziani," as Dante called the Arsenal in Canto XXI of his Inferno, employed, directly and indirectly, between 5,000 and 6,000 people, and in times of crisis, as on

_____
[9] Sivazilyan, *Venezia . . . ,* op. cit., p. 25.

the vigil of the Battle of Lepanto, the shipyard is able to christen one ship per day. Venice at that time is a city of immigrants—we've already seen the role played by the Germans in the development of the local printing trade—and even if they spoke strange languages and their skin color was decidedly on the dark side, they were welcomed for what they could do. Antonio the Armenian is a sort of genius of naval and mechanical engineering: in 1559, at age twenty-nine, he salvages, with all its cargo, a merchant ship that had sunk in the St. Mark's basin, and on another occasion he successfully brings to the surface three precious bronze cannons from the galleass of the nobleman Girolamo Contarini. He has a passion for weapons, and he marries Chiara, the girl next door, the daughter of an arms manufacturer who makes crossbows at the Arsenal.

On October 7, 1571, in the waters off the Curzolari Islands, near the Strait of Lepanto in Greece, the Christian and Ottoman fleets confront each other in the largest and bloodiest naval battle ever fought in the Mediterranean prior to the one between the British and the Franco-Spanish fleets at Trafalgar on October 21, 1805 (evidently October is a propitious month for naval battles). The Christian alliance consists of 208 galleys (106 Venetian, 90 Spanish, including the Genoese squadron of Gianandrea Doria, and 12 from the Papal State), 80,000 men, and 1800 pieces of artillery. The Turks can count on 222 galleys, 90,000 men, and 750 cannons.[10] A decisive role is played by the six Venetian galleasses; riding very high in the water—true floating fortresses—and therefore well protected against fire from the Turkish galleys, they are towed into position between the two fleets and disrupt the Ottoman formation, forcing the Sultan's fleet to split. The galleasses thus showed themselves to be decisive in turning the tide of the battle in favor of the ships under the command of Don John of Austria.

[10] Hermet, Cogni Ratti di Desio, *La Venezia degli armeni*, op. cit., p. 85.

"Antonio Surian, on board the galleass of commander Francesco Duodo, had already deployed on all the attack units cannons of various sizes specially built by him and placed in a totally revolutionary manner, ensuring accurate and rapid-fire volleys that inexorably struck the Turkish ships without missing a shot, alarming the enemy [. . .] No less important is the fact that on that same day, the indefatigable Armenian engineer had saved Duodo's galleass from sinking, by inventing a way to plug an enormous hole in its hull."[11] But there's more: it also seems that the brave Armenian had also invented an effective medication for treating wounds suffered in battle. In the heat of battle he is rebaptized as "the engineer" and dies in 1591, leaving six sons who work for decades in the Arsenal. There are traces of his family until 1655.[12]

Anyway, the surname Surian is fairly common in Venice, further proof of the significant presence of Armenians of Syrian origin. One of these families will be granted a noble title in 1648 (to finance the War of Candia (Crete) against the Turks, the Signory puts up for sale the right of access to the Great Council (Maggior Consiglio); in other words, admission to the patriciate), and a century later the lovely Baroque palace of the Surian, overlooking the Rio di Cannaregio, will become the seat of the French Embassy where, for several years, the secretary of the delegation will be Jean-Jacques Rousseau.

The eighteenth is also the century of the arrival in Venice, from Modone in the Peloponnesus, of the Abbot Mechitar, escaped from the advancing Turks. The Serene Republic will assign him and his religious community the island of San Lazzaro, still the seat of the congregation and for a long time also home to an important printing house, but we will have

[11] Ibid., p. 87.
[12] Sivazliyan, *Venezia,*. . . , op. cit. p. 27.

more to say about that later on. To underscore the continuity of the Armenian presence in Venice, it will suffice to cite the Venetian playwright Goldoni. In scene sixteen of his comedy *The Antiquarian's Family*, written in 1749, Brighella advises Arlecchino to pretend he is Armenian in order to trick Count Anselmo Terrazzini. "What's it take to pass yourself off as Armenian? He certainly can't understand that language. Just change all the words that end in ira to ara and he'll think you're an Armeno-Italian." Evidently in those days it was more common to hear Armenian spoken in Venice than German or English. And none other than the illustrious Englishman Lord Byron will go every day in his gondola to San Lazzaro for Armenian lessons.

All of this helps to explain how it was that in 1512 Armenian publishing made its debut in Venice and not somewhere else. "From that point on the art of printing developed in parallel with the ancient art of writing, with results that were equally splendid."[13] Compared to books printed in other languages, books in Armenian have an extra obstacle to overcome in order to reach their natural market: distance. Sending the printed works to the East is costly and sometimes life-threatening, because of the Barbary pirates,[14] who are based on the coast of North Africa, particularly in Tunisia.

We have already discussed the *Friday Book* and its virtues in combatting bad fortune. Hakob publishes four other works, addressed to both the Armenian residents in Venice and the Armenians living in the Levant. These four books run averse to the dominant publishing trend at the time, which was centered on the classics or religious books. Hakob prints literature that is completely profane, addressed to a readership of seafaring

[13] Gabriella Uluhogian, *Lingua e cultura scritta*, in Adriano Alpago Novello (ed.), *Gli armeni*, Jaca Book, Milan 1986, p. 124.
[14] R.H. Kévorkian, *Le livre arménien imprimé*, in *Le livre. . .* op.cit. p. 71.

merchants who shuttle back and forth between the Adriatic and the Eastern Mediterranean, and who can become not only readers but also promoters of his books. The fact remains, in any event, that thanks to his intuition the Armenians become the first Eastern population to adopt Gutenberg's art,[15] still another first to be remembered and to be ascribed to the extraordinary preeminence of Venice in the early years of the sixteenth century.

It is not known what became of Hakob, whether the characters that he had engraved were used only for five titles (rather unlikely) or were later reutilized. Nor is it known if other Armenian books were published in Venice in the fifty years that separate Hakob's last book, the *Tałaran*, from Abgar's *Tomar,* far in 1565. In the sixteenth century seventeen Armenian books were printed: eight in Venice, six in Constantinople, and three in Rome. In the next century, 160 titles will be published, the majority of them in Venice. From 1512 to 1800, Venice will be home to nineteen printing houses, owned by Armenians and not, which print in Armenian[16] and publish "some 249 volumes of optimum quality, in terms of both content and printing technique."[17]

Having left the world's first Armenian publisher to his mysterious fate, we now jump to the second half of the sixteenth century, when the Counter-Reformation is in full swing. A secret council of the Armenian apostolic church, meeting in Sebaste (the birthplace of Abbot Mechitar) decides to send to Rome, to Pope Pius IV, the nobleman Abgar Dpir, originally from Tokat, in northern Anatolia (Dpir means "sacristan," and it is more a title than a surname). The purpose of his diplo-

---

[15] Hermet, Cogni Ratti di Desio, *La Venezia degli armeni*, op. cit., p. 79.
[16] Sivazliyan, *Venezia . . .* , op. cit., pp. 25, 29, 39.
[17] Sivazliyan, *La nascita . . .* , op. cit., p. 94.

matic mission is to ask the Holy Father "to take action in defense of the Armenians subject to Muslim rule."[18]

The Armenian envoys disembark in Venice in 1564 and are received by the Signory before leaving for Rome. In the Eternal City, the Pope welcomes the delegation warmly, but as for aid there's nothing to be done. The mission is substantially a failure. Abgar returns to Venice and becomes a printer-publisher using Armenian print characters cut in Rome with papal authorization and a recommendation from the pope's nephew, Carlo Borromeo, who would later become Archbishop of Milan.[19] The first Venetian work printed by Abgar is a perpetual calendar, in 1565, after which he publishes a precious psalter (psalm book) in 272 sheets with beautiful woodcuts, of which only two exemplars have survived (conserved in Venice and Milan). The second engraving shows Abgar himself kneeling before Doge Girolamo Priuli. The caption reads: "He came to the beautiful port of the capital city called Venice under the reign of Doge Girolamo, where we have made this new book."[20] He is credited with having established in Venice the first known Armenian printing house (it is not certain whether Hakob at the beginning of the century printed on his own or used the presses of some other publisher), at a time when, as Hermet writes, "holy and erudite books printed in the national language were to take on decisive importance for the future birth of the Armenian people."[21] But Abgar Dpir remains in Venice for only a couple of years: in 1567 he moves his publishing enterprise to Constantinople. In the Ottoman capital with the help of his son Sultanshah, he installs in the courtyard of an apostolic church the first printing house in all

[18] Hermet, Cogni Ratti di Desio, *La Venezia degli armeni,* op. cit., p. 81.
[19] Hermet, Cogni Ratti di Desio, *La Venezia degli armeni*, op. cit., p. 81.
[20] Ibid., p. 82.
[21] Ibid.

of the Levant; the first thing he publishes there is an elementary Armenian grammar.[22] A fundamental function of the Armenian book will be its use as a didactic instrument in favor of minority populations living within territories ruled by others. In Venice Dpir's legacy will be taken up by Houhannes Terzentsi, who in 1587 publishes a new book of psalms. The Armenian publishing business continues throughout the seventeenth century (1681 is the year of publication of the *Bargirk' Taliani*, a fantastic Venetian-Armenian dictionary and conversation manual meant primarily for a readership engaged in commerce with phrases such as *ligate assieme e fate balla* (tie together and make a bale) or *voi volete bon mercà, io voglio vender caro* (you want cheap, I want to sell at a high price) transliterated into the Armenian alphabet), until the boom of the eighteenth century, when on the wave of the publishing activity of Abbot Melchitar San Lazaro will see the installation of the printing house that—right up to the early 1990s—will be the most important Armenian printing house in the entire world.

Now let's move on to another Venetian first (twenty-six years before Hakob begins his activity), the official debut of the Greek book *Batrachomyomachia* (The War of the Frogs and Mice), published in 1496 in the monastery of Saint Peter Martyr on Murano. It is a poem in hexameter verse attributed in the Hellenistic and Renaissance eras to Homer, but today believed to be the work of an anonymous poet. This is the first book printed entirely in Greek, though books partially in that language had already been printed: grammars, generally bilingual, composed partly in Greek and partly in Latin. The most celebrated of these grammars are the *Erotemata*, by Manuele Crisolora, published without a date but believed to have been

[22] Ibid.

printed in 1471 by Adam de Ambergau.[23] The study of Greek was a fad that took the cultivated classes in Renaissance Italy by storm and was accompanied by success in publishing: from 1500 on, Greek grammars go into numerous printings, attesting to the interest of Italian humanists in the subject.[24] For the Greeks, as we have already seen for the Jews and the Armenians, the Venetian debut of publishing in their language stems from their longtime presence in the lagoon. Venice has a special relationship with Greece that goes back to the times in which the then future Serene Republic was only a group of islands inhabited by fishermen and salt panners that wanted to be left alone. The islanders don't want to have too much to do with the Holy Roman Empire, which rules on the mainland, so they decide to become a province of the Byzantine empire. The most important points of reference for the Venetians are not the Roman Pope and the Empire in Aachen (Aix-la-Chapelle) but the Basileus in Constantinople and the Greek Orthodox Exarch in Ravenna. This can be verified simply by looking at the city's churches: St. Mark's Basilica has nothing to do with the austere Romanesque cathedrals of central Europe but is the descendant of Constantinople's Hagia Sophia, sparkling with gilded mosaics. In the fourteenth century the Turks step up their attacks against the Byzantine territories and the Greeks desperately seek support in the West to stave off the rising Ottoman tide. Emperor John V Palaeologus goes to Venice in 1370. A member of his entourage is Demetrio Cidone—Dimityrios Kydonis—a refined diplomat who is

[23] Manosous Manoussakas, *Libri greci stampati a Venezia,* in *Venezia città del libro*, Venice, Isola di San Giorgio Maggiore, 2 September – 7 October 1973, p. 31.
[24] Destina Vlasi Sponza, *I greci a Venezia: una presenza costante nell'editoria (secc. XV-XVI)* in Abbiati (ed.). *L'attività editoriale dei greci durante il Rinascimento italiano 1469- 1523*, Greek Ministry of Culture, Athens, 1986, p. 5.

among the first to spread Greek culture in Europe. Cidone returns to the Serene Republic in 1390, and again in 1394-95 with Manuele Crisolora, the first teacher of the Greek alphabet to arrive in Italy from Byzantium,[25] and one of his students, Guarino Guarini, from Verona, who accompanies him when he returns home, will be the first Italian to study Greek in Constantinople.[26]

We have already mentioned Crisoloro's grammar, which was part of the Greek fad of the 1400s, a fad that was fueled by the humanists Leonardo Giustinian and Francesco Barbaro. In 1416 Barbaro invites Giorgio di Trebisonda (Trapezuntios) to Venice to copy his collection of manuscripts. Trebisonda accepts the invitation with pleasure and he also goes to Padua, where he teaches Greek to the bishop, Pietro Marcello (and studies Latin with Guarino Guarini and Vittorio Da Feltre), before he moves on to Florence and Rome, where he becomes the apostolic secretary (a prestigious post which the Pope reserves for intellectuals from all nations). "His literary production in Greek and Latin is vast and influenced the humanist movement of his era."[27]

But it was not until several years later that there arrived in the lagoon the Greek who more than any other would leave his mark on Venetian history by donating to the Venetian government the initial nucleus of the Marciana Library (founded in 1468), the only institution of the Serene Republic that is still extant and operating. Bessarione comes to Venice for the first time in 1438, with Emperor John VIII Palaeologus and Patriarch Joseph II. The entourage of the highest Byzantine civil and religious offices is quite numerous, consisting of some

[25] Manosous Manoussakas, Costantino Saikos (eds.), *L'attività editoriale dei greci durante il Rinascimento italiano 1469-1523*, Greek Ministry of Culture, Athens 1986, p. 5.
[26] Vlassi Sponza, *I greci* . . . op. cit., p. 71.
[27] Ibid., p. 73.

600 people who pass through Venice on their way to the Council of Ferrara and Florence. The council had been called to sanction the unification of the churches of Rome and Constantinople and the role played by Bessarione so impressed the Pope that he named him cardinal. A refined humanist, Bessarione establishes himself in Rome in 1440, where he tries to promote a crusade against the Turks. He will not succeed in this undertaking, but he will succeed in collecting Greek manuscripts. Thanks to his acquisitions and the work of copyists, his collection will number some 800 manuscripts, which will be donated in 1468 to the Republic of Venice, recognized as a worthy custodian of the precious patrimony.

In the meantime an epoch-making event occurs. In 1453 Constantinople is taken by the Ottoman soldiers of Mehmet II, known as the Conquistador, and becomes the new capital of the Turkish Empire. A lot of Byzantine intellectuals leave their ex-capital, knowing that they will never return. Venice is a hospitable refuge where several of their compatriots already live, and where the Greek exiles will contribute to the birth of Greek printing, working as engravers of Greek characters, publishers, printers, proofreaders, and editors of books in collaboration with Italian printers who, to satisfy the growing demand, devote themselves to the publication of classical literature.[28] Others settle in Crete—a Venetian possession from 1204 to 1669—and it will be the children of this grand Mediterranean island who will set the standard for Greek publishing.

The panorama of the Hellenic presence in Venice would not be complete without citing the Confraternity of the Greeks. Founded in 1489, it still exists today as the Hellenic Institute. The church of Saint George of the Greeks and the nearby museum of the icon are situated at the foot of the

[28] Ibid., p. 74.

Bridge of the Greeks, in demonstration of the fact that even the city's place names record the importance of this age-old ethnic presence.

Indeed it is two men from Crete who are the pioneers of Greek printing. We don't know much about them other than what they wrote in the colophons of the books that they published. Laonikos and Alexandros are priests and both are natives of Chania. Laonikos publishes the *Batrachomyomachia* in 1486, while Alexandros, also a publisher and eventually the bishop of Arcadi:

> prints his Psalter (The Psalms of David), the first religious book in Greek, on November 15 of that same year. The typographical characters of the two books are the same, which indicates that they came out of the same printing house and they are modeled on ancient liturgical manuscripts. The fact that they are printed in black and red could mean that these two printers intended to print a series of religious books; a plan that never comes to fruition.[29]

After making their contribution, Laonikos and Alexandros disappear, swallowed up in the abyss of history, but they are the initiators of a prolific tradition. As Manosous Manoussakas writes:

> No other city in the world is the equal of Venice in its service to the publishing of Greek books and consequently to the progress and development of Greek culture.[30]

The torch of Hellenic publishing then passes into the hands of another Cretan, Zaccaria Calliergi, who is born in Rethimon

[29] Ibid., p. 77.
[30] Manoussakas, *Libri greci . . .* , op. cit., p. 93.

in 1473, to one of the island's most powerful noble families. In 1490, he arrives in Venice, where he forms a partnership with Nicola Vlastò, another Cretan nobleman, "right hand man of Anna Notarà, the daughter of the last Byzantine prime minister, Luca Notarà."[31] Notarà moves to Venice with all of her property and becomes a generous financial backer of the first Greek printing house to open in the Serene Republic. The Calliergi surname is destined for a long life in Venetian history, although it will undergo some modifications in subsequent transcriptions. For example, in 1572 a certain Antonio Calergi dies and leaves a library of 800 volumes, at the time a remarkable collection[32]; and, in 1883, Richard Wagner will die in Ca' Vendramin Calergi, today the location of the Municipal Casino.

Zaccaria Calliergi was the most prominent Greek printer, and his capabilities were numerous and unusual: calligraphic copyist of codices, skilled designer and engraver of print characters, erudite editor and commentator of classical texts, proofreader and publisher of refined taste.[33] He also avails himself of cultivated collaborators such as Marco Musuro, another native of Rethimon, who in later years will become one of the most important collaborators of Aldus Manutius and also professor of Greek at the University of Padua, where he will have Erasmus of Rotterdam among his auditors. Zaccaria and Nicola's willpower, Marco's learning, and Anna's money make possible the 1499 publication of one of the masterworks of Renaissance printing,[34] the *Mega Etymologikon* (*Etymologicum magnum* in Latin). It takes six years for the first Greek printing house to bring to press the first Greek lexicon, "one

[31] Manoussakas, Staikos (eds.), *L'attività* . . . , op. cit., p. 127.
[32] Zorzi, *La circolazione* . . . , op. cit., p. 133.
[33] Manoussakas, Staikos (eds.), *L'attività* . . . , op. cit., p. 127.
[34] Vlassi Sponza, *I greci* . . . , op. cit., p. 78.

of the most important monuments of Byzantine literature."[35]
The costs soar, but in the end they turn out to be proportionate to the beauty of the work: the characters engraved by
Calliergi are of the finest quality, the decorations "imitate the
most beautiful Byzantine manuscripts,"[36] every page is printed
twice, in red and black, and this will turn out to be the first edition (*editio princeps*, for bibliographers) on which all succes-
sive works will be based. The Calliergi-Vlastò partnership is
limited to four books; it concludes in 1500, with Galen's
Terapeutica, a fundamental text for all the physicians of the era.
Calliergi moves to Padua, where he goes back to working as a
manuscript copyist. Vlastò sells the remainder of his books to
Manutius, while their splendid characters are purchased by the
Giuntas, who will use them in 1520.

The most important Renaissance publisher, Aldus Manutius,
has deservedly been given a chapter to himself, but here we can
trace his decisive influence on Greek publishing. Manutius
arrives in Venice in 1489-90 with the specific intention of publishing the Greek and Latin manuscript codices that Cardinal
Bessarione has left to the Serene Republic. "The first dated
book (28-11-1494) off the presses of Aldus," writes Vlassi
Sponza in his book on the Greek presence in Venice, "is the
Grammatica by Costantino Lascaris, but it is likely that the
very first book printed by Manutius is another, printed without
any chronological indication and put into circulation around
1495: the *Galeomyomachia* (The War of the Cat and the Mice)
by Theodoro Prodromo, edited by Aristobulo Apostolio,
known as Arsenio Apostolio."[37] Manutius needs people with a
thorough knowledge of Greek and is lucky to find that Musuro
is just the man he needs. "Marco Musuro, the greatest philo-

[35] Manoussakas, Staikos (eds.), *L'attività* . . . , op. cit., p. 130.
[36] Manoussakas, *Libri greci* . . . , op. cit., p. 90.
[37] Vlassi Sponza, *I greci* . . . , op. cit., p. 79.

logical genius of modern Hellenism, rendered an inestimable service to the European Renaissance with his expert teaching and, above all, with his critical editing of the first editions of ancient Greek writers published for the first time by the famous Venetian printing house of Aldus Manutius."[38] The handwriting of his friend Marco Musuro is the model[39] on which Aldus has his cursive Greek characters engraved by the Bolognese engraver Francesco Griffo.

Another essential collaborator is Giano Lascaris, a native of Constantinople, but the most surprising contribution comes from Giovanni Grigoropulo, who owes his fundamental role in the history of Hellenic publishing to a murder. A "manual laborer of letters,"[40] copyist, son and brother of copyists, he earns a reputation as a scrupulous proofreader. He arrives in Venice in 1494 to try to obtain the release of his brother Manuele who, because of an involuntary homicide, has been exiled on the island of Karpathos. Damages must be paid to the victim's family and an order is obtained from the Venetian authorities. Giovanni battles stubbornly for seven years in the city, which at the time is his capital. He achieves his objective in 1501 and continues working with Manutius until 1504. After that year, it is uncertain whether he died or went back home.[41]

Aldus is urged by his Greek collaborators to publish the indispensible texts of the Hellenic world,[42] which is probably the explanation for another curious fact: in addition to his other noted accomplishments, Manutius is arguably the first to

[38] Manoussakas, Staikos (eds.), *L'attività* . . . , op. cit., p. 102.
[39] Horatio Brown, *The Venetian Printing Press 1469-1800*, John C. Nimmo, London 1891, p. 46.
[40] Manosous Manoussakas, Costantino Staikos (eds.), *Le edizioni di testi greci di Aldo Manuzio e le prime tipografie greche di Venezia*, Fondazione per la cultura greca, Athens 1993, p. 82.
[41] Ibid.
[42] Vlassi Sponza, *I greci* . . . , op. cit., p. 79.

have printed Greek liturgical texts of the Orthodox Church.[43] Evidently Manutius fears that the Roman Catholic Church will not look favorably on the publication of passages from the Orthodox liturgy, and so he does it secretly; in many cases these texts were printed anonymously, clandestinely, without a title, hidden among other writings of a religious, grammatical, or poetic nature.[44]

Manutius dies in 1515, but the activity of his printing house goes on. Then, according to Sponza, "Andrea Cunadis, a merchant from Patras, a member of the Confraternity of the Greeks since 1516, lends his name to the editions of religious and neo-Greek books, requested not only by members of the confraternity, who were constantly increasing in number, but also by Orthodox Greeks in the Levant."[45] Cunadis is only a publisher in the narrow sense—he doesn't do any printing himself but relies on the printers Nicolini da Sabbio, originally from Brescia. When he dies, in 1523, his legacy is taken up by his father-in-law Damiano di Santa Maria, a fabric merchant, who continues to publish with the Sabbios until 1550. In the thirty-two-year span of this partnership forty-nine books are published: thirty-one liturgical texts, seventeen literature texts, and one (the work of Saint Basil) in Latin and Greek. For the first time, books are printed in Greek not only for a refined readership in Italy but also for the Greek-speaking and Orthodox populations of the Levant.[46]

The range of publishing activity expands and so in 1544 the humanist from Corfu Nicola Sofiano, prints a manual of

[43] Reinhard Flogaus, *Aldus Manutius and the printing of Greek liturgical texts*, in Lisa Pon. Kraig Kallendorf (eds.), *TheBooks of Venice. Il libro veneziano*, Biblioteca nazionale marciana/La Musa Talìa/Oak Knoll Press, Venice – New Castle 2008, p. 230.
[44] Ibid., p. 229.
[45] Vlassi Sponza, *I greci* . . . , op. cit., p. 80.
[46] Ibid.

astronomy in modern Greek and translates Plutarch into neo-Greek so he will be more easily accessible (but the publication is edited by others). Understandably, as the years go by, printing in modern Greek steadily becomes more important with respect to classical Greek. The first book in neo-Greek, printed in 1519 by Calligieri, has been lost, as has the second, printed in 1524 by Cunadis, but then neo-Greek production intensifies and the works that have survived become more and more numerous. In that same period publishers begin printing works by living Greek authors, mainly from the Ionian islands, whereas Cretan literature will have its heyday in the next century, primarily because, as mentioned earlier, Venice loses Crete definitively in 1669, and a large number of Cretans take refuge in the lagoon. In the seventeenth century "Venice becomes the cultural capital of the Greek world and it also exercises an incalculable influence on the political rebirth of Greekness."[47] Venetian printing houses will continue publishing works in neo-Greek—in the mid-eighteenth century, 20,000 to 30,000 books were exported to the Levant every year—and the activity will go on even after Greek independence, in 1821, all the way up to the beginning of the twentieth century.

[47] Simonetta Pelusi (ed.), *Le civiltà del libro e la stampa a Venezia*, Il Poligrafo, Padua 2000, p. 24.

6.
The Wind from the East

The Balkans begin at the Rennweg," Prince Metternich, the Prime Minister of Austria was fond of saying. Rennweg was the name of the street he lived on in Vienna. Long before Metternich, Venetians knew that elsewhere was right outside the door. Venice is Europe's port to the East, and you don't even have to leave the Venetian state to find yourself in the East: among its subjects living in the Balkans the Serene Republic counts numerous communities— Catholics in Dalmatia, Orthodox in the Bay of Kotor, and Venetian Albania—who speak Slavic languages. These communities that need liturgical books and their capital city is obviously ready to supply them: the communities are part of the domestic market, so there are no cost-inflating customs duties to pay. And then there's the export market: in its role as the giant multinational of publishing, Venice is willing to work for anyone who shows up with a text to be composed in one hand and some cash in the other. So, although the first two Czech editions of the Bible are printed in Bohemia, the third is printed in Venice in 1506, on the presses of Peter Lichtenstein. It is an Utraquist Bible, written for use by the moderate wing of the Hussite movement, members of which are nevertheless dangerous miscreants in the eyes of the Church of Rome. The Hussites, who take their name from Jan Hus, burned at the stake as a heretic in 1415, had been defeated in Bohemia, after twenty years of war, by the Catholic Church and the high feudal nobility. In the second half of the fifteenth century, however, the moderate wing of the movement, made up of the lesser nobility and the bourgeoisie, adheres to the Protestant Reformation, while the radical wing, the Taborites, made up primarily of peasants, had been crushed earlier.

Again, in this case it is easy to hypothesize that the freedom enjoyed by the Republic in the early sixteenth century played a fundamental role and that the Bohemian Protestants therefore considered it less risky to print their reform Bible in the shadows of Saint Mark's than that of Saint Wenceslaus. Obviously, the book was intended for export and indeed there is only one surviving copy of the Utraquist Bible in Italy today, conserved in Venice at the Cini Foundation.

Up to this point we have focused on Venice's gold medals— first to print a Koran, a Talmud, a book in Greek, and a book in Armenian—but there are also some silvers and bronzes and some smaller caliber golds, such as, for example, the gold for the first Italian translation of the Koran (printed in 1547 by Andrea Arrivabene), while it takes a silver for the printing of the second Bible in vernacular (and the first in Italian); the first vernacular Bible is in German.

But if the easterly wind from central Europe is a light breeze, the one blowing in from the Balkans is an impetuous gale, capable of changing the world of publishing in the lagoon. Venice becomes the center of publishing for the Slavic languages of the south (Yugoslav, to use a word that at the time had not yet been invented): Croatian, Serb, Bosnian. Serbo-Croatian is codified as a language in the nineteenth century and the distinction between Croatian, Serb, and Bosnian—and after independence in 2006, also Montenegrin—comes about only after the decade of war that ravaged the former Yugoslavia from 1991 to 2001. Naturally, nationalists on all sides are ready to demonstrate, documents in hand, that only their language and—God forbid—not the language of the oth-

ers, is the oldest, spoken at least since the Middle Ages, while
the idiom used by neighboring peoples is simply a derivative of
their own. Different alphabets were used for writing, and there
were local variants of the southern Slavic dialects, which gave
rise to the languages we know today.

In our time, the perception of the East knocking on the
door, the East just across the Adriatic, has been distorted by a
century of nationalism and a half century of Communism, and
by the hundred or so years that the southern Slavs and the
Italians faced off against one another to assert their own
national superiority, followed by the fifty years of the Cold
War, in which the superiority asserted was ideological. The
Adriatic has thus been irremediably widened; the sea has
become a barrier between the populations inhabiting its
shores. But in the centuries in which water transport was much
safer and more used than land transport, things were very different. Relationships between the two shores were closer, and
more frequent than those between the coasts and their respec-
tive hinterlands, especially in Dalmatia, where the jagged peaks
of the Velebit range rise up immediately behind the coast line.
It was normal for the inhabitants of the Istrian peninsula to sell
their vegetables at the market near the Rialto, and for centuries
Venice warmed itself with firewood brought over on
Dalmatian fishing boats.

In the sixteenth century the Adriatic is a Venetian lake
(indeed up until the eighteenth century it is called the Gulf of
Venice) that the Republic rules conferring upon it a legal status equal to that of the mainland. This is possible because its
domini da mar (overseas dominions) extended along the eastern shore, the Istrian peninsula, Dalmatia (which also had an
indigenous Ladino tongue, Dalmatic, now extinct; the last person who spoke it died in 1898 on the island of Krk) and
Venetian Albania.

There's nothing strange, therefore, about Venice's Slavic

subjects going to print their books in the city that at the time was their capital, as well as the undisputed queen of publishing. It should also be emphasized that in the evangelization of Slav peoples, conducted by the Byzantines Cyril and Methodius, the written word played an important role: "Cyril placed the translated books on the altar of God, and offered them in sacrifice to the Lord," we read in Simonetta Pelusi's study of the the liturgical books of the Serbs and Croats.[1] The first Croatian book printed in Venice, in 1477, is not however a devotional work but a volume of poems in Latin by Juraj Šižgorić, a humanist from Šibenik, known as Georgius Sisgoreus. The *Elegiarum et carminum libri tres* is also the first book ever published by a Croatian poet.

The first book in Glagolitic characters—the ancient Croatian alphabet—is a missal from 1483, whose place of printing is unknown but is presumed to be somewhere in present-day Croatia, probably Kosinj (today Gornij Kosinj), in the region of Lika, in the Dalmatian interior on the other side of the island of Pag, or else in Modruš, not far from Rijeka. The next book—the second in Glagolitic and the third Croatian book if we count the Latin edition of Šižgorić—is a breviary from 1491. The only extant copy is conserved in Venice, in the Marciana Library. The printing house is unknown, and there is only circumstantial evidence that it was printed in Venice; the geographical attribution has been contested by a contemporary Croatian historian who claims the Croatian book was printed in Kosinj.[2] It should be noted that the region of Lika, where Gornij Kosinj is located, was majority Serb until in a military operation in August, 1995, Croatia

[1] Simonetta Pelusi, *Il libro liturgico per serbi e croati fra Quattro e Cinquecento*, in Ead. (ed.), *Le civiltà del libro e la stampa a Venezia*, Il Poligrafo, Padua 2000, p. 43.
[2] Darko Zubrinić, *Croatian Glagolitic Script*, Zagreb 1995.

won the territory of the secessionist Serbian Republic of Krajina.

There is no doubt, however, about the Venetian origins of the Glagolitic breviary published in 1493 by Andrea Torresani, then future father-in-law of Aldus Manutius, in consultation with Blaž Baromić. Torresani's consultant was born in Vrbnik, on the island of Krk or Veglia, then ruled by the Venetian Republic, and he will become the canon of the cathedral of Senj, in Habsburg territory, where he would later establish what is traditionally considered to be the first printing house in Croatia. It is again Andrea Torresani who in 1527 publishes a luxurious spelling book, richly decorated with woodcuts, printed in red and black, which will be used as a model for designing Glagolitic characters throughout the sixteenth century.[3]

Forty years later, in 1561, another Andrea Torresani, grandson of his namesake, prints a new breviary, edited by Mikula Brožić, pastor and notary public from Omišalj, on Krk. Until fairly recently, it was thought to be a simple reworking of the 1493 edition; but a more careful examination has revealed that Brožić "intervenes in the text, modifying the calendar, adding the offices of the saints and updating the spelling, bringing it more into line with spoken Croatian."[4]

At this point, it is impossible not to note the importance of the island of Krk to the Glagolitic tradition: the editors of the Venetian editions hailed from this island. Located in the Gulf of Quarnero, it is also the closest island to the mainland; only 650 yards of sea separate it from the continental coast (since 1980 it has been joined to the mainland by a mile-long bridge). On Jurandvor, on the southern part of the island, not far from Baška, the oldest known example of Glagolitic writing, the

---

[3] Pelusi, *Il libro* . . . , op. cit., p. 45.
[4] Ibid.

Bašćanska ploča (the Baška Tablet) was rediscovered in the church of Santa Lucia in 1851. Today, the original has been taken to Zagreb and a reproduction is on display in the church. The text of the tablet dates back to 1100 and confirms the donation of lands by King Zvonimir to the Benedictine monks who were the custodians of the church.

But let's return to the printed word. In 1528, a large printing house, one of those multinationals of the book that were then operating in Venice, publishes an important missal, decorated with woodcuts, and edited by Pavao di Modruš. In the span of fifty years, therefore, Venetian presses issued several liturgical books in Glagolitic, but the next missal would not be published until over a hundred years later, in 1631. With the publication of this new missal, however, a lot of things have changed: it is published in Rome, by the Propaganda Fide, the editor is no longer a Benedictine but a Franciscan, Rafael Levaković, from the monastery of Trsat, near Rijeka, the place where legend has it that the house of the Blessed Mother made a stop on its flight from Nazareth to Loreto. Father Levaković introduces into the text numerous eastern Slavic forms, compromising the purity of the language handed down through the previous editions.[5] From a linguistic point of view, there can be no doubt that the Venetian editions are much more rigorous than the subsequent editions issued by the papal presses.

1512, was the year of the first book in Aremenian, as well as the year of the first book in Bosnian Cyrillic, *Ofičje svete dieve Marie* (Office of the Virgin Mary). Nowadays, Bosnian is written in Latin characters, but half a millennium ago the inhabitants of Bosnia—a region in which the Glagolitic alphabet had gradually given way to the Cyrillic—practicing the Latin rite and speaking Croatian, used a special kind of writing, a kind of

---

[5] Ibid.

Cyrillic known as Bosniac (*bosančica*).[6] And it is the Parisian Guillaume Postel—whom we encountered when he was involved with the Arabic characters of Paganino Paganini—who reproduces in print for the first time the Bosnian Cyrillic alphabet and provides its transliteration in Latin characters,[7] while it is Giorgio Rusconi, a Milanese printer with a workshop in San Moisè, who prints the book, followed a few days later by a second book in Bosniac. The editor of the two volumes, Franjo Mikalovic Ratković, comes from Ragusa (present-day Dubrovnik) at the time an independent republic (it will be suppressed by Napoleon in 1808, but in 1776 it is the first sovereign state to recognize the independence of the United States of America).

Venice is a setting for the activities of foreign figures (French, Milanese, Ragusans): the reprints of the two books in 1571 and the publication of a new liturgical book, the work of a partnership, mentioned in the colophon of the volume, between the enigmatic Jakob Djebarom, about whose identity many hypotheses have been proposed without ever arriving at anything certain, and Ambrosio Corso, from Syracuse, already known for having marketed the Vuković editions a decade earlier. Contrary to almost every other sector of Venetian publishing, for which the seventeenth is a gloomy century, for Bosniac printing it is the golden age, especially with the publication of the works of Matija Divković, from Jelaške, a Franciscan who becomes a chaplain in Sarajevo. The printing of texts in Bosnian Cyrillic continues in Venice until 1716; many editions are issued by the presses but only some of them are conserved in Venice, demonstrating once again that production was totally addressed to the export market.[8]

[6] Ibid.
[7] Ibid.
[8] Ibid., p. 46.

Now we come to the largest language group of the Balkans, Serbian, for which the role of Venetian publishing was even greater than for Croatian or Bosniac. In this case, however, we must note its precise political objective: the liturgical books printed in Venice for Orthodox Serbs are meant to support the cause of independence for the lands recently conquered by the Ottoman empire (Serbia had already lost its independence, following the battle of Kosovo Polje in 1389—June 28th—of that year is the founding date of Serbian nationalism). In 1496, the Turks took possession of the last free piece of Orthodox-Serb land, the kingdom of Zeta (present-day Montenegro) the home of Božidar Vuković, the thirty-year-old scion of a noble family. Born near Podgorica, Vuković worked in the printing shop of Djuraj Crnojević. In all likelihood he is a high-ranking officer of the state at the court of the voivode Ivan Crnojević, and, rather than submit to the conquerors of his homeland, he decides to flee the capital of Cetinje. He goes to Venice, where he takes on a mission: supply liturgical books to the Orthodox churches pillaged by the Ottoman troops. By all accounts, he prints his first book in 1519, his last in 1540, and in the span of these twenty years Venice becomes "one of the most important centers for the printing of liturgical books in ecclesiastical Serbian Slavic.[9] His business will then be carried on for several years by his son Vićenco (in other transcriptions, Vicentije) and what would become for many years the only Serbian printing house in the world will keep its presses running through the first half of the seventeenth century. The Vuković printing house becomes the leading book supplier for the Serbian Orthodox Church, with a distribution network that extends from the Adriatic coasts of Dalmatia and Albania to the Balkan interior.

Until well into the nineteenth century, the most important Serbian cultural centers are all to be found outside of their

[9] Ibid., p. 48.

homeland, in Greece (Mount Athos) and in Hungary (Sremski Karlovci and Novi Sad, in Vojvodina, which became a region of Serbia after the First World War), as well as in the Orthodox communities of Budapest, Vienna, and Venice, the westernmost point reached by Serbian culture.

Vuković marries a Venetian and changes his name to Dioniso Della Vecchia, using his wife's surname. For a few years his son Vićenco limits himself to reprinting his father's works, but in 1561 he publishes his own first important edition, with the collaboration of Stefan Marinović, from Shkodër, in Venetian Albania. But the younger Vuković isn't able to make the business inherited from his father profitable and he sells it to a Bulgarian, Jacov Krajkov, who had come to Venice in 1560. Krajkov prints four editions until, in 1572, he sells the printing house to Giuseppe Antonio Rampazzetto, who in 1597 publishes the last Venetian book in Cyrillic of the sixteenth century.

In the seventeenth century only one ecclesiastical Cyrillic book is published in Venice—in 1638—because Venetian Cyrillic publishing is taken over by the polyglot printing house in the Vatican, initiated under Gregory XIII. Venice will manage to regain a certain level of importance, however, in the eighteenth century, thanks to the work of the Greek printer Demetrio Teodosio, who publishes in Greek, Armenian, and Karamanli (Turkish with Greek characters we'll look into that), and after purchasing the Cyrillic characters he starts printing books for Serbs of the Orthodox faith.

A final note: although Croatian bibliographers, as we have seen, tend to "Croaticize" Venetian Glagolitic publishing, the Serbs recognize the contribution made to their culture by the editions printed in the Serene Republic. As the Serbian scholar Lazar Plavšić writes:

> It must be emphasized that the Venetians, independently of the motives which pushed them to make possible

the development of our printing, objectively helped us: first, to enter the circle of those peoples among whom the art of printing had already begun to make inroads as early as the last decade of the fifteenth century; second, to conserve, by printing books, our nationality, and to develop our capacity for writing and our spiritual and temporal culture in the conditions of slavery in which we found ourselves under the Turks.[10]

---

[10] Lazar Plavšić, *Srpske štamparije od kraja XV do sredine XIX veka*, Belgrade 1959, o. 220; quoted and translated by Persida Lazarević Di Giacomo, "La letteratura serba 'in esilio' a Venezia tra la fine del '700 e l'inizio dell'800," in *PaginaZero-Letterature di frontiera*, 9 (2006).

7.
GEOGRAPHY AND WAR

A merica was discovered by the Spanish under the command of an admiral from Genoa, Christopher Columbus; it got its name from a Florentine, Amerigo Vespucci. Canada was explored by the English under the command of a Venetian, Giovanni Caboto (John Cabot). The first circumnavigation of the globe was done by the Portuguese, but the account was written by a subject of the Serene Republic, Antonio Pigafetta. In an era in which riches are being found elsewhere but the brains needed to find them are still where they have been for centuries, old Mediterranean Europe shows itself to be an active participant in the new geographical discoveries and the charting of oceanic navigation routes. And it is the Venetians who make a fundamental contribution to the spread of knowledge about the newly discovered lands, and, while they're at, the old ones too.

That the people of Saint Mark's Republic played a key role in the history of navigation is undisputable; it's sufficient to recall that they gave the name to the wind rose. The direction of the winds was determined from an imprecisely defined base point in the Mediterranean, northwest of Crete: the one that blew from the Maestra (Mistress), or Venice, was called the Maestrale (Mistral). This interpretation is not universally agreed upon; there are some who maintain that the "Maestra" was Rome, but it is far too easy to rebut that the sailors wondering about the Levant in their boats certainly didn't belong to the pope. More than one Venetian also stuck their noses out-

side of the Mediterranean, the brothers Nicolò and Antonio
Zen, for example, who sailed the North Atlantic in the late
fourteenth century, reaching the Faroe Islands, Iceland, probably Greenland, and perhaps exploring the Canadian coasts of
Newfoundland; or Alvise da Mosto (known as Cadamosto)
who departs from his palace on the Grand Canal and, in 1455,
at the head of an expedition of Portuguese, discovers the Cape
Verde Islands and sails up the Senegal river. Some Venetians
also sail in the opposite direction, like Nicolò de' Conti, from
Chioggia, who in 1421 visits Sumatra and then Burma and
Vietnam.
The story of how we came to know about de' Conti's exploits
is an odd one. He had converted to Islam, and when he returned
to Christianity, Pope Eugene IV compelled him, as penance for
his apostasy, to narrate his explorations to the pope's secretary,
the humanist Poggio Bracciolini, who transcribed the account.

Anyway, in order to navigate you need charts, and you also
need charts for waging war; topography, after all, is a military
science. This explains why Venice—well supplied with ships
and cannons—placed so much importance on geographical
and military publishing, obtaining for itself a near monopoly in
the latter and an indisputably strong position in the former. In
the sixteenth century cartography became a sort of collective
frenzy, a "map mania that was then at its peak, not just among
professional cartographers, but among general readers as well.
Unprotected by copyright, thousands of maps and charts were
copied, modified, or simply picked for their choicest parts."[1]
The first geographical treatise ever published is *Navigationi
e viaggi*, by Giovanni Battista Ramusio, from 1550. It is also the
first extensive collection of historical documents that is not

[1] Andrea di Robilant, *Venetian Navigators. The Voyages of the Zen B
rothers to the Far North,* Faber and Faber, London 2011, p. 182.

merely a miscellany of laws and decrees; thus, it is the first example of a documentary history of geography and journeys. It is also the second known exemplar (after *Novis Orbis* was published in Basel in 1532) of a literary genre of what we might today call travel narrative.[2] As is always the case, Ramusio's work is not a solitary mushroom springing up in the woods following a storm but the final fruit of a long flowering, the consequence of the fact that Venice has become the Italian center of distribution for publications related to geographical discoveries.[3]

Venetians had been involved in cartography for quite some time, since long before the invention of printing gave new lifeblood to the enterprise. Their contribution over the centuries to progress in geographical knowledge stems from both their wide-ranging activities and the city's appeal as an economic and cultural center.[4] Venice's capabilities in this regard are unequaled. For example, the Serene Republic's ambassador to Madrid, a member of the Contarini family, will be "the only one able to explain the loss of a day that occurred during Magellan's circumnavigation of the globe."[5]

Let's begin at the beginning. Fra Paolino Minorita, born in Venice in 1275, becomes bishop of Pozzuoli, near Naples, and designs in his *De Mapa Mundi,* a round planisphere picturing a Europe surrounded by ocean. Next, in the first decades of the fifteenth century, Andrea Bianco Veneziano draws nautical charts with a series of instructions for applying to navigation

[2] George Bruner Parks, *Ramuso's Literary History*, "Studies in Philology," 52 (1955), 2, p. 127.
[3] Massimo Donattini, *Giovanni Battista Ramusio e le sue 'Navigationi'. Appuntii per una biografia,* Critica storica," 1980-81, p. 79.
[4] Eugenia Bevilacqua, *Geografi e cosmografi*, in *Storia della cultura veneta*, vol. III, t. II, Neri Pozza, Vicenza 1980, p. 356.
[5] Ibid., p. 364.

some rules of trigonometric calculation.[6] In the seventh chart, which represents north-central Europe, there are some islands on the far side of Norway that do not appear in the works of previous authors, and which are probably related to information obtained during the voyages of the Venetian Zen brothers.[7] But the undoubted primary mover in those years is Fra Mauro. Around 1450 in the Camaldolese monastery on the island of San Michele (the very same monastery where in 1987 history's first printed Koran is rediscovered), Mauro draws "the biggest medieval cartographic monument"[8] ever made, his *Mappa mundi*, rich in decorations and explanations, which survives in a single copy, conserved in the Marciana Library in Venice. This was not his only production; his was in all probability an organized cartographic laboratory where several people worked (including Andrea Bianco, mentioned above) and which produced another world map, commissioned by Alphonse V, King of Portugal, to whom it was sent in 1459,[9] the year that Fra Mauro died.

But meanwhile we have come to the period of the great geographical discoveries, feats accomplished by the Spanish and the Portuguese, as we have said. The Venetians are knocked out of the game, they watch in stunned silence as the world is redrawn, and in February, 1504, the merchant galleys bearing the lion of St. Mark return home empty from Alexandria because all the spices had already been bought by the Portuguese, who had taken the long route around Africa. (But this is not a death blow—after a few years spices will be flowing into the port of the Queen of the Adriatic at the same rate as before). The Venetians look on, keep playing on the mar-

[6] Ibid., p. 359.
[7] Ibid.
[8] Ibid., p. 360.
[9] Ibid.

gins, think—mistakenly—that the Iberians are simply the continuation in the West of what they have already established in
the East and that, therefore, an equilibrium will be established
between the two branches of world trade. (Instead it will be
Great Britain's overwhelming entrance on the scene that will
turn everything on its head and put the Mediterranean out of
the game once and for all).

The Venetian Republic does not immediately become the
distribution hub of the network of new geographical knowledge; Columbus's first voyages across the Atlantic appear to
have caught Venice's printers unprepared. News of the discovered lands comes to Europe with the letter that Columbus
writes in February, 1493—his ships not yet back in port—
addressing it to Luis de Santangel, Finance Minister of the
crown of Aragon and the principal fundraiser for the voyage. In
May, 1493, in order to claim sovereignty over the new lands, the
Catholic Spanish monarchs have the letter translated into Latin
and printed in Rome. Within the next year the letter goes
through nine editions, in Rome, Paris, Basel, and Antwerp, but
is not translated into German until 1497, as though Northern
Europe were not all that interested in the discovery.[10] The
Republic of San Marco enters the scene on the occasion of
Columbus's final voyage, May, 1502-November, 1504. The only
news of that voyage comes in the form of a letter from Jamaica,
written by the navigator to the Spanish sovereigns in 1503. At
first the letter circulates in manuscript form; the first printed
edition comes in 1505, and is made in Venice. Although the
printers have to try to regain their lost ground, the same is not
true for the diplomats, who immediately understand the
epochal importance of the Columbian enterprises. The
Venetian authorities want to find out what the Spanish have

[10] Numa Broc, *La geografia del Rinascimento*, Edizioni Panini, Modena
1989, p. 17.

accomplished, and the efforts of Angelo Trevisan, in 1501 the secretary of Domenico Pisani, ambassador of the Serene Republic in Madrid, turn out to be fundamental. He copies down the transcription of Columbus's letters and commissions Palos, with the decisive assistance of Columbus, to make a map of the coasts of the American continent to be sent back to Venice. He adds to the letters further details gleaned from the oral accounts of Columbus, to whom he is tied by "great friendship" and who, he points out, "at present finds himself in difficulty here, in the bad graces of these sovereigns, and with little money."[11] In light of this passage, it certainly seems possible that the Genose admiral may have been helped through the tough times by a gift of some Venetian ducats. Trevisan's letters are published in Venice in the anonymous volume *Libretto di tutta la navigatione de' Re de Spagna de le isole et terreni novamenti trovati*, printed by Albertino Vercellese, a native of Lissone, a town in the Brianza region not far from Milan. But the writings of Columbus have a very meager readership (they will come into favor in the nineteenth century). The immediate consequence of his paltry publishing success is that America comes to be called "America," and not "Columbia."

Today, if you ask anyone, "Who discovered America?" the answer is obvious: Christopher Columbus. But if the same question had been asked in the sixteenth century the answer would have been different, not Columbus but Amerigo Vespucci. One of the most widely circulated geographical texts of the Renaissance is a letter written by Vespucci[12] that essentially informs Europe of the existence of a new continent, and the most widely distributed edition of this letter is published in the territory of the Serene Republic, in Vicenza.

---

[11] Giuliano Lucchetta, *Viaggiatori e racconti di viaggi nel Cinquecento*, in *Storia della cultrua veneta*, vol.III, t. II, Neri Pozza, Vicenza 1980, p. 435.
[12] Broc, *La geografia del Rinascimento*, cit., p. 17.

In 1502, Vespucci wrote to Lorenzo de' Medici, Florentine ambassador to France. Immediately translated into Latin, the letter is printed in Paris (1503) and in Venice (1504) under the title *Mundus Novus*. It goes through eleven Latin editions before 1506 and no less than fifty in the first half of the sixteenth century. In a word, a best seller. America's birth certificate. Proof that in Germany Vespucci is better known than Columbus is confirmed by Martin Waldseemüller, who, in 1507, in his *Cosmographiae Introductio,* publishes the *Quatar Navigationes* by Vespucci, with this introduction:

> A fourth part of the world has been discovered by Amerigo Vespucci [. . .]. I don't see any reason not to call this part *Ameriga*, or land of Amerigo, or *America*, after the clever man who has discovered it.[13]

So America is born, but in order for the world to be aware of it news of the happy event must be broadcast. The task will be taken on by a humanist from Vicenza, Fracanzio da Montalboddo, who in 1507 publishes *Mondo novo e novamente ritrovati da Alberico Vesputio fiorentino*, and the fifth of the six books reproduces the letter of the Tuscan admiral. This work, along with Waldseemüller's *Cosmographiae*, becomes the main source for early Renaissance geographers. America, therefore, owes its name to the intuition of a German and to the circulation of Vespucci's letter, which only the Venetian publishing trade could guarantee. As Massimo Donattini observes, "The most favorable conditions for the union between publishing and geographical discoveries were achieved in Venice."[14]

Europe at the time is caught up in a fever pitch rush for new

---

[13] Ibid.
[14] Donattini, ,*Giovanni Battista Ramusio*, op. cit., p. 71.

geographical knowledge, and Venice steps up to the role of distribution center for the new breakthroughs. Between 1492 and 1550, ninety-eight works in some way related to the New World are published in Italy: fifty of them are printed in Venice, and second place, with just fifteen works, goes to Rome.[15] Geographical discoveries are recorded in the correspondence of banking houses and in the dispatches of ambassadors accredited at the courts of Portugal and Spain, and only one state of the time could avail itself of both structures at the highest levels: the Serene Republic of Venice. "The great voyage-organizing countries (Spain, Portugal) were not the main information distribution centers," writes Numa Broc. "In this field, Italy seems to have played the role of the real clearing house."[16] After Venice and Italy come Germany and France, with England now momentarily absent but getting ready to join the game in the second half of the century.

The book considered to be the world's first book of islands (*isolario*) is made in Venice in 1528, the work of Benedetto Bordon (or Bordone). Born in Padua around 1450 to a modest family, Bordon is a man of many talents: in addition to being a geographer, he is an able illuminator, drawer, and painter (though his paintings, which we know about through wills and testaments, have all been lost. As an illuminator, he is presumably involved with Aldus Manutius, as we saw in chapter two, in the engraving of the woodcuts for the *Poliphilo*). Toward the end of the century he moves to Venice, where he stays until just before to his death, in February, 1530. He has three daughters and two sons, one of whom in all likelihood is the philologist known as Giulio Cesare Scagliero.[17] In 1508 he requests a print-

[15] Ibid.

[16] Broc, *La geografia Rinascimentale*, op.cit., p. 21.

[17] Myriam Billanovich, *Bordon (Bordone) Benedetto*, in *Dizionario biografico degli italiani*, vol. XII, IEI, Rome 1970, p. 511.

ing license for a series of woodcuts to be brought together in the work *Tutta la provincia de Italia* (lost) and to print a *mappa mundi*. His most important work sees the light twenty years later, in 1528. *Libro di Benedetto Bordon nel qual si ragiona tutte le isole del mondo* (The Book of Benedetto Bordon in which all the islands of the world are discussed) is dedicated to his nephew Baldassare who, probably as a medical officer, has sailed all over the Mediterranean "on the powerful warships of the Venetian Signory and the Catholic King." Jammed with "beliefs and myths beyond reality [. . .] with little information worthy of faith,"[18] Bordon's book changes its title in its first reprinting from *Libro* (book) to *Isolario* (Islandary), and goes through five editions in twenty years, until 1547. Aside from adding the word "*isolario*" to the Italian vocabulary, the volume has another indubitable claim to fame: Baptizing that part of North America with the name Labrador, which grows out of Bordon calling it "*Terra del laboratore*" (land of the worker) in honor of the slaves who were brought there.

Bordon dies, as poor ever, two years after the release of his book, and never sees its success, since the first reprint is in 1534. But his nautical charts and his city plans will know great good fortune. His errors were macroscopic; his Brazil, for example, is a little island not much bigger than the Azores, and North America is drawn as a totally separate island, but Bordon is also the first to report the conquests of Francisco Pizarro in Peru, and he draws a plan of the "great city" of Tenochtitlan with a pyramid plainly visible in the center, probably basing it on the Italian version of the account by Hernan Cortes, translated by Nicolò Liburnio and printed in Venice in 1524 (an anonymous translation had been printed two years earlier in Milan). Present-day Mexico City, at the time sur-

---

[18] Donattini, *Giovanni Battista Ramuso*, op.cit., p. 69.

rounded by the waters of Lake Texcoco, was a perfect example of the concept of the island. He describes terrifying situations, like the island of the Cannibals, near Cuba, whose population conducts raids on nearby islands to capture the inhabitants, "and having taken them, they cook them and eat them," but only the men; they take the women with them, make them pregnant, and then, immediately after the birth, they eat the child, obviously more tender than the leathery adult males. In the next chapter, however, he moves on to more reassuring descriptions of Sicily, Malta, and Ischia.

Antonio Pigafetta, from Vicenza, writes his account of Ferdinand Magellan's circumnavigation of the globe in French because he dedicates it to the Grand Master of the Knights of Rodi, Philippe de Villiers de l'Isle-Adam, but it is the edition printed in Venice in 1536, signed with Maximilianus Transylvanus, that makes his *Il viaggio fatto da gli Spagniuoli a torno a 'l mondo* a work that is well known and highly respected.

We have already mentioned the work of information-gathering carried out by the diplomats of the Serene Republic, but we must recall that the Republic also employed a highly efficient secret service, perhaps the best of its time, with an extensive network of informers who constantly sent reports back to the capital. The aforementioned ambassador, Domenico Pisani, aside from availing himself of the efforts of Trevisan, sends Giovan Matteo Cretico to Lisbon, with the assignment to report on Portuguese affairs in India. There are numerous surviving reports from the ambassadors sent to the Iberian Peninsula in those years. Each report contains news regarding the East and West Indies.[19] Sometimes it is the ambassadors themselves, and not just their secretaries, who gather materials, like Pietro Paqualigo in Portugal in 1501, or Andrea Navagero in Spain. Navagero plays a fundamental role in providing the necessary

[19] Donattini, *Giovanni Battista Ramusio*, op.cit., p. 76.

sources for compiling the first geographical treatise of our era, *Navigationi e viaggi*, by Giovanni Battista Ramusio.

Giovanni Battista's father, Paolo, leaves Venice in the second half of the fifteenth century, in the period in which the Serene Republic is attempting to take possession of the coast of Romagna, to the south of Venice. Giovanni Battista is born in 1485 and in 1505 he enters the Ducal Chancery as a secretary, embarking on a brilliant career that will see him become secretary to the Senate in 1515 and to the Council of Ten in 1533. He travels, going to France in the entourage of Ambassador Alvise Mocenigo, then to Switzerland, Rome, and perhaps also to Africa. But his great passion for geography is the fruit of the concourse between chance and a political assignment:

> In 1530, a Jew named David, who calls himself the son of the king, preaches in Venice the return of the Jews to the Promised Land. Ramusio is charged with examining him and unmasking the mystification if he should find any. Ramusio goes to speak with him and reports back to the Senate ("about forty-years-old, . . . very drawn and thin . . . rich and dressed in silk and has some jewels on his fingers, the Oriental look") [. . .] and he makes, it seems, a good impression: he is erudite in his interpretation of the Bible [. . .] and an excellent horseman and warrior.[20]

For seven years the Jew has been going around to European and African courts, and Ramusio does not take him as a braggart. On the contrary he takes a passionate interest in the man and, above all, in the lands he has visited. He starts to develop an interest in exotic literature, so much so that the Senate does

---

[20] Marcia Milanesi, Introduzione a Giovanni Battista Ramusio, *Navigazioni e Viaggi*, Einaudi, Turin 1978, p. XV.

not hesitate to ask for expert opinions from its secretary. Ramusio is friends with Pietro Bembo, who was also interested in geography and possessed a number of precious *mappa mundi* and astrolabes, which were in fashion among the cultivated men of the time,[21] and in 1495 he published a work of geography, *De Aetna*, "the fruit of observations made directly during an excursion on the [Sicilian] volcano"[22]

His interest in "geographic discoveries and their contribution to a new knowledge of the earth, and in nature and its phenomena," is a common interest[23] of Ramusio and all of his humanist friends, but at the same time it allows Ramusio to distinguish himself from them, being more illustrious by birth and literary glory. The secretary of the Senate, with his interest in cosmography, geography, and history, is undoubtedly more pleasing to the Venetian governing class than those "loafers" who devote themselves to useless things, such as literature and poetry, instead of boarding ships and going to make money in commerce.

Meanwhile Ramusio also tries to act as a mediator between Sebastian Cabot and the Signory. John Cabot's son wants to put his talents as a mariner at the service of the land of his origins and tries to shift from serving the British Crown to serving the Serene Republic. He would like to come to Venice to present his plans in person, but Ramusio's efforts to persuade are not successful, and he concludes that men, insensitive to ideals, explore the earth only "to satiate their immense cupidity and avarice."[24] In any case, the friendship between the two must be solid, since Sebastiano Caboto names Ramusio curator of his interests in Venice.[25]

[21] Lucchetta, *Viaggiatori . . .* , op. cit., p. 483.
[22] Bevilacqua, *Geografi e cosmografi*, op.cit., p. 372.
[23] Milanesi, Introduction . . . , op. cit., p. XVI.
[24] Lucchetta, *Viaggiatori . . .* , op. cit., p. 489.
[25] Donattini, *Giovanni Battista Ramusio*, op. cit., p. 79.

Ramusio's fame as a geographer is such that the Signory assigns him the task of drawing the four geographic charts that adorn the Sala dello Scudo of the Doge's palace. Those plans had more than just a decorative function; they recalled the grandeur of the Republic and the centrality of Venice to the foreign visitors who waited in that room to be received. The earliest news of these charts dates to 1339, during the dogeship of Francesco Dandolo, but Giovanni Battista Ramusio is charged with redoing them, along with Jacopo Castaldi. The four large maps (Asia Major, Asia Minor, Africa, and Europe) still occupy the same place today, even though their attribution to Ramusio is purely nominal since—nearly erased by time— they were entirely redone in 1762 by Francesco Grisellini.

Ramusio initially approaches geographical publishing in the role of translator. In 1534 he translates and publishes the "account of the conquest of Peru by an anonymous follower of Francisco Pizarro, completed with another by Francisco Xeres,"[26] and some scholars claim to see his hand in the anonymous translation of Pigafetta published two years later. Meanwhile Ramusio goes about collecting every sort of geographical account he can get his hands on. The aforementioned Navagero is a generous supplier. Francesco Contarini, Venetian ambassador to the court of Charles V in Flanders, brings him the account in Old French by Geoffroy de Villehardouin on the conquest of Constantinople. The Spanish ambassador to Venice, Diego Hurtado de Mendoza, brother of Antonio, viceroy of Mexico, gives him an account of Montezuma, the last Aztec emperor, and he also receives material from Gonzalo Fernández de Oviedo, alcaide of the fortress of Santo Domingo and historian of the Indies.

Ramusio edits the first Italian edition of Oviedo's *Sumario* and he will reprint it, together with the Spanish author's

[26] Milanesi, Introduction . . . , op. cit., p. XVII.

Historia general, in the third volume of his own *Navigationi*.[27] As a good Venetian, Ramusio has no contempt for a good business deal, and in 1537 he forms a partnership with Oviedo (whom he will never meet in person) and Antonio Priuli, procurator of Saint Mark (the second highest office of the Republic, after the Doge), for the marketing of products from the West Indies ("liquors and sugars"). The contract is signed partly in Santo Domingo and partly in Venice, and it is not known how the venture turned out because the archive of the notary, Pietro de' Bartoli, was destroyed in a fire.[28] All that's known for sure is that, during his lifetime, Ramusio triples the landholdings that he inherited. That a contribution to his increased wealth came from the income derived from his transoceanic enterprise is certainly plausible, but it remains a hypothesis.

The gathering of material needed for the publication of his work goes ahead for at least twenty years, and the end result is *Navigationi*: "Some sixty-five firsthand accounts of voyages undertaken by men from all different countries toward the various corners of the world, from ancient times all the way up to his own time, organically distributed over three volumes *in folio*."[29] The first volume of *Navigationi e viaggi* comes out in 1550, the third in 1556, the second not until 1559, when Ramusio has already been dead for two years. The reason for the order is that the printing forms for the second volume, evidently already prepared, disappeared during a terrible fire that devastated the printing house of Tommaso Giunta. Based on some brief references in some letters, we know that there was supposed to be a fourth volume, planned but never completed.[30] As was his wont, Ramusio published the work anony-

---

[27] Ibid., p. XIX.
[28] Donattini, *Giovanni Battista Ramusio*, op. cit., p. 85.
[29] Lucchetta, *Viaggiatori . . . ,* op. cit., p. 486.
[30] Milanesi, Introduzione . . . , op. cit., p. XXV.

mously, and only after his death and the publication of the second volume does the publisher reveal that he is the author.

The first volume concerns Africa, the Moluccas, and Japan with reference to the voyage of Magellan. This is the most frequently reprinted volume, the one that appeals most to the patriotism of the subjects of Saint Mark, since it deals with an economic activity of vital importance for Venice: the trade in Indian spices and African gold.[31] Throughout the volume there are expressions of "the preoccupation, intense and preponderant in Venice at the time, for the fate of that trade which for generations had strongly favored the power and wealth of the Republic."[32] The second volume is devoted to continental Asia, Persia, China, Muskovy, and Scandinavia. This is where Marco Polo's *Il Milione* is transcribed and reproposed, emphasizing the role played by Polo and all the Venetian voyagers to the Orient in previous centuries. The third volume concerns the New World and it is the least successful, probably because Venice and the Italian peninsula feel estranged from those exploits and those horizons. It comes out in the second half of the sixteenth century, the period in which the Mediterranean and Levantine contributions to the Venetian economy were consolidated.[33] The fourth volume was supposed to deal with South America (extracting it from the third) and the mysterious continent of the austral hemisphere of whose existence everyone was convinced of but that nobody had ever discovered.

The *Navigationi* achieve a wide circulation in Europe. The French discoveries in the Gulf of St. Lawrence, for example, are better documented in Ramusio's third volume than in *Brief Récit*,[34] a work by the French navigator, Jacques Cartier, who

---

[31] Donattini, *Giovanni Battista Ramusio*, op. cit., p. 38.
[32] Ibid., p. 59.
[33] Ibid., p. 61.
[34] Broc, *La geografia del Rinascimento*, op. cit., p. 26.

explored Newfoundland in 1534. Ramusio's major innovation is that he doesn't organize his collection of accounts on a chronological basis but uses a spatial criterion not based on continental masses but on areas of homogenous human occupation.[35] Furthermore, the author of the first geographical treatise in history turns our customary way of viewing the world inside out: "Venetian, and thus citizen of a state whose 'territorial base' was the sea, he sees the world as a succession of seas surrounded by land."[36]

The *Navigationi* also owe their success to their publication in the vernacular, at a time when the common language of science is Latin.[37] Ramusio packages a mass market product at a time when the Tuscan vernacular, destined to become Italian, is rather widespread in Europe. The materials collected by Ramusio will continue to be the standard texts for some parts of the world (Arabia, North Africa) well into the nineteenth century. After him, travel accounts will fill entire libraries, but they will always be separate texts rather than organic collections.

Thanks to Ramusio's volumes, Venice becomes the center of production and sales for geographic charts and maps. This is also the period when some larger publishing enterprises take shape, such as the house of Michele Tramezzino, printer and publisher, who with his brother owns a shop in Venice that operates under the sign of the Sybil, and another in Rome.[38] The first modernly conceived atlases are printed; the printer Bolognino Zaltieri puts together in Venice a collection of fifty plans and views of the city. It seems that this publisher had also compiled a collection of geographical maps, a proper atlas, of which, no known copies exist.[39] Almost all the engravers and

[35] Milanesi, Introduzione . . . , op. cit., p. XXV.
[36] Ibid.
[37] Ibid., p. XXXII.
[38] Bevilacqua, *Geografi e cosmografi* . . . , op. cit., p. 365.
[39] Ibid.

printers in Venice work for the largest cartographer in six-teenth century Italy, Giacomo Gastaldi,[40] a Piedmontese from Villafranca who moves to Venice in 1539 and remains there until his death, in 1566. He is named cosmographer of the Republic. In 1548 he publishes Ptolemy's *Geographia*, with twenty-six Ptolemaic maps and thirty-four new ones.

"In 1485, the year Ramusio was born," writes Marcia Milanesi in her introduction to an edition of *Navigazioni e Viaggi* published in 1978, "the Portuguese have still not reached the Cape of Good Hope and only seven years hence will Columbus set foot, without knowing it, on the fourth part of the world. In 1557, the year of Ramusio's death, the geographical maps are drawn with totally new forms [. . .] Of this passage—of the transformation that that the image of the world underwent in little more than half a century—Giovanni Battista Ramusio is the first historian."[41] But all of this glory and vivacious commerce will not last long. The flourishing of geographical accounts and cartographic pub-lishing in Venice declines in the closing years of the sixteenth century, corresponding to the declining power of the Republic. The great geographic discoveries, opening new routes to immense lands, had brought about the marginaliza-tion of the splendid Gulf of the Adriatic, whose position was by now deleterious.[42] "Ramusio's legacy [. . .] will fall to the Englishman Richard Hakluyt: his *Principal Navigations*, pub-lished immediately after the victory over the Invincible Armada, opens a new chapter of European expansion."[43] By now the world has truly changed, and the torch passes from the Republic of Saint Mark to the realm of Saint George.

[40] Ibid.
[41] Milanesi, Introduzione . . . , op. cit., p. XXI.
[42] Bevilacqua, *Geografi e cosmografi* . . . , op. cit., p. 372.
[43] Donattini, *Giovanni Battista Ramusio*, op. cit., p. 100.

At the beginning of this chapter we noted that cartography is intimately related to war. For combat, whether on land or sea, you need charts. And sixteenth century Venice is not only the city of Titian, Tintoretto, and Veronese, of Sansovino and Palladio, in short a cradle of the arts. It is also a military power. Even more than that, it was *the* superpower of the age. The prowess of its navy was beyond dispute. The Turks managed to beat the Venetians only when they heavily outnumbered them; for skill and expertise the commanders and artillerymen of the Serene Republic were unrivaled. But even on land the Venetian troops were a tough nut to crack. In order to stop them just shy of the gates of Milan, all of the military powers of the age had to form an alliance against them.

Venice was a superpower whose behavior was comparable in many ways to that of the military giant of our own time, the United States. For example, Venetians routinely went about their daily business bearing arms, much more so than any of their contemporaries, and the Republic was one of the most important arms exporters of the time. The forges of Brescia produced body armor, blades for swords, and lance tips, and firearms were assembled there too. In the area around Brescia, in Gardone Val Trompia, and in Friuli, in Pontebba, gun barrels were manufactured, and Beretta, in Gardone, is still one of the world's most important producers of light firearms. Verona produced equipment for the cavalry, while in the valleys to the north of Brescia and in Montovun in Istria, shafts for lances, halberds, and partisans (a kind of lance with a triangular tip with two wings at the base) were cut and modeled. The only supplies that Venice had to import were the more sophisticated kinds of breech-blocks for pistols and harquebuses, sulfur and part of the saltpeter needed for gun powder, and copper for its bronze cannons.[44] Venice itself

---

[44] John R. Hale, *Industria del libro e cultura militare a Venezia nel Rinascimento*, in *Storia della cultura veneta*, op. cit., p. 266.

produced light arms (arrows and spears), and its bronze cannons were cast at the Arsenal. The armory of the Arsenal alone (sacked and pillaged by Napoleon) was believed to be capable of outfitting ten thousand soldiers and, with the smaller more selective armory of the Council of Ten, constituted a well-known attraction for important visitors. The target-shooting matches at the Lido attracted as many as eight hundred contestants from all social classes.[45] Furthermore, arms were widely distributed throughout the Venetian state, arms possession was normal, and the government of Venetia was more willing than any of its rival governments to trust its citizens, an attitude encouraged by the lack of revolts aboard the realm's ships where every man, from oarsman to patrician commander, was armed in case of combat on the sea.[46]

Obviously, this enormous and variegated military force must be governed, and consequently "no other governing class had such a well-motivated interest in military questions as the Venetian patriciate,"[47] and the nobility are generally educated people who read. Moreover, the patricians, in rotation, serve as military commanders on land and sea before going on to hold political offices that determine military policy—the Senate, the Council of Ten, the College—bringing their military experience in the field with them. The patricians in command are always assisted by secretaries and accountants, they too are educated, and thus potential readers. Finally, we must not forget the mainland nobility that traditionally supplies the personnel for the high command of the ground forces (while the Venetian patriciate provides the commanders for the fleet.)

This explains why the domestic market for military texts is rather vast, without taking into account those who have an

[45] Ibid., p. 267.
[46] Ibid.
[47] Ibid.

interest in such issues for scholarly or legal purposes.[48] And it also explains why "from 1492 to 1570 there were 145 works printed in Venice related to military issues [. . .]. Not counting new editions and reprints, Venetian printers in this period produced sixty-seven new titles."[49] In the same period, the rest of Europe together published only sixty-four (with the rest of Italy, excluding Venice accounting for the lion's share, twenty-two, while England produces just fourteen and France ten). "Venice's supremacy in this field is surprisingly evident"[50]; equally surprising, however, is the total absence of works devoted to naval war (perhaps the Venetians thought they had nothing to learn in that field). To be sure, military publishing was not the only sector in which Venice was the head of the class—the city also led in the publishing of Bibles, law books, classical texts and translations, medicine, geography—but the novelty lies in the fact that "the unusually high percentage of military books did not derive from the presence of some renowned scholar in this field, in the same way that the presence of Regiomontanus helped to make Nuremberg the European center for the printing of original works on mathematics. Nor was there a particular printer who solicited the demand, as Aldus Manutius did for reasonably priced classical texts in Venice at the beginning of the sixteenth century."[51] Military publishing, in short, is an enterprise of the first water, and there were a lot of printers who dived into it head first, though no one established a dominant position in the market: the first fifty-three original titles (to which must be added ten re-editions and four translations) were edited by thirty-one different printers. One publisher,

[48] Ibid., p. 268.
[49] Ibid., p. 245.
[50] Ibid.
[51] Ibid., p. 246.

Gabriel Giolito de'Ferrari, prints ten titles, but he is certainly not specialized in military publishing, given that he is described as being the most active of the Venetian printers of the time.[52]

Giolito also promotes an unprecedented publishing initiative which appears to be the prototype of the serial works printed in installments in the nineteenth century, and he begins the use of the word that is still well known in the publishing world today, "series." Giolito de'Ferrari uses *"ghirlanda"* (garland) to indicate a number of volumes in the same format issued in sequence, exactly what publishers today designate as a series. From 1557 to 1570 he publishes a series of volumes, all in italic characters and in the same format, of thirteen Greek historians, along with a parallel series of military books.[53] In the end, the volumes will constitute a collection "with which you will be able to adorn your rooms," the publisher declares. That this actually turned out to be the case was demonstrated two centuries later, in 1773, when one of these collections was sold, the one belonging to the library of British Consul Joseph Smith.

This is a period of epochal transition, in which artillery takes on an ever more important role and the defense strategies of cities are compelled to adjust to it. There is a gradual shift from machicolation-based, vertical defense to rampart and ditch defense, from towers and high, thin walls to pointed bastions and low, thick walls able to stand up to enemy heavy artillery. During this period, Venetian printers establish a "quasi monopoly"[54] in works about military architecture and the art of fortification.

[52] Ibid.
[53] Ibid., p. 261.
[54] Ibid., p. 275.

154 - ALESSANDRO MARZO MAGNO

All of the sixteenth century states set about modernizing their systems of defense, but "nevertheless it is unclear whether any other state in this period had a restructuring program as vast and amply debated as the one carried out in the Venetian state."[55] Indeed, with the exception of Vicenza, all the important cities of the Venetian state reconstruct their defensive walls in response to modern artillery. In 1499 the Turks entered Friuli and the fires of their encampments could be seen from the top of the bell tower of St. Mark's. The decision was made—not all that quickly—to build a fortress that would make anymore such incursions impossible. On October 7, 1593, (the anniversary of the Battle of Lepanto) the cornerstone of the fortress-city of Palmanova is laid. Port defense also had to be modernized, in Dalmatia, in the Aegean, on Cyprus, Crete, and even Venice. Here things happened faster, and from 1554 to 1559 Michele Sanmicheli, a celebrated architect of the time, built the fort of Sant'Andrea, guarding the access to the lagoon at the mouth of the port of the Lido (Palmanova will never be used, Sant'Andrea will open fire just once, in 1797, against a French ship, ironically named *Libérateur d'Italie*. The ship sinks, and Commandant Domenico Pizzamano will be arrested to placate Napoleon).

Missing from the authors of works of military architecture, the dominant category of Venetian military books,[56] is the most famous architect of the era, Andrea Palladio, who never takes an interest in fortifications, although he nurtures a remarkable interest in the training and organization of armies.

But he doesn't stop at pure theory, he puts his passion into practice, organizing an "old-fashioned training"[57] session at the expense of a specially constituted formation of recruits—

[55] Ibid.
[56] Ibid., p. 274.
[57] Ibid., p. 266.

explorers and galley oarsmen. That an architect of villas and churches could bark orders over an improvised training field and count on an audience that included experts in the art of war attests to the existence of a relatively substantial readership of military books.[58]

The unchallenged leader in books on fortifications, Venice is also first in books on artillery, and establishes its preeminence "with no need to reprint books first published elsewhere.[59] In the middle two decades of the sixteenth century, only two works on artillery are printed outside of Venice, and one of them is printed in Brescia, within the borders of the Venetian state (the other is printed in Nuremberg in 1547). But artillery also means ballistics, and, therefore, mathematics. A certain interest in mathematics was widespread in Italy, but more specifically it was in Venice that this interest took the form of a plethora of books on the art of war.[60] Not coincidentally, the first Latin translation of Euclid dates back to 1505.

After this overview of the theoretical apparatus of the sixteenth century's superpower, it may be worth pausing to reflect on the kinds of books that were not published there—those regarding naval warfare. This absence arouses "a certain surprise, if one takes into account how numerous were the Venetians who had experienced life on board ship, of the continuous nature of the state of war and anti-piracy activities, of the experimentation of new ships and new ways for arming and outfitting them."[61] Actually, a book ready to be printed, but never published, did exist and had, although only in manuscript, quite an impact. The book was *Della militia maritima* by Cristoforo da Canal "the most imaginative and combative of

[58] Ibid.
[59] Ibid., p. 276.
[60] Ibid., p. 277.
[61] Ibid., p. 279.

the [sixteenth century] Venetian naval commanders."[62] The nobleman-commander, or *sopracomito*—galley commanders were always noblemen—was born in 1510 and died in 1562 from wounds suffered in combat at sea. Apart from a brief stint as quarter-master general in Marano Lagunare, he spends his entire life in the fleet. He is the first to use convict rowers on galleys instead of free men (*buonavoglia* or volunteers) and he is the first to command an armed galley with an entire crew of convicts. His innovation is so successful that the Italian term for galley, *galera*, transitions from designating a ship to designating a jail. Cristoforo da Canal dies without seeing the publication of his treatise on maritime war which is "much admired but never sent to press."[63]

One of the reasons for this absence of naval warfare books from Venetian military publishing may be the fact that combat on the open sea was avoided whenever possible and the main task of the fleet was instead to transport troops and supplies in support of land operations. Nor must we forget the fleet's role as a deterrent: Venetian ships were sent to the hot spots of the Mediterranean to show the flag and make it understood that it was better to avoid having anything to do with them, a forerunner of sorts of the "fleet in being" that would characterize naval deployment policy up to World War I.

[62] Ibid., p. 260.
[63] Ibid.

8.
MUSIC PUBLISHING

The image of a city all lutes and madrigals might be a stereotype but it's not all that far from the truth. The Venetians of the sixteenth century are defined by the German painter Albrect Dürer as "connoisseurs of art and good lute players"[1] while Cassandra Fedele, that rare figure of a female humanist, becomes famous as a poetess and musician. In 1533 Andrea Gabrieli is born, destined to become the organist at St. Mark's and, together with his nephew Giovanni, one of the best-known musicians in the world.

So the Venetians can play, and they can sing too. The vibrato is in fashion and continues to be so for several centuries, so much so that when a sleepless Richard Wagner walks the streets of nineteenth century nighttime Venice in search of lost repose, he finds instead the inspiration for the finale of Act Two of *Tristan and Isolde*, by listening to the singing of the gondoliers. In the first half of the twentieth century it was not rare to hear the Venetian milkman announce himself with a musical refrain, or the pile-driver singing to keep his rhythm as he planted the mooring piles in the bottom of the canal. All that singing meant that people knew music and therefore that collections of songs and sonatas were not a niche product for a small elite but, on the contrary, publications with an ample

---

[1] Agostino Vernarecci, *Ottaviano de'Petrucci da Fossombrone, inventore dei tipi mobile metallici fusi della musica nel secolo XV*, romagnoli, Bologna 1882, p. 38.

readership. This to underline that, from the very beginning, Venetian music publishing had enormous potential in the domestic market.

Contrary to other sectors, which developed quickly and soon reached their peak, printed music follows a strange sort of roundabout itinerary before Venice finally becomes its undisputed capital. In this case there are two individual print shops, Scotto and Gardano, who alone publish "more than two thousand music editions, a figure representing more than the total output of all contemporary Italian and northern European music printers combined."[2] Scotto and Gardano amounted to two printing dynasties: "their contributions to the commercialization of music printing along with their prodigious outputs established the Houses of Scotto and Gardano as the two most important music publishing firms in Renaissance Europe."[3] Nevertheless, despite reaching such heights, they are not the first to print music in Venice, nor the first to use movable type to print polyphonic music (much more complicated than Gregorian chant). This last achievement is credited to Ottaviano Petrucci, considered by many "the Gutenberg of music."

The first attempts to print notes are made immediately following the first edition of Gutenberg's Bible. A couple of years later, in 1547, also in Mainz, Johann Fust and Peter Schöffer publish a Psalter with the lines printed on a press and the notes added by hand. But it will be the opposite procedure, tracing the lines of the musical staff by hand and then printing the notes over them, that will prevail.

The first attempt to print music with movable type has been dated to 1476, when a certain Ulrich Han publishes a missal in

[2] Jane A. Bernstein, *Print, Culture and Music in Sixteenth Century Venice*, Oxford University Press, New York-Oxford 2001, p. 115.
[3] Ibid. p. 140.

Rome (yet another German immigrant in Italy). The music in
this case, however, it is important to note, is Gregorian chant,
which has a simpler system of notation than polyphonic music;
only four lines and a smaller variety of notes. "Liturgical music
was simpler to print, and thus flourished first. The nature of
chant, with its relatively narrow range and lack of rhythmic differentiation, made it far easier to reproduce in print than [. . .]
complex polyphonic music. . . ."[4] In Han's missal, however,
"the musical effect is not thrilling, being the result of a printing with roughly designed wooden forms of irregular dimensions."[5]

Music proved to be one of the most challenging typogra-
phies of all. Besides requiring a different set of symbols, it presented technical difficulties that had not been encountered
before. Liturgical chant can be transcribed using three different notation systems: Roman, Gothic, or Ambrosian.
Normally, the lines were printed in red and then the sheets
were passed through the presses to impress the notes in black,
but often the inside of the notes on the line were blackened by
hand. Even in the era of the incunabula, however, Venice was
the leader; in the 1480s it issues more than seventy-six editions
or more than half of all Italian music incunabula. Some seventeen Venetian printers participated in the production of music
books. Giunti was the leading printer of liturgical music books
until 1569, when Pope Pius V granted another printer an
exclusive privilege to print the Tridentine missal.[6]

The revolution, in any event, is on its way and once again it
will be brought to Venice by an immigrant. Ottaviano Petrucci
is a native of Fossombrone, near Pesaro, in the Marches, born

[4] Mary S. Lewis, *Antonio Gardano Venetian Music Printer 1538-1569*,
Garland Publishing, New York-London 1988, p. 4.
[5] Franco Mariani, *I cinquecento anni della stampa della musica a caratteri
mobile*, Civitanova Marche 2001.
[6] Ibid.

on June 18, 1466. He proves himself to be "an innovator, a dis-seminator, and in some measure the initiator of the great explo-sion in musical literacy."[7] His biographer draws a curious par-allel: in the music revolution, Ottaviano Petrucci is Karl Marx (the one who conceives it) while Antonio Gardano is Lenin (the one who enacts it).[8] We know very little about his life before he became a printer, in his thirties, a rather advanced age at the time. His family is not poor; they own land outside of the city, but in 1493 Ottaviano sells it. We don't know why, nor do we know when and why he moves to Venice. We know only that in 1493 he asks the Signory for a privilege for print-ing music, and from this we deduce that he must have already been in the city for a while. We have no idea as to when and where he learned how to print, though some have hypothe-sized Urbino[9]; but it could also have been in Venice, where since 1480 his fellow townsman, Bartolomeo Budrio, from Fossombrone, has been running a printing shop in association with Antonio della Paglia, from Alessandria, and Marchesino di Savioni, from Milan.[10] There is also another native of Fossombrone living in the Serene Republic at the time: a maes-tro of the lute by the name of Francesco Spinacino (Petrucci will print a book of his). A printer and a musician in the city where the first printer of polyphonic music will work. We don't have proof, but perhaps their moving to Venice at around the same time is not just a coincidence.

Between the request for the privilege and the actual print-ing of the first book three years go by, an unusually long inter-val, which, perhaps, is justified by the technical difficulties encountered in engraving the notes and symbols necessary for

[7] Stanley Boorman, *Ottaviano Petrucci. Catalogue Rasinonné*, Oxford University Press, Oxford-New York 2006, p. 3.
[8] Ibid.
[9] Vernarecci, *Ottaviano . . .* , op. cit., p.29.
[10] Boorman, *Ottaviano Petrucci . . .* , op. cit., p. 27.

polyphonic music, placing them correctly on the staff, and making sure that the whole thing doesn't move. It is no coincidence that polyphonic music finishes almost last in the race to print. In any event, the publication of the first music book in movable type seems to have been an affair totally dominated by immigrants to Venice from the Marches, since Petrucci is helped in the composition by Petrus Castellanus, whom recent studies have identified as a Dominican monk from the monastery of SS. Giovanni e Paolo, a native of the Marches, who will become *Maestro di cappella* in 1505.[11]

It is May 15, 1501 when the *Harmonice Musices Odhecaton*— better known as *Odhecaton*— sees the light. It is a collection of *chansons*, some in Latin and some in Greek, written primarily by Franco-Flemish composers. According to the title, there should be a hundred *chansons* but in reality there are only ninety-six. The text is composed in sharply defined Gothic characters, printed in brilliant black ink, which have been conserved unchanged on the pages that we are still able to read five centuries later. The metal characters, whether in lead, tin, or an alloy, were evidently engraved by masters of the art; it wasn't difficult to find them back then in Venice, where the major printers placed great importance on the quality of the characters used for their works.[12] A few fragments of the original have survived along with an incomplete copy conserved in Bologna, at the civic museum of musical bibliography. This publishing enterprise must have been successful because nine months later Petrucci publishes a second title. He evidently recognized an untapped demand for printed editions of polyphonic music and had some sort of assurances that an up-to-date repertory would be available to him[13]: the printer from

[11] Ibid., p. 33.
[12] Mariani, *I cinquecento anni . . . ,* op. cit.
[13] Lewis, *Antonio Gardano . . .* , op. cit., p. 5.

162 - ALESSANDRO MARZO MAGNO

Fossombrone, in short, is able to give his readers the hits of the moment, and music lovers repay him for the effort by buying his editions.

Petrucci uses a very costly printing technique: each sheet passes through the press three times, the first to impress the lines, the second the notes and symbols, and the third the lyrics. He uses characters that are very small and sharply defined, obtaining a level of quality that is unmatched; even his reprints are excellent, indistinguishable from the first pressrun, "which made Petrucci's work a true masterpiece and its maker a true artist,"[14] while in the editions published by other printers it is fairly normal that the reprints are not on a par with the first edition. Additionally, unlike the work of other printers, whose books had relatively few pages of music, Petrucci's volumes consisted entirely of music.[15]

No one could equal the precision with which Petrucci aligned the notes on the staff nor rival the elegant look of his pages of music. Petrucci designed his music books to resemble manuscripts, in keeping with the custom at the time.[16] But his system has a fundamental problem: it is enormously expensive. His printed volumes are probably as expensive as many manuscripts.[17] Moreover, obtaining the desired precision by passing the sheets through the press three times is a very labor-intensive and time-consuming procedure that does not allow for large pressruns: it is believed that they didn't go beyond 150 copies. Circulation is thus limited perforce to the same small elite that commission manuscripts—the natural consequence is the search for less costly printing methods. We must assume that the potential market is appetizing, given that more than a

[14] Mariani, *I cinquecento anni . . .* , op. cit.
[15] Bernstein, *Print . . .* op. cit., p. 20.
[16] Ibid. p. 21.
[17] Lewis, *Antonio Gardano . . .* , op. cit., p. 5.

few printers try to take advantage of it, such as Jacomo
Ungaro, a letter engraver, and a former apprentice in the
Manutius printing shop, who in 1513 asks for a privilege for
"having found the way to print figured chant."[18]

In any case, commercial success smiles on Ottaviano
Petrucci, and he appears to have invested part of his profits in
his hometown, since Duke Guidobaldo grants him the honor
of being elected to the Council of Fossombrone, access to
which is only allowed to the wealthy. In 1511—let's not forget
that at the time Venice was no longer in control of the mainland after the defeat in Agnadello in 1509, and will not regain
possession of it until 1516—Petrucci decides to move his business home. In Fossombrone, Petrucci continues to devote himself to printing, but not just of music. In 1513 he publishes the
most important work of Paul of Middelburg, the city's bishop:
De recta Paschae Celebratione, better known as *Paulina*, a treatise on the correction of the Roman calendar and the calculations for determining the exact date for Easter. It is a prestigious
volume, with beautiful decorations and marvelous initial letters,
and a sharply defined text with a great typographical effect,
which invites admiration as a superb example of fine printing.
Especially noteworthy in the *Paulina* is the beauty of the font,
designed by Francesco Griffo, who in those years is working in
Fossombrone.[19]

The printer invests the profits from his printing business in
a related sector: papermaking. He owns at least two paper
mills, one in Sora, near Fossombrone, and one in Acquasanta
di Fossombrone which, passing through a series of owners, will
continue to operate until 1862. Petrucci dies in 1539—as far as
we know, in Venice—after a life at the forefront of the dynamic

[18] Renato Fulin, *Documenti per servire alla storia della tipografia veneziana,*
"Archivio Veneto," 23 (1882), p. 86.
[19] Mariani, *I cinquecento anni . . .* , op.cit.

Venetian printing industry and after having held in his native city an uninterrupted series of public offices.[20] His is one of the many cases of underappreciated illustrious sons of Italy. As the inventor of movable-type music printing, he certainly deserves to be remembered with something more than a piazza in his native Fossombrone and two streets, one in Urbino and one in Fiumicino, in the province of Rome.

An alternative to Petrucci's printing method is the technique developed by Andrea Antico, an Istrian musician from Montona (then part of the Venetian state, today the town is called Motovun, located in Croatia), who lives in Rome. He designs a mixed method: engraving the notes in wooden matrices using woodcut techniques and composing the text below the lines in movable type. He moves to Venice in 1520 and works as an engraver with the principal printers of the era, especially with Ottaviano Scotto. He publishes his own editions, and his system has the advantage of requiring just one passage of the paper through the press, as well as the ability to reuse the matrices, but in the end it will not turn out to be cost-competitive.[21] Indeed, although the printing procedure undoubtedly takes less time, the work of carving the notes into the woodblocks requires hours and hours; the only substantial difference from the multiple-impression method is in the pressrun: many more copies could be printed in the same amount of time. Recent studies estimate that the cost of a music book printed by Antico was one-third the cost of a book by Petrucci, and therefore the Istrian printer should have been able to approach commercially profitable production costs. Nevertheless, the time required for carving the notes limited the quantity of titles that could be published. Both craftsmen, Petrucci and Antico, produced editions of surpassing beauty

[20] Ibid.
[21] Bernstein, *Print* . . . , op. cit., p. 21.

and clarity; however, they made only limited headway toward meeting the needs of the potential market for printed music.[22]

This time the answer does not come from Venice but from London, where, for the first time, music is printed with a single passage of the sheets through the press. The single-impression printing method is developed between 1519 and 1523 by John Rastell, who will not, however, manage to turn his invention into a profitable business. Instead, commercial success will reward the efforts of a Parisian, Pierre Attaingnant (or Attaignant), the royal music printer, who in 1528 transforms the publication of books with notes and staffs into an activity just as potentially lucrative as the printing of words and woodcuts. His method is very simple: the staff is divided into vertical sections within which the notes and symbols are placed. The various sections are then mounted one next to the other to reach the desired length. The points where the staffs come together can be seen and the final result doesn't come close to the refinement and elegance of the editions of Petrucci and Antico, but it costs infinitely less. The aesthetic brilliance of earlier music books was sacrificed in favor of mass production. It was now cheaper, faster, and easier to produce music books than ever before.[23] "The process," writes Jane Bernstein in *Print Culture and Music in Sixteenth Century Venice*, "made not only quantity production possible, but inexpensive quantity production possible for the first time."[24] It appears that Attaingnant's editions were still more expensive than nonmusic books, but they had a pressrun of around one thousand copies.

Single-impression music printing is like an electric current that radiates throughout Europe, but it will not be capable of

[22] Lewis, *Antonio Gardona* . . . , op. cit., p. 6.
[23] Bernstein, *Print* . . . , op. cit., p. 22.
[24] Lewis, *Antonio Gardano* . . . , op. cit., p. 6.

turning on the light until it reaches Venice. From Paris it goes to Lyons and then to Germany, Nuremberg, Wittenberg, Frankfurt, and Augsburg, and in 1537 it arrives in Naples, to then sail back up the peninsula and dock, a year later, in the Serene Republic. In her study of Antonio Gardano, Mary Lewis writes, "It was in Venice that the commercial possibilities of music printing, and particularly of the single-impression process, were most consistently and fruitfully realized. [. . .] the growth in the numbers of those who could read music took place over a considerable length of time"[25] in a city that had numerous centers of musical instruction, both lay and religious. The Venetians also introduce a series of innovative techniques, developing special tools for music printing; probably the wood galley tray that framed the composed page had notches and grooves to keep the lines of music aligned, and some have hypothesized that large pins were used to keep the lines from moving out of line on the sheets.

The Venetian environment was propitious. In fact, during the first part of the sixteenth century a collector market emerged that was attuned to the purchase of music by great composers[26]: while in principle the publishers limited themselves to describing the book's contents, at the end of the 1530, they start specifying the names of the composers included in the collections and then publishing books with the compositions of a single artist. The academies of art and literary societies that proliferate in Renaissance Italy constitute another important source of readers. The Philharmonic Academy of Verona, founded in 1543 and still with us today, has conserved its library nearly intact: its collection of ancient music contains some 230 printed works, most of which are sixteenth century madrigals. Finally, let's not forget that for noblemen and gen-

[25] Ibid., p. 7.
[26] Ibid., p. 13.

tlemen it is normal to spend the after-dinner hours singing and playing music, and therefore it follows that music books become an item of daily use. When supply meets demand the music printing industry passes from an artisanal phase to a period of vast commercial expansion. This is the period in which the two great dynasties of music publishing, Gardano and Scotto, publish over 850 editions in thirty years, a figure that surpassed the total output of all other European music printers combined.[27]

The new system of music printing is brought to Venice by a Frenchman, Antonio Gardano. But before we talk about Gardano let's talk about Ottaviano Scotto, the founding father of the other music publishing dynasty, who started a bit earlier. Scotto is born in Monza, near Milan, and in the 1470s he opens his first printing shop in Venice, in San Samuele, a neighborhood known today as home to Palazzo Grassi, the headquarters of the Pinault Foundation and prestigious art exhibits. Scotto also publishes non-musical editions, and he is an important innovator. "He is the first printer to use quarto and octavo formats for liturgical books. These small formats not only made liturgical books more affordable but also allowed new possibilities for the clergy since the bulk and weight of large folio volumes meant they couldn't be moved from their lecterns."[28]

Ottaviano Scotto dies on December 24, 1498, and is buried at San Francesco della Vigna. His gravestone is still visible on the floor of the cloister of the Franciscan monastery (the one whose library conserves the first Koran). The business continues under Ottaviano II but the boom arrives with Girolamo, who will be the head of the Scotto house for thirty-six years. "Active as a publisher, bookseller, and composer from around

[27] Bernstein, *Print* . . . , op. cit., p. 22.
[28] Ibid., p. 116.

1536 until his death in 1572, Girolamo issued more than 400 music publications, containing a huge repertory that ranged from Masses to motets and madrigals, chansons, and instrumental music by all the leading composers of the day. The influence of the Scotto press as printer and publisher extended beyond music into other fields, in particular philosophy, medicine, and religion, where it published a number of books equal to the firm's music production."[29]

Girolamo is a leading figure in the Venice of his time, so much so that he behaves like a typical patrician, investing the proceeds from his bookselling business in the agricultural sector. The Scotto family owns properties in Venice, Padua, and Treviso. The dynasty dies out in 1615, with the illegitimate son of Melchiorre Scotto, Baldissera. When Baldissera dies he is not buried in the family tomb at San Francesco della Vigna and he has no right to pass on the family's wealth to his heirs, so the properties are sold at auction.[30] "During its 134 year history, the House of Scotto printed more than 1,650 editions, while the Gardano press, which endured for seventy-three years, produced some 1,425. In both cases these figures matched or far exceeded the other great printing houses of Venice. Indeed the Scotto and Gardano Houses were not just important presses; they were the most renowned music publishing houses of Renaissance Europe."[31]

About the founder of the other dynasty, Antonio Gardano, we know very little of his life before he begins his printing career on the lagoon, in 1538. He is French (all of his editions will be signed Gardane until 1555, when he Italianizes his surname, continuing, however, to sign Gardane on notarized con-

[29] Jane A. Bernstein, *Music Printing in Renaissance Venice*, Oxford University Press, New Yorl-Oxford 1998, p. 4.
[30] Bernstein, *Print . . .*, op. cit., p. 128.
[31] Ibid., p. 12.

tracts)[32] but we don't know from where, perhaps the Midì. Near Aix-en-Provence there is a town named Gardanne. But if he learned the art of printing in France then it had to have been in Paris or Lyons, likely Lyons, because in that city, in 1532, at age twenty-two, he publishes his first composition, a Mass, as part of a collection. When he arrives in Venice he is not a printer but a musician, and he is often referred to as a "French musician," and one letter mentions a music school, which he may have directed. He will continue composing all his life, but will publish only a third of his works. He opens a shop in Calle della Simia, in Rialto (during the city's nineteenth century urban renewal it was widened and transformed into the present-day Larga Mazzini), and the first work that he prints is not a music edition but a collection of letters, the *Pistole vulgari* by Nicolò Franco, former secretary of Pietro Aretino. That the sixteenth century polemicist and his assistant had had a falling out can be deduced from a letter from October 7, 1539, which Aretino writes to Ludovico Dolce, spewing contempt for poor Franco: "The Sodomite, from the writer of my letters he becomes their emulator, from which he made a book that, with its failure to sell even one copy, has ruined the Frenchman Gardano, who lent him the money to print them."[33] Aretino exaggerates; in fact the *Pistole* must not have sold all that badly since Gardano reprints them in 1542. But from this letter we also learn two other things: confirmation that the printer is of French origin and that in those times a partnership between author and publisher was not so unusual.

It is fairly common for printers and booksellers in cities throughout Italy, lacking in specialized equipment and

---

[32] Claudio Sartori, *Una dinastia di editori musicali. Documenti inediti sui Gardano e i loro congiunti Stefano Bindoni e alessandro Raverii*, Olschki, Florence 1956 (Extract from "La Bibliofilia"), p. 178.

[33] Pietro Aretino, *Lettere*, in *Opere di Foligno, Aretino, Doni*, Volume II, Ricciardi, Milan-Naples 1976, p. 546.

machines for printing music, to commission editions from Venetians. Even a leading cultural center such as Florence has no specialized music printers until the 1580s.[34] Furthermore, certain editions required complicated operations, like the printing of a work for the Roman Curia in 1516, for which Ottaviano Scotto finances the publication and distributes the 1,008 copies of the pressrun, Andrea Antico composes the musical text and engraves the woodcuts, and Antonio Giunta does the printing. Giunta is not a partner in the enterprise but is paid for his services.[35] It is the composers themselves who best understand the profound influence of the publishing industry and try to turn it to their advantage. They eagerly sought out reliable and competent printers who could print their works quickly and correctly, as we learn from Heliseo Ghibel, who thanks Ottaviano Scotto popularizing out his motets.[36] And we can't forget the importance of religious music. For example, the monastic community of San Giorgio Maggiore paid the Venetian printer Girolamo Scotto 550 lire to produce 500 copies of a music edition in 1565.[37]

But let's return to Antonio Gardano, who in 1538 publishes his first music book, *Venticinque canzoni francesi* (Twenty-five French Songs), and from that moment on devotes himself to music publishing. In that same year he marries the sister of Stefano Bindoni, a famous Venetian bookseller.[38] (In the male chauvinist tradition we always know the names of the fathers and brothers of the women referred to in the documents but almost never the names of the women themselves.) The couple will have six children; four boys and two girls. The

[34] Bernstein, *Print . . .* , op. cit., p. 80.
[35] Ibid., p. 75.
[36] Ibid., p. 100.
[37] Brian Richardson, *Printing, Writers, and Readers in Renaissance Italy*, Cambridge University Press, Cambridge 1999, p. 65.
[38] Sartori, *Una dinastia . . .* , op. cit., p. 177.

Frenchman's publishing success is highlighted by his decision, in 1548, to move the printing shop to the Mercerie, then, as now, the city's most important commercial artery. Antonio Gardano dies on October 28, 1569, at the age of sixty, as noted in the *Necrologi di sanità* conserved in the Archive of the Frari, in Venice. His gravestone can still be seen on the floor of the church of San Salvador (where we also find the tombstone of Caterina Corner, Queen of Cyprus and Armenia). His profession as a printer evidently enriched his family: his will lists fifty-four agricultural fields in the areas of Mirano and Camposanpietro (today in the provinces of Venice and Padua), a house in Padua, and a good number of those luxury items that the Venetians of his day were crazy about: carpets, candelabras, mirrors, precious fabrics, men's shirts, pillows, table linen, for a total value of 1,200 ducats. By way of comparison, in the same period the annual salary of the Mastro di Cappella of Saint Mark's is 200 ducats. If it is true, as Pietro Aretino claims, that in 1539-1540 Gardano risked going into ruin, that means that over the next thirty years he accumulated a remarkable fortune from music publishing.[39]

The plague of 1575-1577 (when a fourth of the city's population dies and the Signory, as a votive offering, commissions Andrea Palladio to design the church of the Redeemer, on the Giudecca) deals a harsh blow to the Gardano House, which goes from sixteen editions in 1576 to just three the following year (the House of Scotto went from sixteen to five). From 1575 to 1611 Angelo Gardano issues at least 813 music editions, doubling his father's output. He dies at seventy-one, on August 6, 1611. The business is taken over by his son-in-law, Bartolomeo Magni, and stays in operation for almost the entire century under the name of Magni until, in 1685, it disappears, and with it Gardano's legacy.

[39] Lewis, *Antonio Gardana . . .* , op. cit., p. 33.

It's not known what early relations between Scotto and Gardano were like, but some of their contemporaries let on that the two men behaved like two roosters in a chicken coop, each pirating the other's editions whenever possible. But by 1541 the mood between them seems to have improved, and later on Scotto and Gardano frequently publish editions with similar, if not identical, content, suggesting they had reached some form of equilibrium between competition and cooperation.[40] The partnership between the two, with occasional flare-ups, will continue for many years.

"The real money in music publishing lay not with the printing of books but with their distribution. As highly successful book merchants, Gardano and Scotto maintained efficient marketing systems involving established networks of publishers, printers, and booksellers that stretched far beyond the confines of Venice."[41] The two great Venetian houses send their *procurators* (in modern terminology, sales reps) all around Europe to take orders for their books and arrange for shipment. In this extensive network of relationships, which is the basis of the European book trade, family ties are a big help, and so it is fairly common that the most important reps are close relatives of the publishers. As wealthy merchants, Scotto and Gardano also act as brokers for the shipping of works published by the city's smaller printing houses.

We have already mentioned the distribution outlets for the book trade but it is worth returning to them in order to understand the dimensions of the market. The resident population of Venice alone is able to absorb from 500 to 1,000 copies of each music edition, a figure that is sufficient to justify publication. But even at that time there were a lot of tourists in

---

[40] Lewis, *Antonio Gardanoi . . .* , op. cit., p. 32.
[41] Bernstein, *Print . . .* op. cit. p. 85.

Venice, for the most part pilgrims waiting to embark on a ship bound for the Holy Land. In all likelihood, one of these tourists is the German woman Maria Pfaffenperg, who proudly writes in her music book: "*Anno 1577. In Venedig, dis Beuch gehört mir*" (this book belongs to me).[42] Another important outlet is the Kingdom of the Two Sicilies, especially Naples and Sicily, places easily reached by sea, more than other northern Italian cities are by land. Numerous Scotto and Gardano editions are conserved in the libraries of Naples, Messina, and Palermo: the Venetian printers "dominated Italian music printing."[43] Another fundamental market was central and northern Europe. The music edition catalogues of the 1565 Frankfurt book fair show thirty-two Venetian editions, one from Rome, one from Louvain, and one from Wittenberg.[44] In short, a quasi monopoly, with compositions evenly divided between sacred and profane, a sign that northern Europe appreciated the songs from the South at least as much as they liked High Mass.

Through the third decade of the sixteenth century, the best route for reaching the markets of the North was the water route, operated by the so-called *muda di Fiandra*, which stopped at Southampton before going on to its final destination in Flanders. The name *muda* was given to several convoys of merchant galleys with fixed navigation routes (for example to Alexandria, Syria, or Constantinople), which the government put up for auction each year. The *muda* of Flanders ceased operations because the waters it had to cross were infested with pirates, and it was replaced by more costly safer land routes. Books, and all other goods, are shipped for as long as possible on the Po and Adige rivers, to transfer points to

[42] Ibid., p. 87.
[43] Ibid., p. 88.
[44] Ibid., p. 90.

roads going through the most important Alpine passes: Brenner, St. Gotthard, and Great Saint Bernard. As we have seen, the necessity of opening new land routes will not prevent Venice from maintaining its position as the most important center of the European book trade for many years to come.

9.
CURES FOR THE BODY:
MEDICINE, COSMETOLOGY, AND GASTRONOMY

The first cookbook bearing a specific place and date of publication, the first printed text of cosmetology, the books needed by every physician of the era to learn the basics of the profession, all are achievements of Venetian publishing in the late fifteenth and early sixteenth centuries. Medicine, cosmetology, and gastronomy share a devotion to the care of the body and even today they occasionally overlap. It is only natural that they intersected even more when herbs and potions were commonly used for healing purposes and certain foods were attributed curative capacities, which, more often than not, they did not possess. And while bleaching one's hair had no medical implications, there nevertheless existed salves and ointments that could serve both to cure physical maladies and make one's appearance more aesthetically pleasing.

The medical book trade is an attractive business, profitable and stable over the long term. Where there are doctors there is also a demand for books so they can learn their profession and keep themselves up to date. It is not surprising, then, that Venetian printers, attentive as they are to everything that might generate profits, throw themselves into the sector. Already in the incunabula era the production of medical volumes was abundant and in the sixteenth century it grows even more so as the various medical specialties gradually distinguish themselves from each other. At the start, printing is reserved for manuscripts from classical antiquity and the most important medieval masters; later on, the presses begin to issue editions of treatises compiled by contemporary physicians.

To get an idea of the situation of medical publishing in Renaissance Venice the place to start is with the father of medicine: Hippocrates. His *Corpus*—a collection of seventy works in ancient Greek (most probably not all of them his)—circulates in manuscript form for centuries, and in 1526 it is printed in Greek in the printing shop owned by Manutius's heirs and Andrea d'Asola (the preceding year they had also published the works of Galen in Greek). A Latin version of *Corpus* had already been issued in Rome in 1525, and some extracts had been printed almost twenty years earlier (Venice 1508).

Printers are keenly interested not only in the works of classical authors but also in the works of the Medieval and Arab masters of medicine. For example, Bruno da Longobucco's *La cyrogia del maestro Bruno* (The Surgery of Master Bruno) is issued in 1498 and it is an instant success, with five reprints by 1549. Bruno da Longobucco (or Longoburgo) is born at the beginning of the thirteenth century in Calabria. He reveals this himself at the end of his principal work, *Chirurgia magna*, one of the most consulted medical treatises of the Middle Ages. He finishes writing it in 1253, in Padua, where he probably teaches at the university. That is also where he writes *Chiurgia parva*, a compendium of the larger volume. *Chirurgia magna* is later translated into Italian, French, German, and even two Hebrew versions, one by Hillel ben Samuel, from Verona, and one by a Spanish Jew, Jacob ben Hehuda. The book is a proper textbook in which Bruno da Longobucco reports not only "what he had learned from classical and especially Arab surgery [. . .] but also describes surgical operations and techniques which he experimented for the first time."[1]

---

[1] Enrico Pispisa, *Bruno da Longobucco,* in *Dizionario biografico degli italiani*, vol. XIV, IEI, Rome 1972, p. 644.

Another outstanding figure, Guglielmo da Saliceto, explains in his treatise on surgery how in Bergamo and Paris, he successfully treated two soldiers whose wounds were so severe that they had been left for dead. The fame of this man of medicine is great, and the success of his manuscript is proportionate. Guglielmo comes into the world in Saliceto di Cadeo, near Piacenza, around 1210. He teaches in Bologna and practices in various places until, in 1275, we find him as a physician in the employ of the City of Verona. We know this detail because in the same year in the same Venetian city, he finished writing his *Chirurgia* (Surgery), which will be printed in Venice for the first time in the vernacular in 1474 and the next year in Latin in Piacenza. The work inaugurates the tradition "of medicine as a science, not merely a mechanical art, but the union of theory and practice."[2]

The French physician Guy de Chauliac, born sometime between 1280 and 1300, falls ill during the terrible black plague epidemic in 1348 and his description of his symptoms, written after his recovery, is the first to distinguish between the bubonic and pneumonic plagues. He admires Bruno di Longobucco, calling him one of the most important physicians of the thirteenth century, and he is the custodian of the tradition of medical practice first enunciated by Guglielmo da Saliceto. *De Cirogia* (On Surgery), by Chauliac, is first published in Italian translation in Verona in 1493, and its numerous reprints demonstrate that it quickly became a reference text. A student of his from Bologna, Pietro Argellata, who is listed in Mario Crespi's Biographical Dictionary of the Italians as an "excellent surgeon, skilled in hernia operations, renal calculosis, the skull, and bone resections,"[3] writes another work entitled *Cirurgia* (Surgery), in which he discusses ulcers, skull

² Graziella Federici Vescovini, *guglielmo da saliceto* in *Dizionario biografico degli italiani*, vol. LXI, IEI, Rome 2003, p. 33.
³ Mario Crespi, *Argellata, Pietro,* in *Dizionario b iografico degli italiani*, vol. IV, IEI, Rome 1962, p. 114.

fractures, hernias, wounds, and warts, and argues that bone marrow is meant to nourish the bones and prevent them from breaking. The work very quickly becomes famous; the first printed edition is issued in 1480 in Venice, the second edition in 1497.

The first illustrated medical book also appears in this context of publishing works by Medieval masters; the so-called *Fascicolo Ketham* comes off the presses in February 1494 (1493 according to the Venetian calendar). This medical compendium is composed of six different medical treatises printed and bound together for the first time in Germany in 1491. It takes its name from the German physician Johannes de Ketham, who was simply the owner of the manuscript. The Venetian edition is translated into the vernacular and illustrated by beautiful full-page engravings, sometimes unnerving, as when a pathologist is pictured preparing to section a cadaver with an instrument that today would be considered more appropriate in the hands of a butcher than a physician. In any event, these images will have an enormous influence on medical publishing throughout Europe: through the first half of the sixteenth century the illustrations in medical books will be modeled on those in the *Fascicolus*. The father of modern anatomy, the Fleming Andras van Wasel, though he teaches in Padua, has the first edition of his fundamental work, *De humani corporis fabricai,* printed in Basel. Five years earlier, in 1538, he had published in Venice six anatomical tables; print reproductions of drawings that he used to illustrate the dissection of cadavers.

At the end of the fifteenth century Venetian printers add the major Arab authors to their repertory. As early as 1479, they publish the *Breviarum medicinae,* by Yuhanna bin Serapion, known as Serapione the Younger, and another fundamental text, the treatise by Ali ben Abbas, is issued in 1492.

Venice is certainly not one of the top-ranking centers in the practice of the art of medicine—Bologna and Padua are more advanced—but neither is it that far down on the list, especially because there is a great demand for doctors aboard its military ships and because Venetian physicians often serve abroad in the diplomatic seats of the Republic of Saint Mark. For example, Giulio Doglioni, professor of medicine at the University of Padua, dies while he is treating a pestilence in Aleppo, where he is in service to the Venetian consulate. Or Cornelio Bianchi, from Marostica, who served in Damascus in the consulate of the Serene Republic in 1542-1543, and who will become famous for treating plague victims in Venice in 1576.[4]

Meanwhile the printers start publishing works by contemporary physicians such as Alessandro Benedetti, founder of the anatomy school in Padua who builds the first anatomical theater, a temporary wooden theater that could be dismantled. He distinguishes himself because in his lessons he uses only cadavers, refusing to adopt the common practice of vivisecting the bodies of convicts who had been sentenced to death.

Benedetti is a native of Padua and he receives his degree there in 1450. He spends fifteen years or so between Crete and Modone, in the Peloponnesus, the Greek territories of the Venetian Republic, and then returns to his hometown, where he teaches medicine and anatomy. He becomes the chief medical officer of the Venice-Milan-Mantua alliance that confronts Charles VIII of France at Fornovo (July 6, 1495) and his account of the war is published by Aldus Manutius in 1496, with the title *Diaria de bello carolino*. After the war he goes back to teaching in Padua, moves to Zara, and then dies in Venice on October 31, 1512. His major scientific achievement is having stimulated a new interest in anatomical research. His lessons on the constitution of the human body invariably attracted a large

---

[4] Giuliano Lucchetta, *Viaggiatori e racconti di viaggi nel Cinquecento*, in *Storia della cultura veneta,, vol. III, t. II,* Neri Pozza, Vicenza 1980, p. 433.

audience,[5] and one of them was attended by the Emperor Maximilian I of Austria. Benedetti's *Historia corporis humani*, especially important for the science of anatomy, is printed in Venice in 1493 and republished in several other editions, including one in Paris (1514) and one in Cologne (1527), and then in anthologies.

Girolamo Fracastoro, a humanist physician from Verona in contact with all the major figures of his time—Pietro Bembo, Andrea Navagero, Aldus Manutius—is born sometime between 1476 and 1478, studies in Padua, and reaches the high point of his career in 1545, when he is named chief physician to the Council of Trent, and it is his report on the Council, signed by Balduino de' Balduini, that provokes its transfer to Bologna caused by the onset of an epidemic of petechial typhus. His first printed work, *Syphilis sive de morbo gallico,* is published clandestinely and fraudulently in Venice, and then in a corrected and official edition in Verona in 1530. This is the work that definitively established the name of the disease as syphilis, or the "French disease," since it was brought to Italy by the soldiers of Charles VIII. His *Opera omnia* is published posthumously by Giunta, in Venice, in 1555.

Gabriele Falloppio (or Falloppia) is the Renaissance physician best known by gynecologists for having given his name to the tubes that connect the ovaries to the uterus. A native of Modena, he studies anatomy, the plague, and syphilis and, called to the University of Pisa by Cosimo de' Medici, he conducts experiments with poisons (he administered opium to death-row inmates and was accused of subjecting them to vivisection). In 1551, at age twenty-eight, he moves to Padua, where he remains until his death in October, 1562. His works are first sent to press, using his students' notes, in 1563, in

[5] Marco Crespi, *Benedetti Alessandro*, in *Dizionario biografico degli italiani*, vol. VIII, IEI, Rome 1966, p. 245.

Venice (on ulcers and tumors) and in Padua (on the French diseases or syphilis).

The father of modern sports medicine and physical therapy is Girolamo Mercuriale. His *Artis Gymnasticae* is issued in 1569, printed by Giunta. Mercuriale is born in Forlì in 1530, teaches in Padua, and becomes a celebrated physician who in 1573 is called to Vienna to treat Emperor Maximilian II. Three years later, in 1576, he commits a terrible blunder when he is called to Venice by the Senate and declares, in open and heated contrast with the Venetian doctors, that the epidemic then in progress is not bubonic plague. He is wrong and the final death toll comes to more than 50,000 dead, or a third of the population. But the blunder doesn't cost him his job; on the contrary, his appointment is renewed and he is given a pay raise. His lessons on the plague will be collected and published by a student (most of the works that have come down to us are lessons collected and printed after the fact by students). He studies pediatrics (his is the first treatise on breastfeeding), dermatology (he writes the first work that classifies skin diseases), and toxicology (he becomes one of the foremost experts on poisons in his time). But it is his work on athletics, Giuseppe Ongaro tells us in his entry in the *Biographical Dictionary of the Italians*, that is "his best known and most original work, the fruit of almost seven years of study and research in the museums and libraries of Rome. It is the first complete treatise on sports medicine in which the athletics of the ancients are compared to modern athletics, of which Mercuriale is the true precursor. He examines gymnastics from the historical and medical as well as the more general hygienic perspective."[6] He dies in Forlì in 1606.

Military surgery also has a sixteenth century founding

---

[6] Giuseppe Ongaro, *Mercvuriale Girolamo*, in *Dizionario biografico degli italiani*, vol. LXXIII, IEI, Rome 2009, p. 620.

father, the Venetian Giovanni Andrea Della Croce, who is born in 1515 (or perhaps in 1509). His fate seems to have been pre-determined: his grandfather was a surgeon in Parma and his father was a barber, the latter occupation involving practices that were at times very similar to those practiced by physicians. It is uncertain whether Della Croce ever got his degree in Padua, but we know that he sat for the highly selective examinations for admittance to the College of Surgery in Venice. He is sent to Feltre, but after eight years there he returns to Venice, where he is named physician to the fleet. Thanks to his experience aboard military ships, he specializes in the treatment of abdominal firearm wounds. He publishes an initial treatise on this subject in 1560, which is later included in his larger work, printed in 1573 in Latin, and in the next year, with the title *Chirurgia universale e perfetta* (Universal and Perfect Surgery), in the vernacular (1571 is the year of the Battle of Lepanto and interest in the medicine of war is at its height): the Latin edition goes through two reprints, and the vernacular edition three. The fame of the Italian military surgeon crosses the Alps and his work is translated into several languages. He dies in Venice in 1575, probably of the plague.

The first significant modern treatise on pharmacology was penned by Doctor Pietro Andrea Mattioli, born in Siena in 1501, who translated and expanded on the work of the Greek Pedanius Dioscorides. Born in Celicia and active around 60 CE, Dioscorides was perhaps the greatest physician of antiquity, so great that Dante puts him in limbo ("And I saw the good collector of the qualities, Dioscorides I mean; and saw Orpheus, Tully, Livy, and Seneca the moralist"). His five books, the most complete compendium of medicinal remedies of the classical age, are divided into 827 chapters, and describe 625 species of plants, 85 animals, and 50 minerals. The first print edition is the Greek edition by Aldus Manutius, in 1499. But it is Mattioli who transforms this work into the authentic corner-

stone of pharmacology as we know it today. During the thirteen years that he resides in Gorizia he translates it and
expands it, adding to it all of his pharmacological knowledge
and expertise. Mattioli himself asks the Signory for a privilege
for the first translated and expanded edition, which is printed
in Venice by Nicolò de' Bescarini in 1544. It is one of the greatest publishing successes of the century, selling as many as
32,000 copies,[7] in some thirteen editions. The Sienese physician having escaped to Rome after the sack of Siena in 1527,
takes refuge first in the province of Trent and then in Gorizia.
The first revised edition of Dioscorides is printed without illustrations, which appear in the third edition (1550) and are then
replaced by beautiful, large engravings in the eleventh; the text
includes numerous translations in French, Czech, and
German, in addition to the Latin, and there are a number of
pirated editions, often replete with errors. "The book is the
best known botanico-pharmaceutical text of the sixteenth century," says Cesare Presti in the *Biographical Dictionary of the
Italians*. "It contains the description of the medicinal virtues of
hundreds of new plants, a large part of which unknown in as
much as they are imported from the East and from the
Americas, and others botanized by Mattioli himself during his
explorations of the Val di Non and on Mount Baldo."[8] To be
sure, this fundamental text of modern pharmacology can
sometimes make your nose curl, for example when it suggests
using dried cockles, chopped up and sprayed with citron
liquor, to keep your eyelashes from growing too long, or when
it recommends, as a remedy for renal colic or bladder pain,
roast snails, ground up with their shells, to be eaten mixed with

---

[7] Brian Richardson, *Printing, Writers and Readers in Renaissance Italy*,
Cambridge University Press, Cambridge 1999, p. 66.
[8] Cesare Preti, *Mattioli (Matthioli) Pietro Andrea* in *Dizionario biografico
degli italiani*, vol. LXXII, IEI, Roma 2009, p. 308.

wine or myrrh, or dried and ground hippopotamus testicles to cure snake bite, or roast mice, pulverized and added to the baby's food, to prevent excessive salivation, and finally a nice enema of boiled electric ray to combat sciatica. Mattioli's career benefits enormously from his publishing success; Ferdinand I of Habsburg calls him to his court in Prague as personal physician for his second son.

Even today pharmacology and cosmetology sometimes overlap, and this was even more common in the sixteenth century. Venice, it should be emphasized, is not only the cradle of cosmetic publishing but also of cosmetics in general. Face powder, *cipria* in Italian, is none other than "powder from Cyprus," as it is called by Eustachio Celebrino in his treatise of 1525, one of the most important cosmetology texts of the century (the island will remain under Venetian control until 1571). And in all likelihood today's women who highlight their hair with blond streaks fail to realize that they are using a technique that started in Renaissance Venice. One of the aesthetic obligations of sixteenth century ladies was to have reddish-blond hair. Strawberry blondes were so much the fashion that Tiziano Vecellio (Titian) painted the flowing manes of his women a color that from then on would be called "Titian blond." To obtain the longed-for tint, the daughters of Venetian high society wiled away hours and hours during the summer months on their roof-terraces (wood platforms situated on the rooftops, meant to be used for hanging out the laundry) dressed in nothing but a lightweight white tunic, on their heads a hat with the skull cap cut out (called a "solana") and in their hand a sponge that they used to constantly wet their hair before spreading it out to dry in the sun. Presumably the liquid used at the start of the craze was simple chamomile tea, effective in bleaching hair, but as time went on the cosmetics treatises began to include accounts of increasingly complicated—and who knows how efficacious—mixtures, such as "blond water for perfect hair," by Celebrino, or the recipe provided in 1562 by Giovanni Marinello—"boil in clear water ashes of vines with barley hay"—to which, if you wish, you can add licorice wood ground with cedar—and so on, all the way to, at the close of the century, the rankest smelling concoctions cooked up by amateur wizards, with ever more improbable ingredients, such as pigeon dung, tortoise blood or boiled Spanish flies[9] (which a century and a half later Giacomo Casanova would use—dried and pulverized—as an aphrodisiac).

Very little is known about Eustachio Celebrino except for what we can deduce from his editions. It is from Udine, and presumably he was born at the end of the fifteenth century. He goes to live in Perugia, where he makes woodcuts for a local printer, though we know that in 1523 he is in Venice to work on engravings for a manual of calligraphy. In 1525 he writes and publishes an "entirely calligraphic pamphlet."[10] He devotes himself to "frankly commercial works that aim to win the attention of a large audience with popular topics such as health, etiquette, and foreign languages."[11] So, in 1525, the same year that the calligraphic pamphlet is published, along with a Turkish conversation manual and another on table-setting, he publishes what is believed to be the era's first text on cosmetics: *Opera nova piacevole la quale insegna a fare varie composizioni odorifere per adornar ciascuna donna* (A pleasant new work which teaches how to make various odoriferous compositions to adorn all women); a copy is conserved in the town library in Roverto. This too is a mixed treatise that provides indications on how to treat the "Frenchish disease," "sores and pains," while "the various smooth ointments or perfumed waters were indicated by Celebrino for 'making or

[9] Giuliana Grando, Bepi Monico, *Profumi e cosmesi nella Venezia del '500*, Centro internazionale della grafica, Venice 1985, p. 10.
[10] Marco Palma, *Celebrino, Eustachio*, in *Dizionario biografico degli italiani*, vol. XXIII, IEI, Rome 1979, p. 361.
[11] Ibid.

maintaining a beautiful face' or 'to oil the hands and make them beautiful,' 'to consolidate and restore the countenance,' to ensure that the 'skin doesn't crack' to 'color the face.' It is interesting to note how [. . .] the aesthetic canons were no different than current ones."[12] Indeed, the remedies are used for removing spots from the face and to soothe sunburn, eliminate wrinkles, whiten teeth and strengthen gums, freshen breath, grow hair and keep it from turning white, remove body hair, make beards grow for boys who are in a hurry to become men. There is even a recipe for "invigorating the vulva," probably meant for courtesans who needed to tone up the body part that earned them a living.

But cosmetics, in any event, are not the exclusive prerogative of the female sex; they are also used by "those brazen Ganymedes who wave their hair in the feminine guise, burnish their curls, and sprinkle their soft cheeks with a thousand perfumes to make the basset hounds run to the honey," as Tommaso Garzoni writes in his *Piazza universale di tutte le professioni del mondo* (Universal piazza of all the professions in the world), printed in Venice in 1535, proof that the third sex and transvestites were already much appreciated back then.

In 1540, Giovanventura Rosetti, born in Venice to a family originally from Vicenza, publishes one of the earliest known treatises on chemistry, for use by fabric dyers, an activity that is widely practiced in Venice and also quite remunerative, given that Venice's red fabrics were the most prestigious in Europe and the Levant. His biggest publishing success, however, is his *Notandissimi secreti de l'arte profumatoria* (Most noteworthy secrets of the perfumatory art). After the first edition, in 1555, three more editions were published, the last in Venice in 1678, a sign that among the ladies of the era it was very much the fashion to perfume themselves on the basis of Rosetti's suggestions.

[12] Grando, Monico, *Profumi e cosmesi . . .* , op. cit., p. 10.

Marinello also publishes a small treatise on cosmetics that is 319 pages long, *Gli ornamenti delle donne* (Women's ornaments), which furnishes the recipe for soaps for washing the hands and explains how to use pigeon blood to eliminate redness in the eyes, as well as describing an "unction that makes the lips vermillion," which seems very much like lipstick, and another "that gets rid of dandruff," a claim that will reappear in countless TV commercials centuries later.

Beyond medical and cosmetic remedies, Renaissance Venice also becomes the capital of publishing concerned with what we ingest, and its curative or pleasure-provoking qualities; there is no other city that publishes as many books on gastronomy, as Françoise Sabban and Silvano Servetri underline in their book on the Renaissance table:

> Sixteenth century Italy generates a level of publishing activity on the arts of the table that has no equal in other European countries and that it will not reach again for centuries. These works, which for the most part focus on serving at table and the organization of banquets, are in a certain sense the technical version of a 'didactic' literature founded on the dominant values of court society, intent on forging a superior man whose model is defined by Baldassare Castiglione in his *Book of the Courtier* (1528). A cult book of the European aristocracy, it was an enormous publishing success, with no fewer than thirty-eight editions appearing during the course of the century in Italy alone.[13]

It is worth saying a few words about this book, published for the first time in the printing house of the heirs of Manutius and Andrea d'Asola. It is a treatise in the form of a dialogue whose

---

[13] Françoise Sabban, Silvano Serventi, *A tavola nel Rinascimento*, Laterza, Rome-Bari 1996, p. 15.

protagonists (one is Pietro Bembo) explain, during an evening set in the palace of the Duke of Urbino, how the perfect gentleman must behave at court: of noble blood, vigorous, expert in arms and music, a poet, an able conversationalist, a devotee of painting and sculpture. "It is also convenient to know how to swim, jump, run, throw rocks"; his voice must be "sonorous, clear, sweet, and well composed," Castiglione writes. Then it is necessary that the courtier "in each of his operations be cautious, and always accompany everything he says or does with prudence." All, naturally, within a framework of grace and elegance. The same principles are also valid for the lady of the palace.

The volume is an overwhelming success, likely the most widely read book of the Renaissance. It is translated into six languages and printed in twenty different European cities. The French translation, published in 1537, is promoted by François I in person, who reads it and considers it a model for his court. The English version is dated 1561, edited by Sir Thomas Hoby, and has a profound influence on the court of London.

But let's now turn to the era's books on gastronomy, which operate according to a strange sort of political distinction between principalities and republics. Informing the public about what the prince eats serves to underline his detachment from the people and it therefore legitimates his power. Shedding light on the delicacies of the Episcopal dinner table also has a useful function: those were times when many religious vocations were corroborated by an excess of unused gastric juices.[14] On the other hand, in commercial oligarchies, where winning the trust of the people was of fundamental importance for maintaining power and, consequently, an arrogant ostentation of excessively expensive habits could produce

[14] Orazio Bagnasco, *Prefazione*, in *Catalogo del fondo italiano e latino delle opera di gaastronomia*, B.I,N.G., Lugano 1994, p. 6.

negative effects, the situation was entirely different.[15] Such considerations are clearly confirmed by the fact that while Venice produces an enormous quantity of gastronomic texts, it prints not a single one that deals with the specific gastronomy of the city. This remains the case, until the start of the nineteenth century, for too many centuries, that is, to be considered a fortuitous coincidence. It just wouldn't do to propagandize the kind of life led by the dominant class and therefore, even without there being some kind of law on the subject, nothing was published.[16]

Until the period of the French Revolution we know very little indeed about the eating habits of the subordinate classes, and that little doesn't come from books on gastronomy but from literature. For example, from the works of Giovanni Boccaccio, who recounts that the lower classes ate animals that died of disease and drank wine that had turned to vinegar; or Carlo Goldoni, who writes in his *Donna di garbo* of Rosaura giving Arlecchino a recipe for polenta: "We'll fill a beautiful pot with water, and we'll put it over the fire. When the water starts to murmur, I'll take some of that ingredient, in powder as lovely as gold, called yellow flour; and little by little I'll go dissolving it in the pot, in which you with a skillful twist of the hand will go on making circles and lines. When the stuff is thickened, we'll take it off the fire, and the two of us together, with a spoon for each, will make it pass from the pot to a plate. Then we'll sprinkle it bit by bit with an abundant portion of fresh, yellow and delicate butter, then an equal amount of fat, yellow, and well-grated cheese". In any case, the problem of the subordinate classes was not how to cook food, but how to get the food to cook.[17]

[15] Ibid.
[16] Ibid., p. 7.
[17] Ibid.

Cooking was a matter for the rich, and Renaissance gastronomy is based on a sort of Bible, a book that will influence the recipes of the court and aristocratic kitchens in half of Europe. The book is *De honesta voluptate et valetudine* by Bartolomeo Sacchi di Piadena, known as Platina, printed for the first time in Rome between 1473 and 1475 in a clandestine edition without place or date, while the first official edition is printed in Venice on December 15, 1475. The book exerts enormous influence on the culinary history of early Renaissance Europe because the transcription of Platina is translated not only into Italian but also into German and French.[18]

This exceedingly important work, the first printed cookbook in circulation, is the summa of gastronomic knowledge in the second half of the fifteenth century. It is an essay on the art of cooking strictly tied to dietetics, nutrition hygiene, nutrition ethics, and the pleasures of the table; it will shape all gastronomic literature of the sixteenth century (almost exclusively Italian) including many voluminous general treatises.[19] The recipe collection of the *Honesta voluptate* is not the work of Platina but the copy of a manuscript by Martino da Como, chef of the patriarch of Aquileia until 1465. It is a work of plagiarism—Platina does not cite his source—which was not unmasked until fairly recently, by a study of the manuscript of Maestro Martino conserved in the Library of Congress in Washington.

At table we eat, but we also drink, and so in Venice, in 1535, Ottaviano Scotto publishes what is considered to be one of the first treatises of enology, *De vini natura disputatio* by

[18] Richard Westbury, *Handlist of Italian Cookery Books*, Olschki, Florence 1963, p. XII.
[19] Anna Alberati, Mirella Canzian, tiziana Plebani, Marcello Brusegan, *Arte della cucina e alimentazione nelle opere a stampa della Biblioteca Nazionale Marciana dal XV al XIX secolo*, Istituto poligrafico e zecca dello stato, Rome 1987, p. XI.

Giovanni Battista Confalonieri, which analyzes the characteristics of wine and describes its various typologies.

Meanwhile cookbooks gradually evolve into treatises on the art of banqueting. One of the most celebrated of the era is *Libro novo*—first edition published in Ferrara in 1549, but all of its nine subsequent editions, from 1564 to 1621, in Venice, in which Cristoforo da Messisbugo, seneschal at the court of the Estensi in Ferrara, shows himself to be the most clever and skillful manager of the needs of the court. His treatise, in addition to offering 315 recipes, recounts the characteristics of a Renaissance feast, its ostentatious display and sumptuousness cadenced by a series of guided sequences, giving it a sense of harmony and balance: menu, music, dance, theater, conversation, surprises, all deftly modulated by the refined art of receiving.[20] To see that these banquets were far more elaborate than your garden variety dinner party, you need only take a quick glance at Messisbugo's menus: fifty-six partridges, three hundred oysters, twenty-five peacocks, large and small, eighty thrushes, eighty turtle doves, and so on.

In modern terms, seneschal, or steward, is a title that combines and expands on the figures of the chef and the maître d'. He is the superintendant of noble and aristocratic kitchens. He is responsible for selecting, training, and directing the cooks and servants, preparing the daily meals for his master, with whom he maintains a personal relationship, ordering and taking delivery of supplies, and organizing banquets in every detail. The seneschal is not a simple servant but a courtier, a gentleman by birth. Therefore, unlike chefs, for whom it is prohibited, he can dress in the best of fashion, and so wear a beard, mustache, and wig.[21]

Another seneschal is Domenico Romoli, known as Panuto,

[20] Ibid.
[21] Ibid., p. XII.

who in his work published in Venice, in 1560, *La singolare dottrina* (The Singular Doctrine), describes the courses, the banquets, and the salutary properties of the ingredients. Scappi, "secret chef to Pius V," as it says in the introduction, also writes a volume entitled *Opera* (1570), in which he describes "the compendium of his experience at the pontifical court, he recounts his responsibilities as chef, describes the space and layout of the kitchen (a description accompanied by a series of celebrated engravings), and presents recipes, seasonal menus, and dietetic regimens for the infirm."[22]

The other key figure in the Renaissance kitchen is the aforementioned carver. His task is to cut and distribute the servings of meat on the plates of the table companions; a figure far more accomplished and elevated than even an expert modern waiter. His is an authentic art that becomes a ballet, an acrobatic performance, of strength and balance. Again, it is Sabban and Serventi who tell us, "the carving of the meat, which is carried out under the gaze of the diners, is a crucial moment of the meal and constitutes the carver's opportunity to display his dexterity [. . .]. The cut must be performed 'in the air,' which means that the portion of meat stuck with the fork is to be sliced while keeping it suspended over the plate [. . .]. This requires a perfect mastery of the art, which [. . .] is acquired only after years of daily practice."[23] *Il Trinciante* (The Carver), by Vincenzo Cervio (1581), is a sort of manual for those who perform this activity, which seems much more a ritual or ceremony than the simple act of serving at table. The task of satisfying the diners at a Renaissance feast is reserved to the first two courses, while subsequent courses, and particularly the roast meats, perform a function which is primarily choreographic. When the roasts are brought to the table they are

---

[22] Alberati, Canizan, Plebani, Brusegan, *Arte della cucina . . .*, op. cit., p. XII.
[23] Westbury, *Handlist . . .*, op. cit., 24.

already cold, after being put on display and passed under the expert hands of the carver. After gazing in amusement at the acrobatics with which the roasts are brought to the table, the diners nibble languidly at a slice or two.

In addition to gastronomic treatises on real food, there are those that are concerned with mythical or imaginary food, such as manna. In 1562, the Neapolitan physician and philosopher Donato Antonio Altomare publishes in Venice a little book called *De mannae*, whose forty-six pages explain everything about this mythical food item, first mentioned of in Exodus.

The Serene Republic always keeps an attentive eye on what is happening in the rest of the world. The first book including a description of the cocoa plant and how to prepare chocolate is published in Venice 1565. Written by a Milanese, Girolamo Benzoni,[24] *La historia del mondo nuovo* contains a recipe decidedly ahead of its time; it will take another hundred years before that bean imported from America will become a popular drink. Evidently, as so many times before and since, the author and his publisher were visionaries.

---

[24] Westbury, *Handlist* . . . , op. cit., p. 24.

10.
PIETRO ARETINO AND THE BIRTH OF THE AUTHOR

A genius. A pornographer. A pervert. A refined intellectual. Pietro Aretino has been called all of these and more. And, at the end of the day, all of them are justified. He published what can be defined as the first pornographic book in history. And he, "the scourge of princes," invented the figure of the author-celebrity, the writer-star that droves of nameless readers throng to see. Unlike a lot of his contemporaries, he writes not to please but more often than not to satirize. Nor does he write to instruct or teach. His is a militant use of writing, and in this sense too he turns out to be a surprisingly modern writer.[1]

In his Venice years he himself becomes a tourist attraction, in a sort of osmotic relationship with the place that gave him notoriety. "Venice's proverbial 'liberty' is the *humus* without which his vigorous literary development would not have been feasible," writes Giuliano Innamorati in his entry on Aretino in the Biographical Dictionary of the Italians.[2] And Aretino returns the favor to the city by attracting additional visitors. He goes there to live in 1527 and for two decades he becomes one of its attractions. He dies in 1556 and is buried in San Luca; the church still exists but his tomb has been lost. He makes

[1] Fabio Massimo Bertolo, *Aretino a la stampa. Strategie di autopromozione a Venezia nel Cinquecento*, Salerno, Rome 2003, p. 12.

[2] Giovanni Aquilecchia, *Pietro Aretino e altri poligrafi a Venezia,* in *Storia della cultura veneta*, vol. III, t. II, Neri Pozza, Vicenza 1980, p. 62.

friends with the most famous personalities of his day: Titian, who paints his portrait (conserved in Florence, in Palazzo Pitti), Sebastiano del Piombo, Sansovino, and even Emperor Charles V.

In the centuries since then, however, history has been to cast him aside. A gentlemen who wrote things such as the *Sonetti lussuriosi* (Salacious Sonnets—"let's fuck, heart of mine, let's fuck soon/since to fuck is what all of us are born to do; /and while it's the cock that you adore, it's the vulva that I love more") could not but be relegated to the attic during the nineteenth century, the most boring, bigoted, and moralistic century of the last millennium. Aretino was spoken about little and badly, and even today his literary merits are not highly esteemed and he is certainly not celebrated as one of the important figures of Italian culture.

Aretino is born in Arezzo in 1492, then moves to Rome, to Mantua, then back to Rome and later on, back to Mantua. His fame as a satirist explodes after the death of Pope Leo X and the unexpected election to the papal throne of the Fleming Adrian VI. During his second Roman sojourn Aretino obtains directly from the pope the release from prison of the engraver Marcantonio Raimondi, who had reproduced sixteen erotic drawings by Giulio Romano. Aretino seems to want to demonstrate that he can get away with anything and he writes sixteen sonnets to accompany the drawings of Giulio Romano.[3] He also suffers an assassination attempt, a knifing, that doesn't kill him but leaves him with seriously mutilated hands. At this point the mood in Rome has turned against him and he returns to Mantua, this time as a fugitive. He becomes an attraction at the court of the Gonzaga, family where he most surely does not

[3] Giuliano Innamorati, *Aretino, Pietro*, in *Dizionario biographico degli italiani*, vol. IV, IEIO, Rome 1962, p. 92.

hide his homosexual loves nor does he disdain, now and again, a hetero relationship.

He arrives in Venice in 1527 and a couple of months later the lansquenets of Charles V of Habsburg sack Rome, an event that Aretino had predicted and that, in his hatred for the papacy, he welcomes with great satisfaction. The Venetian Signory lets him do as he pleases and Doge Andrea Gritti even supports him. Pietro Aretino will say that the women in Venice are so beautiful that they make him neglect his gay lover. At age thirty-five the lagoon city becomes his chosen fatherland: he rents a house in Rialto, from Domenico Bolani, on the corner of Rio San Giovanni, on "the most worthy side of the Grand Canal," a house that soon came to be known as "Aretino".[4] What Aretino saw from the windows of his house has been immortalized in a painting by Francesco Guardi, *Canal Grande e ponte di Rialto*, whose point of view seems to be from the three-arched window on the first floor of the building. The palace—Ca' Bollani Erizzo—built in the 1200s—still exists, even though there remains very little of what was there at the time of Aretino, apart from the three-arched windows on the first and second floors from which the writer loved to contemplate the comings and goings of Venetian life (and when he did so he could be seen by the crowds of his admirers gathered on the Rialto bridge). For some time in 1944 the house was inhabited by the father of futurism, Filippo Tommaso Marinetti..

Aretino stays in the house for twenty-two years, not least because he pays the rent in the form of sonnets instead of money, until 1551, when the owner gets tired of it and evicts him. The ineffable Pietro moves to a place close by, in Riva del Carbon, in a house that he rents from Leonardo Dandolo, but only after convincing the Duke of Florence to pay the annual rent of sixty scudi. Until just a few years earlier, that same sec-

[4] Ibid., p. 96.

tion of shoreline overlooking the Grand Canal had been the home of the other illustrious Pietro of the era, Bembo (who died in Rome in 1547).

In 1553, the King of France, François I, makes him a present of a three-pound gold chain whose links are in the form of serpent's tongues. This royal jewel will become Aretino's symbol, present in every portrait of him. The writer becomes so famous that the Serene Signory assigns him diplomatic missions. His popularity peaks in 1543, when he is added to the Venetian delegation charged with welcoming Holy Roman Emperor Charles V. The envoys from the Republic meet up with the imperial procession between Verona and Brescia and Charles V, upon being informed that Aretino is part of the group, invites him to ride beside him. When they arrive in Peschiera, Charles entertains Pietro in a long confidential colloquium, after which he calls him "one of his dearest Italian friends."[5] That all of this helps to sell his books is beyond doubt.

But now let's return to the point when Aretino, no longer a young man, arrives in Venice, "uncertain of his own future, in less than brilliant economic conditions."[6] It is March, 1527. He arrives as a tourist and ends up never leaving. It is highly probable that he chose Venice because "it was the city which, due to the number and variety of its printing houses, could ensure the greatest diffusion of his message [. . .]. Aretino's previous contacts with publishers were limited to a few sporadic episodes."[7]

Now we come to the episode that is intimately tied to publishing, what comes to be considered the first pornographic book ever published, *Sonetti Lussuriosi* (Salacious Sonnets).

[5] Aquilecchia, *Pietro Aretino* . . . , op. cit., p. 71.
[6] Guido Davico Bonino, *Lo scrittore, il potere, la maschera.* Liviana, Padua 1979, p. 64.
[7] Bertolo, *Aretino e la stampa* . . . . , op. cit., p. 16.

He writes them in Rome, probably in 1525, in one of those typical excesses that define his personality. As mentioned above, Giulio Romano, Rapahel's favorite student, executes a series of sexually explicit drawings, pornographic by contemporary standards, which Marcantonio Raimondi reproduces in sixteen obscene engravings that can be printed and replicated. The papal authorities are not at all pleased and they throw Raimondi into prison. Aretino uses his prestige to have him released. At this point, anyone with a modicum of good sense would have been satisfied: he has obtained the result he wanted; his friend has been released. But Pietro doesn't have a feel for limits and he ups the ante, writing sixteen sonnets that are meant to serve as captions for the illustrations. Thus are born the *Sonetti lussuriosi* which caused his expulsion from Rome and what seems at the beginning like an exile in Venice. It is here, far away from the Roman Inquisition that he sends the book to press, with its obscene images and verses. The place and year of printing (Venice, 1527) are only presumed by the experts,[8] because the only surviving copy has come down to us without the frontispiece and the two sonnets published on the back of it.

This book (there is a poor quality microfilm copy of it in the British Library) was owned by Walter Toscanini (son of Arturo, the orchestra director) and was sold at auction at Christie's in New York in 1978, seven years after the owner's death. Bound together with three other works (also obscene, in the style of the author but probably not by Aretino) it sold for 32,000 US dollars. The auction house did not reveal the name of the buyer.

We don't know the commercial results for the Venetian pressrun of *Sonetti*, but they are presumed to have been quite good, given that the new editorial line is not abandoned,—on

---

[8] Pietro Aretino, *sonetti sopra I "XVI modi"*, edited by Giovanni Aquilecchia, Salerno, Rome 2006.

the contrary. Venice and Aretino, however, are still just sniffing each other out. According to the Italian scholar Guido Bonino: "A Roman courtier of uncertain birth [. . .] with a penchant for ostentatious display and exhibitionism could not at first sight be introduced to government circles. What probably cast a favorable light on Aretino was the tactical potential which his frenetic manipulations, between this and that powerful figure, could be made to express, if wisely managed, in favor of the Republic."[9]

At this point, Pietro Aretino sets to work on what has been called "the most ill-famed book of sixteenth century Italy"[10]: *Ragionamento* (Discussion), 1534 and *Dialogo* (Dialogue), 1536 bound together in the *Sei giornate* (Six Days). At the beginning of the 1530s, the "scourge of princes" is a polemicist, a well-known personality—thanks to the *Sonetti* he personifies the role of the licentious celebrity—but still not the writer he would like to be. So he calculates how to win just recognition as a writer, setting in motion a coldly orchestrated career plan.[11] He consciously sits down at the drawing board to design a book that would bring him notoriety. Pietro Bembo, thanks to his *Asolani* (1505), had already made the amorous dialogue famous, and in his *Prose della vulgar lingua* (1525) he promoted the use of the vernacular as a literary language. Aretino's book will be a dialogue in the vernacular, and it will speak about love, but physical rather than spiritual love. Its female protagonists will not be the ethereal damsels of the Renaissance who play the lute while singing sweet verses but the rather more "material girls," who use their bodies to earn a living. So, based on this total reversal of roles, Aretino conceives the "bawdy dialogue," or the parody of the amorous dia-

[9] Davico Bonino, *Lo scrittore* . . . , op.cit. p. 68.

[10] Gianfranco Folena, "Introduzione a Pietro Aretino," *Sei giornate*, Laterza, Bari 1969.

[11] Davico Bonino, *Lo scrittore* . . . , op.cit. p. 71.

logue in fashion at the turn of the century. The way was thus paved for the birth of the *Sei giornate* (Six Days), "one of the essential documents of the sixteenth century,"[12] which, by way of the pornographic dialogue, offers Aretino the perfect instrument for the literary expression of his social and ideological non-conformism.[13] The dialogues, which unfold over a span of six days, are divided into two parts. In the first three days— *Ragionamento della Nanna e dell'Antonia*—set in a Roman garden, Nanna, an ex-meretrix, explains to her friend Antonia the three social states of women: nuns, wives, and prostitutes. The objective is to decide which is the best for Pippa, Nanna's young daughter, and in the end it is agreed that "the career of the courtesan is the most secure and, at bottom, the most honest."[14] In explaining the prostitute's profession, Aretino does not refrain from inserting the occasional sado-maso scene, on the second day, for example, "He had her get down on the floor on her hands and knees and after running his belt through her mouth like a bit, jumped on her, digging in his heels, and rode her like he rode his horse." And he has Nanna explain what a whore is supposed to do: "And putting it in my hand, he said: 'Do it yourself, I'm not even gonna move' and almost in tears I answered: 'What is this big hunk of a thing? Do other men have them this big?'"

The second three days, published in 1536, have a rather explicit title which must have scandalized moralists and conservative minded people even more: *Il dialogo di messer Pietro Aretino nel quale la Nanna [. . .] insegna alla Pippa sua figliuola a esser puttana* (The dialogue of Mister Pietro Aretino, in which Nanna explains to her little girl Pippa how to be a whore). The mother gives her girl some sound advice: "Once

[12] Innamorati, *Aretino, Pietro . . .*, op. cit., p. 98.
[13] Aquilecchia, *Pietro Aretino . . .*, op. cit., p. 74.
[14] Innamorati, *Aretino, Pietro . . .*, op. cit., p. 98.

you've got his pestle in hand, squeeze it real tight until it starts
to get agitated, and when it's good and hot, stick it in the hub."
No surprise then, presented with compositions such as these,
that an eyebrow or two was raised, "that succession of cou-
plings, rapes, incestuous intercourse, sodomies [. . .] is the alle-
gory of a world unhinged, plummeted into its own desolation,
disheveled in its innumerable orgasms: the world of Disorder."[15]
Aretino sends the *Ragionamento*, the anti-amorous dialogue
par excellence, the most provocative and obscene book in our
literary history, to press some twenty-nine years after the
Asolani. For him, the rush of unauthorized reprints and the
veto of the ecclesiastical authorities (it was even put on the
index) are just so many confirmations of the success he has
achieved. From here on out he would be known as "the infa-
mous Aretino."[16]

The symbiosis of writer and city is total. In no other place
in sixteenth century Europe could Pietro have become the
Aretino, in almost no other place could he have written such
things without landing in jail, in no other place could he have
found a publishing network able to guarantee him the pressruns and distribution. As Bonino writes: "Taken all together,
the first Venetian editions of Aretino represent a significant
sampling of what publishing could be in a dog-eat-dog world
of unbridled competition, replete with counterfeit editions,
with or without false editorial indications."[17] This is the real
measure of success, when a point is reached at which plagiarized and counterfeit editions damage the author on the one
hand while fueling his popularity on the other. Further evidence of the resonance of this new literary genre is to be found
in the sheer number of imitations; whores become the protag-

[15] Davico Bonino, *Lo scrittore . . .* , op. cit., p. 84.
[16] Ibid., p. 80.
[17] Bertolo, *Aretino e la stampa . . .* , op. cit., p. 18.

onists of a quantity of lesser works of which Aretino is undoubt-
edly the inspiration, from *Puttana errante* (The Wandering
Whore), 1530 to *Zaffetta* (1531), from *Tariffa delle puttane*
(Whore Fees), 1535, to *Ragionamento del Zoppino fatto frate e
Ludovico puttaniere* (Dialogue between Friar Zoppino and
Ludovico the Whoremonger), 1539.

The other side of the coin is that once the claws of the
Inquisition take Venice in their clutches, the works of Aretino
will experience three centuries of underground existence and
the critical attention shown them will consistently be damp-
ened by a tendency to self-censorship."[18]

At this point, Pietro is a famous writer; he has knowingly
inaugurated a literary genre and, just as knowingly, "he founds
a new publishing tradition, the tradition of the book of letters,
which for the rest of the century and beyond will become stable and constant."[19] His is not a collection of various kinds of
letters but, rather, an organic ensemble especially composed for
the collection. *Il Primo libro delle lettere* (The First Book of
Letters), which is published by Marcolini in January, 1538 will
be Aretino's biggest publishing success, and he is fully aware of
it: "The first letters to be printed in our language are my off-
spring, which I enjoy as I feel myself being transfixed by the art
of imitation."[20] The book sells well not only because of its content but also because of the way it's packaged. It was meant to
be "recognizable and identifiable from the time it was placed
on the bookseller's shelf. It could not look like just any book
because Aretino was staking his reputation and his future in
Venice[21] on it," and in fact it was a large format *in folio*, decorated and expensive, destined for the hands of a small elite.

Pietro Aretino plays a fundamental role in the launch of his

[18] Davico Bonino, *Lo scrittore* . . . , op. cit., 81.
[19] Bertolo, *Aretino e la stampa* . . . , op. cit., p. 13.
[20] Ibid., p. 14.
[21] Ibid., p. 23.

publisher's printing house, though not under its subsequent owner. His twenty-five years of activity are interrupted just once, for three years (1546-49) when he moves to Cyprus to free his wife from the clutches of his most prized author—Francesco Marcolini, from Forlì, who probably arrived in Venice in the same year as Aretino, underwrote 126 titles, for an annual average of around six works. For his part, the writer appears to be very focused on self-promotion, to what today we would call his "platform" and to editorial marketing. He has an ongoing relationship with his readers "to request, thank, solicit, advise, exhort, condemn, in short to offer himself as the supreme authority, the prince and king of virtue, on exhibition before all of his readers."[22]

At this time, the primary beneficiary of book sales is the publisher. Often the author is underpaid or not paid at all. In the case of Aretino, obviously, it can't be this way, but even so Pietro cedes his rights to Marcolini. He procures his money from other sources, for the most part from donations punctiliously solicited. As Fabio Bertoli writes in his book on Aretino's publishing success:

> The fundraising system put into place by the volumes of *Lettere* provided for the usual channel of offer and request, addressed to the usual benefactors, with the usual petulance [. . .]. The novelty is that the circuit, in some ways asphyxiated, of manuscript distribution, was now opened up by printing to numerous other addressees, like a sort of continually updated modern mailing list. After the publication of the volumes of *Lettere*, Aretino was able to expand the number of possible donors, who in turn would benefit form their elevation to the Parnassus of the correspondents of the Divine.[23]

[22] Ibid., p. 25.
[23] Ibid., p. 29.

A person as extravagant as Pietro Aretino cannot help but lead a costly existence, especially considering the substantial number of servants and parasites who gravitate to him. "An approximate calculation of the income declared on several occasions by the author yields an estimated average annual income of about 1600-1700 scudi, of which [. . .] about 600 are annuities—received in the form of an imperial pension and pensions granted by the Marquis of Vasto and the Prince of Salerno—and another thousand 'I procure myself each year with a notebook of paper and a bottle of ink.'"[24] A sensational result, there can be no doubt, which puts Aretino's income on a par with that of many of today's best-selling authors.

[24] Ibid., p. 29.

11.
DECLINE, COME BACK, AND SWAN SONG

"Now, what news on the Rialto?" asks Solanio to open Act III of Shakespeare's *The Merchant of Venice*. A commercial power lives on news. In the sixteenth century, newspapers as we know them didn't exist yet, so in order to provide itself with advance news the Serene Republic invented modern diplomacy. It established the world's most extensive network of ambassadors and consuls, which would become the model for the British diplomatic corps (although not the Italian one). The world's first stable embassy is the Venetian embassy in Rome, instituted in 1431, on the occasion of the election of Gabriele Condulmer, a former Venetian subject, as Pope Eugene IV. The Republic's representatives to the Holy See will reside at Palazzo Venezia, destined to become famous throughout the world for its balcony from which Benito Mussolini will deliver his speeches to the cheering crowds in the piazza below.

Who can say if Shakespeare knew that right there at the Rialto, about fifteen years before he wrote *Merchant,* that history's first printed periodical was born. It is conceived by a money changer of Umbrian origins, Panfilo Brancacci who, in partnership with two of the largest publishers of the time, Jacopo Giunti and Bonifacio Ciera, starts to print currency exchange rates and commodity prices on thin strips of paper which could easily be bound to ordinary correspondence.[1] The

[1] Mario Infelise, *Prima dei giornali. Alle orgini della pubbloca informazione,* Laterza, Rome-Bari 2002, p. 80.

new publication is certainly something very different from a periodical as we understand it today, though it is printed and distributed at regular intervals; the first known copy bears the date of March 14, 1585, but publication had probably already begun some time before that.

This was happening right in the heart of the period when the Venetian book trade came under the suffocating dark cloud of the Roman Inquisition, but the first green shoots of what will become an editorial rebirth are starting to emerge. This second flourishing will belong not only, and not even primarily, to the book trade but rather to the press and public information sector. Already in the 1600s, but especially in the 1700s, the resurgence of the Venetian publishing industry will come about in large part through the newspapers. The very word "gazette" has Venetian origins: it is the name of the coin used to purchase a newspaper that cost exactly that amount. One of the first newspapers, in the modern sense of the term, is Venetian, the *Gazetta veneta*, founded in 1760 by Gasparo Gozzi, which prints news and portraits of famous people. Even before that, however, in 1696, Apostolo Zeno, from Verona, started printing a literary journal in Venice. And the first woman editor of a newspaper in Italy is Elisabetta Caminer, who in 1777 takes over the reins of the *Giornale enciclopedico,* founded by her father.

But before this recovery phase, the Venetian publishing industry went through some decidedly dark times.

As we have seen, the boom of the Venetian book trade between the late fifteenth and early sixteenth centuries was based primarily on three factors: available capital, commercial relationships, and freedom of expression. In the second half of the sixteenth century all three of these contributing factors were on the wane. By this time, the commercial demobilization of the Venetian patriciate is well on its way, and capital is being redirected toward real estate, agriculture, and the initial stage of industrial activity permitted by the abundant presence of water—and therefore of hydraulic energy—in the Alpine foothills. The network of inland villas, apart from providing luxurious country resorts for their fabulously wealthy owners, are centers of agricultural and industrial production, and they are changing the rural landscape of the Venetian hinterland. The chief architect of this change is Andrea Palladio, the most formidable villa designer of all time (his style will influence the British Victorian mansion as well as the White House and Capitol, in Washington, to the point that the U.S. Congress will vote on December 6, 2010, to approve Resolution 259, naming him as the father of American architecture). Palladio is born in Padua in 1508 and dies in 1580 in Maser, near Asolo, which is home to his marvelous Villa Barbaro, which has frescoes by Paolo Veronese. Palladio is also involved in publishing. He contributes to the translation and commentary,—and he illustrates—of the first critical edition of Vitruvius's *De architectura*, printed in Venice in 1556. Nevertheless, his architectural activity has negative repercussions for the book trade. Having a villa designed and built by him, or by one of his numerous emulators, requires such a huge economic commitment that there is little room for other investments.

Also at this time, the opening up of Atlantic navigation is definitively shifting the most important trade routes outside of the Mediterranean. Because of its geographic position and also because its patriciate fails to fully understand the revolution in progress, Venice remains excluded from the new routes, and its port loses much of its traffic to the ports of northern Europe. That part of the continent, besides its strategic position on the Atlantic, is also the part where sovereigns have signed on to the Protestant Reformation and where, therefore, freedom of the press is not threatened by the Roman Inquisition. It is no coincidence that these are the years when the torch of the publishing industry passes from Venice to the cities of northern Europe.

There is also another factor that should not be neglected: the loss in stature of the Italian vernacular and of the Venetian dialect. For a while, the economic and cultural strength of Venice and Florence made Italian a sort of bridge language. The letters that Elizabeth I of England exchanges with the Turkish Sultan Murad III are, at least in part, written in Venetian. Then, in the span of just a few decades, French definitively displaces the idiom of the Republic of Saint Mark, becoming the new international language.

Toward the middle of the sixteenth century, the Roman Inquisition manages to extend its influence as far as Venice. The Holy Office in the Serene Republic is reorganized in 1547, and the new tribunal has sufficient authority and firmer determination to eliminate Protestant literature than the overworked Heads of the Ten and the Executors against blasphemy,[2] the public magistrates who should have been responsible for carrying out the task.

On July 12 , 1548 some 1,400 volumes found in the home of a clandestine bookseller who had wisely dropped out of sight are thrown into the flames between Rialto and Saint Mark's Square. This is the turning point. A second bonfire of Protestant books will be organized for November 21st. A year later, in 1549, Monsignor Giovanni Della Casa, apostolic nuncio in Venice, compiles the first *Catalogo di libri dannati et proibiti* (The First Catalogue of Condemned and Forbidden Books), listing 149 items.[3] But the patriciate—led by Nicolò da Ponte, later named Doge—opposes the measure and it is not implemented (two years later Della Casa would write his famous *Galateo*—Book of Manners—destined to enjoy much

[2] Paul E. Grendler, *L'inquisizione romana e l'editoria a Venezia 1540-1605*, Il Veltro, Rome 1983, p. 131.

[3] Marino Zorzi, Introduction to Simonetta Pelusi (ed.) *Le civiltà del libro e la stampa a Venezia. Testi sacri ebraici, cristiani, islamici, dal Quattrocento al Settecento*, Il Poligrafico, Padua 2000, p. 22.

better fortune). Despite the Doge's resistance, however, this catalogue also marks a turning point: it is issued five years before
the first Roman Index, compiled in 1554. This time too, the
Signory manages to resist the Curia, but when Rome promul-
gates a new index, on December 30, 1558, Venice is forced to
concede. Over 600 authors are condemned and 400 works are
specifically forbidden. The condemned authors include
Erasmus, Machiavelli, Aretino, and Rabelais; all vernacular
Bibles are prohibited. For Venetian publishing this was an
unavoidable and mortal blow.[4]

We have already seen that the first burning of the Talmud
happens on October 21, 1553, to the delight of the apostolic
nuncio. "In the months that follow, the Talmud, along with
other texts, was thrown to the flames in the most remote
Venetian dominions, such as the island of Crete, while all over
Italy Hebrew books were destroyed by the hundreds of thousands."[5]

The bonfires keep on burning: on March 18, 1559, Holy
Saturday, to celebrate the installation of the new Inquisitor,
Michele Cardinal Ghisleri, between 10,000 and 12,000 books
are burned in Venice. Ghisleri is outraged by the refusal of
some Venetian booksellers to publish the Index, and he asks
the Holy Office three times to give him the names of the dis-
obedient printers. The fate of the booksellers was sealed,[6] as
was that of their books.

In 1562, Venice establishes its own rules: every manuscript
must be examined by one religious and two laymen. But this
does nothing but cause delays and increase costs. The process
for obtaining permission to publish takes from one to three
months, the publisher has to pay each of the readers one ducat

[4] Ibid.
[5] Grendler, *L'inquisizione romana* . . . , op. cit., p. 138.
[6] Ibid., p. 163.

for every page examined, and, starting in 1569, he has to provide them with two copies of the manuscript: one unbound copy to be examined and one bound copy to be archived and compared to the printed edition.

Meanwhile the culture of suspicion spreads. In 1565, the simple fact that a worker in a silk-making workshop "reads all the time" is sufficient grounds for a priest to denounce him to the Holy Office of the Inquisition in Venice.[7]

The number of printing presses located in the city declines: by 1588 the number is down from 120 to seventy, in 1596 to forty, in 1598 to thirty-four.[8] Significant figures, but not in themselves conclusive, because the quantity of books printed depends more on the productivity of the single press than on their total number. In fact, an examination of the imprimaturs granted, or rather the number of newly published titles, shows that the high point is reached between 1560 and 1574 (89.3 per year), whereas in the period 1574-1584, when the effects of the plague are felt, the number falls to 45.2 per year, to then rise again to 72.9, between 1585 and 1599.[9] There is certainly a crisis, but it is less serious than it otherwise might seem if we were to consider only the decline in the number of printing presses.

The booksellers try to react. They refuse to disappear, to be swept away by the Inquisition and the shifting of the commercial center of gravity to the north. And so they begin to print what the Counter-Reformation publishing market demands: religious texts. As Paul Grendler points out in his study of publishing in Venice during the Inquisition, "books on religious subjects, amounting to between 13 and 15 percent of new titles in the 1550s, increase to 25 percent between 1562 and 1582, and to 33 percent for the rest of the century. On the other

---

[7] Brian Richardson, *Printing, Writers, and Readers in Renaissance Italy*, Cambridge University Press, Cambridge 1999, p. 46.

[8] Zorzi, Introduzione . . . , op. cit., p. 22

[9] Grendler, *L'inquisizione romana* . . . , op. cit., p. 320.

hand, profane literature in the vernacular, which in the 1550s amounted to 25 to 31 percent of the total, declined to around 20 percent in the following decade, remaining at that level or just shy of it in the decades to come. Instead of books on secular culture, which could be accused of being anti-clerical, irreverent, or obscene, printers now preferred to turn out devotional books. For the entire second half of the century, the sum total of production in these two fields—religious and devotional—continued to oscillate between 43 and 57 percent (for an average of 49 percent) of the total number of titles authorized with an imprimatur."[10]

The Battle of Lepanto (October 7, 1571) also has repercussions for the publishing business, and not only because of the quantity of apologetic and celebratory pamphlets that try to transform a victory that was certainly dazzling but from a military and strategic perspective, relatively insignificant into a epochal event. "It was almost natural that an alliance with the pontiff sealed in the atmosphere of a crusade should reinforce the demand for an Inquisition that was more vigilant and more severe."[11] This is a period of close collaboration between Rome and Venice, though afterward the bonds would loosen and then come completely undone with the interdict fulminated by the pope against the Serene Republic in 1606.

Rome, in any event, behaves like a predator. Not content with controlling the orthodoxy of religious and ecclesiastical books printed abroad, it aims to take over their production, by attempting, for example, to impede the reprinting of first editions issued on the banks of the Tiber:

In the harsh decade 1575-84 Venetian production diminished until it was on a par with the other Italian cities.

[10] Ibid., p. 193.
[11] Ibid., p. 200

In this same period, publishers in Rome and Turin experienced a remarkable expansion, destined to continue even after the Venetian recovery. The printing houses on the lagoon won back their first-place position in the closing decade of the sixteenth century, when their production again exceeded, by only 15 percent however, the total number of books issued in the other Italian cities. At the end of the 1580s, Roman publishing, previously modest in size, becomes the second in Italy."[12] By now Venice's primacy has been definitively lost: in 1600 the city's printing presses will issue only "between 50 and 55 percent of the books printed in the same year in Paris.[13]

The recovery of Venetian publishing, as we said at the beginning of this chapter, does not come about through book publishing but, rather, through journalistic periodicals. News is the lifeblood of a commercial power, but even when Venice's international role declines, the city retains a reading public attentive to world events, perhaps resembling Great Britain today, where, though it no longer has a great colonial empire to govern, its media nonetheless continue to be very interested in what happens abroad.

In fifteenth century Venice, news is spread by way of handwritten reports, complemented by the printed gazettes. But the victory of the latter over the former, the struggle between "reporters" and "gazetteers," is a very long affair, and the triumph of presses over pens is not nearly as immediate as might seem logical to our eyes. For a long time, printed news reports are considered to be simply a different version of public edicts, while handwritten reports are believed to be authentic and not subject to censorship (which was exercised only on works issued

[12] Ibid., p. 323.
[13] Ibid., p. 328.

by printing houses). "It was for this reason that [printed news], at least in governmental environments and at court, continued for decades to be given only conditional credit and to be greeted with great diffidence."[14] Things worked more or less like this: when a ship docked in the port of Saint Mark loaded with goods and pregnant with news, the reporter rushed to interrogate the commander or one of the officers, ran back to the office, wrote down what he had learned, and hung the handwritten sheet outside his door, where a crowd gathered to read it. The gazetteer, on the other hand, had to go to the printer's, compose the text, submit the proofs for authorization, and then print. At this point the news was already old.

We have said that the first periodical in history appeared in the lagoon in the 1580s, whereas the first printed gazette is presumed to have been published in Strasbourg in 1605, but Venice makes a decisive contribution to the growth and development of newspapers. The printing of weekly gazettes becomes the logical outcome of an interest in events that had matured over the course of the century.[15] An essential factor in the growth of the gazettes is the enormous demand for news generated by the wars against the Turks in the late sixteen hundreds: the siege of Vienna in 1683 and the conquest of Buda in 1686. Venice joins the opposition to the Turks in 1684, and in a couple of years has conquered the entire Peloponnesus. In 1687 Venice sieges and conquers Athens, bombarding and destroying the Parthenon, transformed by the Turks into a munitions depot.

The big publishers fail to take advantage of the market for war news, while the small booksellers and printers begin to specialize in it. Guido Bonino paints the following scene:

---

[14] Inbfelise, *Prima dei giornali . . .* , op. cit., p. 79.
[15] Ibid., p. 86.

Between St. Mark's Square and the Rialto it was possible to encounter several street vendors with their baskets, some stands, and even some shops in which material of that sort was readily available [. . .]. They devoted themselves to the printed news trade in an environment of intense competition, partly fueled by the fact that printed flyers were not covered by the protection guaranteed by a printing privilege. So there was no shortage of disputes arising from the intense competition. Once you received the military news you had to print it right away and then run to the piazza to sell it.[16]

The competition between printers is so heated that at least in one case they came to knives, and one of them was wounded in the face by an employee of his rival.

The censors closed an eye, and sometimes two, less regarding the content of the writing, than the procedures for the conduct of their inspections. The official procedure was to go first to the secretary of the three "reformers" of the University of Padua (the three patricians appointed as a board of governors of the university who had jurisdiction over censorship), who would then send the printed pages requiring a license to the three reformers. But the printers didn't have time to waste; they had to get to St. Mark's Square first if they wanted to beat the competition. So they would skip the first step and go directly to the house of one of the reformers to get an authorization.

The outstanding gazetteer of the time was Girolamo Albrizzi, the founder of a dynasty that would dominate production of all kinds of periodical sheets through the first half of the nineteenth century. The son of a rag seller, he was born in 1662 and enrolled in the printers' guild on October 14,

---

[16] Ibid., p. 128.

1685, a year after opening. Behind the church of San Zulian, a printing shop under the sign of the "name of God," which became the seat of his printing and journalistic endeavors.[17] Starting in the spring of 1686, Albrizzi, who is no relation to the patrician family of the same name, publishes the *Giornale del campo cesareo di Buda*, which will become the most successful of the numerous military periodicals of the time, appearing weekly for almost four years. The news arrives from Vienna, provided by the Habsburgian capital's gazetteers, among them Johann van Gehlen, who distinguishes himself by not just passing by the printing shop to pick up dispatches received from others but by going personally to the front to get the news and then printing it in very accurate reports written in correct Italian, without any rhetorical flourishes.[18] It takes about twenty days from the date of the latest news to the moment that the sheet comes off the presses to be distributed in the Venetian market. Albrizzi's paper also has some advertising, initially for other periodicals of his, but eventually also for various products, for example, "the newly discovered true and admirable water of the Queen of Hungary for the health of human bodies,"[19] on sale at his bookshop.

In 1687, Fabio Bertolo writes, "the extension of military operations to the Mediterranean theater, of great interest to the Venetian and Italian public but not covered by the news from Vienna, induces Albrizzi in 1687 to publish another periodical, with the title *Giornale dell'armata veneta in Levante* (Journal of the Venetian Armada in the Levant), all about the Venetian victories in Dalmatia, Albania, and the Peloponnese, based on reports from a source in direct contact with the Venetian fleet. The suspicion that Albrizzi may have exploited dispatches sent

[17] Ibid., p. 131.
[18] Ibid.
[19] Ibid., p. 132.

back to Venice by the high command has been dissipated by comparisons of the letters received at the Doge's Palace and the printed news. The comparison confirms the simultaneity of the drafting of the texts but there are differences in the details described. It appears that Albrizzi had his own correspondents serving with the fleet who were able to send back their accounts using the same means as the official dispatches."[20] It's a shame that the correspondents did not sign their reports, as it would be possible to contest the title of the Irishman William Howard Russell, considered the world's first war correspondent for his 1854 reports to *The Times* on the charge of the British light brigade at Balaclava during the Crimean War.

The conflicts with the Ottoman Turks, starting with the siege of Vienna in 1683 and ending with the peace of Passarowitz (Požarevac, in Serbia) in 1718, and the Venetian conquests during the war in the Peloponnesus, also create new demand for geographical publications. Father Vincenzo Coronelli, a Franciscan from the monastery of the Frari (today the seat of the National Archives), works in Venice from 1678 to 1718. The official cosmographer of the Serene Republic, he also makes two globes, one terrestrial and one celestial, for King Louis XIV of France. He publishes the thirteen volumes of his *Atlante Veneto* (Venetian Atlas) and the twenty-seven volumes of *Teatro della Guerra* (Theater of War), with illustrations of the places where battles took place, as well as the cities and fortresses won from the Ottomans.[21]

Newspapers and periodicals bring us to a time when publishing in Venetia is no longer situated in Venice alone, but has become regional—the eighteenth century, or rather to the "century of the Remondini," so named for the family that

[20] Ibid., p. 133.
[21] Eugenia Bevilacqua, *Geografi e cosmografi*, in *Storia della cultura veneta*, vol. II.. t. II, Neri Pozza, Vicenza 1980, p. 373.

establishes what will become by century's end the largest printing house in Europe in Bassano del Grappa, province of
Vicenza. Indeed, the entry for Bassano in Diderot and
D'Alembert's *Encyclopedie* will read: "City on the River Brenta
known for the great Remondini printing house which employs
a hundred and eighty people and has fifty presses for books
and prints."[22]

The Remondini story is a long and captivating one that
starts in 1670 and lasts for 130 years. They become an illustrious family who can count on friendships with prominent figures such as the playwright Gasparo Gozzi or the next-to-last
Doge of Venice, Paolo Renier, both frequent holiday guests at
the Raimondini houses in Bassano. But fame also brings trou-
bles: from 1766 to 1773 the Remondinis have to defend themselves in a controversy initiated by the chalcographers of
Augsburg, who are annoyed by the expansion of Bassano
engravings into the German market, and in 1772 they are sued
by Charles III, King of Spain, for a print believed to be offen-
sive.

With the same inventiveness and entrepreneurial capacity
that would characterize the commercial success of the Italian
northeast in the second half of the twentieth century, the
Remondinis concentrate on a neglected and residual market
segment and transform it into a profit-maker.

The founder of the dynasty is Giovanni Antonio, but it will
be his grandson Giambattista Remondini who leads the company to its moment of greatest prosperity. The Remondinis
base their business on making prints, which in earlier times
were the exclusive domain of the lowest category of printers:
images of saints, religious scenes, traditional themes of popular iconography. They use the techniques of chalcography

[22] Mario Infelise, *I Remondini di Bassano. Stampa e industria nel Veneto
del Settecento*. Tassotti, Bassano 1980, p. 77.

(copper engraving) to print what will be known throughout Europe with the mocking and slightly contemptuous name of "the Remondini saints."[23] However, as any basic course in economics will tell you, to be successful a company has to diversify its product. And so the saints are joined by prints of animals, like *The Domestic Cat* and *Il Cane Barbino* (Truffle Dog), or else mythical scenes for the poorer classes who were the target consumers of these low-cost illustrations, for example *The World Turned Upside Down* or *The Land of Cockaigne*, "where the less you work the more you gain," or, the joy of thousands of little boys, the "the little soldiers," prints in which the various armies of the era were represented in their multicolored uniforms. From 1730 to 1750 the Remondinis also produce wallpaper, and after 1750 they produce colored fans and playing cards, including Tarot cards that were exported to Spain and, from there, to Madrid's overseas colonies.

At this point the Remondini factory occupies the entire north side of the main square in Bassano, Piazza dei Signori. In the second half of the eighteenth century, they had fifty-four presses at their disposal, of which thirty-two were for copper prints, eighteen for books, and four for gilded paper. There were also all of the collateral workshops: the engraving school, the workshops for the engravers, the illustrators and binders, three workshops for the polishers and perforators, the rooms where the colors and dyes were prepared, the ovens for casting metal characters, and numerous warehouses used to store their products.[24] The Remondinis are also the owners of three paper mills on the River Brenta and one on the Piave (the largest paper mill in the territory of the Serene Republic), which provide them with an indispensable supply of paper.

In the second half of the eighteenth century, Remondini

[23] Ibid., p. 102.
[24] Ibid., p. 72.

starts printing maps and board games,[25] another field in which the Venetian Republic boasts a well-established tradition. The first game book in history was published in Verona in 1603, *Passatempo* (Pastime) followed by a second, *Laberinto* (Labyrinth), of which we know of two Venetian editions, from 1607 and 1616. Unfortunately, the 1607 edition conserved in the Biblioteca Marciana has been lost (probably stolen), but two other editions have been identified, in Florence and London. The 1603 edition of *Passatempo* was unknown and was identified only recently, in 2011, in Brescia, by Roberto Labanti, a systems analyst, and Mariano Tomatis, a mathematician and illusionist, who has also managed to reconstruct how it worked: "The book was used in Italian courts to present a kind of magic trick: a person was invited to think of a figure and indicate in which of four columns it appeared; at the bottom of each column was a reference to another page, giving rise to a non-linear reading itinerary that allowed those who did not know the secret to guess the identity of the chosen figure."[26] *Passatempo* and *Laberinto* are surprisingly contemporary: magical hypertexts that have their own icons but are unavoidably lacking in interactivity. Their creator is a noble Venetian about whom little is known, Andrea Ghisi. The Remondinis, unlike Ghisi, aimed to reach customers who were not rich and cultivated but simple, ordinary people who needed to ensure that their saints, soldiers, and games got to the places where their buyers lived. Their products were carried around Europe by traveling salesmen from the Val Tesino (province of Trent) and from Val Gardena in the South Tyrol, both subjects of the Habsburgs, and by the Slovenes of Venetian Slovenia, subjects of the Serene Republic. It is primarily the *Tesini* (salesmen from Val Tesino) who filled their

[25] Ibid., p. 107.
[26] http://www.marianotomatis.it/?page=libro&b=passatempo

baskets with prints and went around the continent selling them, staying away from home for as long as three or four years at a time, giving rise to the saying "*senza Tesini, niente Remondini*" (no Tesini, no Remondini). The salesmen are given prints on credit and cash for travel expenses and customs duties. On their return home they pay for the goods and repay their loans. Things don't always go as planned, however, and indeed the Remondinis become the largest property owners in the area thanks to the defaults on the mortgages they were given in exchange for the loans.[27]

It's a two-day journey on foot from the Val Tesino to Bassano, so the Remondinis decide to open up an agency in Pieve, which, at the end of the eighteenth century, is valued at 40 percent more than their renowned branch office in Venice.[28] The agency has in stock the entire assortment needed to fill the baskets of the peddlers, who then go off on their rounds in teams. The teams from Venetian Slovenia, by virtue of the fact that they speak a Slavic language, cover primarily Eastern Europe, while the Tesini leave traces of their presence all over the world. Around 1730, for example, they were on the Iberian Peninsula, and from there they sailed to the Americas. In the opposite direction, they got as far as Russia; there are traces of peddlers who sold Remondini prints and games as far away as Siberia and Astrakan. In *The Brothers Karamazov*, Fyodor Dostoevsky's description of the hermitage of the starec Zosima refers to prints that could well be Remondini productions: "Next to the fine and expensive prints were displayed several sheets of the commonest Russian lithographs of saints, martyrs, hierarchs, and so on, such as are sold for a few kopeks at any fair." In the archive in Pieve there are ninety death certificates of Tesini who died abroad between 1724 and

---

[27] Ibid., p. 110.
[28] Ibid., p. 111.

1824: forty in German-speaking countries, eight in Russia, five in Holland and five in Hungary, the others in other European countries and one in Albany, New York.[29]

The most successful of the peddlers start to open shops in various European cities, where they sell Remondini prints. And it is a peddler from Val Tesino, named Simonato, the owner of a shop in Rome, who is the involuntary cause of a long and costly dispute between the Remondinis and the court of Madrid. The man is arrested at the request of the Spanish ambassador after displaying a representation of the *Last Judgment* in which the crest of Charles III of Bourbon, King of Spain, is pictured on the side of the devils. This is the start of long diplomatic-political dispute, which the Remondini manage to resolve after many bagfuls of gold ducats.

The traveling peddlers are useful not only for selling prints but also for supplying, on their return, a precious item: information. The saints, in fact, have an inherent problem: they are different from place to place that, chances are the inhabitants of southern Europe have never heard of Saint Bede the Venerable, and it's easy to imagine that Saint Gennaro doesn't excite much interest among the faithful outside of Naples. The peddlers plying their territories made it possible for images engraved in Bassano to be suitable for the people of so many different nations, and accepted as if they were their own."[30]

The Remondinis print in Latin, Greek, Cyrillic, and Hebrew characters, as well as in Italian, Spanish, Portuguese, French, German, English, Russian, and Greek. The quality of their engravings is poor, but the only thing they're interested in is being able to assemble a vast repertory of images that can be produced as rapidly as possible so they can be sold everywhere. The crisis arrives in the days following the Napoleonic

[29] Ibid., p. 112.
[30] Ibid., p. 103.

invasion, but a few more decades will go by before the printing house closes definitively, in 1860, just a few years before Venetia becomes part of the Kingdom of Italy.

In the eighteenth century Venice cedes its crown as the most important publishing center in Europe to its rivals. Nevertheless, the city remains a formidable player in the production of books in foreign languages. Rather interesting and little known is the story of books printed in Karamanlidic. Today, we are used to linking a language to a certain alphabet: English is written in Latin letters, Hebrew in Hebrew letters, Russian in Cyrillic. In the past, however, the choice of alphabet was often tied to religion. The most outstanding example is Turkish, which could be written with Arabic, Greek, Armenian, Georgian, Hebrew, Cyrillic, or Latin letters, depending on the religion of the people whose native language was Turkish. Another example is Albanian. Until a little more than a century ago, it was written by Muslims in Arabic letters, by Roman Catholics in Latin letters, and by Orthodox Catholics in Greek letters. Similarly, until the dissolution of Yugoslavia, in 1991, Catholic Croatians wrote Serbo-Croatian in Latin letters, while Orthodox Serbs wrote in Cyrillic.

For many centuries there existed a literature at the service of Turkish speaking Ottomans of the Orthodox Christian faith: the so-called Karamanlides. Their texts were in Turkish written in Greek letters. They lived mostly in Asia Minor, in Cappadocia, but also along the shores of the Mediterranean, the Aegean, and Black Sea, and in the cities of Constantinople and Smyrna, as well as on Cyprus and in the Balkans.

The first book in Karamanlidic, *Florilegium of the Christian Faith*, was printed in 1718, probably in Constantinople, but it was not until the middle of the eighteenth century that significant numbers of titles were published: from 1743 to 1800, thirty-one titles were published, twenty-two of them in Venice. 1718 is an important date for the Ottoman book, because the

Turkish book printed in Greek letters is followed, less than a decade later (1727), by a Turkish book in Armenian letters and, finally, in 1729, by a Turkish book in Arabic letters. It follows that *Florilegium* is in all likelihood the very first Turkish book ever printed, in any alphabet. In the nineteenth century the Karamanlidic bibliography was enriched by 432 titles, with the highest concentration of them published in Constantinople and Athens, while in the twentieth century, until 1935, 138 titles were printed.[31] A century earlier, however, the primary place of publication is, without doubt, Venice. Until 1811, relatively few Karamanlidic books had been printed elsewhere (Amsterdam, Leipzig, Bucharest, and Constantinople combined for a total of twelve against the thirty-nine printed in Venice) [. . .]. Until 1780 the leading Venetian printer of Karamanlidic is Antonio Bartoli. Afterward the leadership passes into the hands of the Epirote Nicolò Glici.[32]

Between 1826 and 1935, Venice definitively loses its position as the leading producer of Karamanlidic publications, even though Glici's work is carried on by a Greek printing house, the Fenice. Karamanlidic literature dies out shortly after 1923, when the Hellenic populations of Asia Minor, regardless of their language, are compelled to leave their homes and move to Greece. The last known book is from 1929, printed in Athens; there is some evidence of a 1935 edition, but the book has never been found. Even the use of Turkish by Greek populations is by now almost totally extinct, with just a few elderly people perhaps still able to recall a song or some poetry they learned in childhood.

The fall of the Venetian Republic on May 12, 1797, under the onslaught of Napoleon, and Venice's loss of its status as the

---

[31] Matthias Kappler, *La stampa "caramanlidica,"* in Pelusi (ed.), *Le civiltà del libro* . . . , op. cit., p. 65.
[32] Ibid., p. 67.

226 - ALESSANDRO MARZO MAGNO

capital of an independent state, brought an end to all of its publishing activity, with one notable exception: publishing in Armenian. We have already seen what happened in this sector in the sixteenth century, but even in later centuries Armenian publishing continued to be a rather lively enterprise. The first Armenian edition of the Bible is printed in Amsterdam in 1666, but most of the copies end up at the bottom of the sea on their way to Constantinople. A second edition is printed in the Ottoman capital, but it is a patch-up job and is full of typographical errors. The fundamental edition for the history of the Armenians is the so-called Abbot's Bible, or rather the one printed in Venice by Abbot Mekhitar, in 1735. From 1716 to 1749, Mekhitar, "convinced that one of the highest expressions of his apostolate was printing,"[33] publishes fifty works, sixteen of them original.[34] In 1789 an Armenian printing house is established on San Lazzaro, an island in the lagoon next to the Lido. In its first eleven years it turns out thirty-six volumes: a frenetic pace. Throughout the nineteenth century but especially in the years following the Armenian genocide (starting April 24, 1915) and during the Soviet era, the printing house on San Lazzaro becomes a reference point for the Armenian diaspora throughout the world. School books, liturgical books, and literature are all printed in Venice; the volumes printed on San Lazzaro reach Turkey, enter the Soviet Union, and spread throughout France and the United States, the two countries where the exiles are most numerous. But after the fall of the Berlin Wall in 1989 and the consequent breakup of the Soviet Union in 1991, the Soviet Republic of Armenia becomes an independent state; the first Armenian state in over six centuries, since the end of the Kingdom of Cilicia in 1375. At this point, Venice can no longer

---

[33] Gabriella Uluhogian, *Lingua e cultura scritta*, in Alpago Novello, *Gli armeni . . .* , op. cit., p. 124.

[34] Vahan Ohanian, *La Bibbia armena dell'abate Mechitar*, in Pelusi (ed.), *Le civiltà del libro . . .* , op. cit., p. 95.

hold on to its role, the printing house on San Lazzaro loses the importance, and what had been, only a few years earlier, the most important Armenian printing house in the world is dismantled.

Venetian publishing sings a sort of swan song in the nineteenth and twentieth centuries, with Ferdinando Ongania, one of the first publishers to use photography in art books and to have intuited the remarkable possibilities that it could offer to traditional printing.[35] His *La Basilica di San Marco in Venezia*—sixteen volumes and ten years in the making, 425 illustrations presented in 391 plates—is an extraordinary exploration in images of the city's most celebrated church and establishes him as one of the finest art publishers of his time. Ongania is active between 1871 and 1911, a difficult period following Venice's unification with Italy in 1866, in an impoverished and marginalized city. As a boy he goes to work in the bookshop that the Münster brothers, Ermanno, Federico, and Massimilaino, originally from Hamburg, had opened in 1846, the year Venice's Austrian rulers inaugurated the railroad bridge that radically improved the access to the city and opened it up to growing crowds of tourists.

The bookshop looks out on St. Mark's Square, under the Napoleonic Wing. There the young Ferdinando learns the trade, and when the last surviving brother, Massimilaino, decides to leave, probably in part because he feels out of place in what has become an Italian city, the former sales clerk buys the firm. He and forms a partnership with, Ivan Beloserski, a Ukrainian friend from Kiev, who, however, leaves him on his own one year later.

Ferdinando Ongania thinks of himself as the heir to the great Venetian publishers of the past, but he realizes that in

[35] Mariachiara Mazzariol (ed.), *Ferdinando Ongania a San Marco*, Marsilio, Venice 2008, p. 10.

order not to be outdone by his colleagues and competitors in Milan, Turin, and Florence, he has to identify a new niche market where he can establish himself. He gets a helping hand from technology: all of his publications are "created with the most recent and sophisticated techniques of photomechanical reproduction."[36] The precision of his photographic images and the beauty of his heliographic prints are difficult to achieve even with current techniques. "The young bookseller made Venice the most advanced center of the new printing of images," writes Mariachiara Mazzariol in her book *on Ongania*. "He introduces techniques never previously adopted, such as 'the new system of heliotypy' which [. . .] he proudly claimed to have 'introduced to Italy.'"[37]

In any event, producing photographic works is costly, and to finance his publishing endeavors Ongania doesn't hesitate to display in his store, along with the books, precious antiques, designed to satisfy the whims and the desire for ostentation of wealthy tourists. His books of images are also designed for this type of clientele: elegant, precious, numbered, exclusive, and costly, they have very little text and for the most part are not in Italian. The publication of the multi-volume work on St. Mark's almost drives him into bankruptcy: he hires painters, designers, and photographers to make the images, "and then historians, archeologists, and architects coordinated by Camillo Boito, to provide the necessary information and interpretations for an accurate and complete knowledge of the monument."[38] The enterprise earns him fame and glory in Europe and around the world: he wins medals and prizes in Italy, France, Austria-Hungary, Great Britain, and the United States.

[36] Mazzariol, *Ferdinando Ongania* . . . , op.cit., p. 12.
[37] Ibid., p. 26.
[38] Ibid., p. 27.

Ongania had all the characteristics that energized his sixteenth century predecessors: entrepreneurial intuition, the desire to innovate and experiment, the capacity to use new and cutting-edge technologies. His efforts are crowned with success, but Venice is no longer the metropolis at the center of the world that is was four centuries earlier, and his business suffers as a result. He publishes 145, titles and his great achievement is having had every angle of the city photographed, allowing us to know the appearance even of areas that were later mutilated or demolished. His activity is interrupted suddenly when he dies at the age of sixty-nine, during the night of August 20-21, 1911, in Saint Moritz, Switzerland. He had only recently recovered the enormous investment required to produce the work on the Basilica of St. Mark, and he had finally decided to give himself a vacation in the company of one of his daughters. After his death the store began the process of closing down, and with him died the last genius of Venetian publishing.

INDEX

ABOUT THE AUTHOR

Alessandro Marzo Magno was born in
Venice, Italy, in 1962. He worked as a jour-
nalist for various newspapers and was chief
editor of the foreign affairs desk at *Diario*
for ten years. He has since published ten
books. He lives in Milan with his wife and
two children.

EUROPA EDITIONS BACKLIST
(alphabetical by author)

Fiction

Carmine Abate
Between Two Seas • 978-1-933372-40-2 • Territories: World
The Homecoming Party • 978-1-933372-83-9 • Territories: World

Milena Agus
From the Land of the Moon • 978-1-60945-001-4 • Ebook • Territories: World (excl. ANZ)

Salwa Al Neimi
The Proof of the Honey • 978-1-933372-68-6 • Ebook • Territories: World (excl UK)

Simonetta Agnello Hornby
The Nun • 978-1-60945-062-5 • Territories: World

Daniel Arsand
Lovers • 978-1-60945-071-7 • Ebook • Territories: World

Jenn Ashworth
A Kind of Intimacy • 978-1-933372-86-0 • Territories: US & Can

Beryl Bainbridge
The Girl in the Polka Dot Dress • 978-1-60945-056-4 • Ebook • Territories: US

Muriel Barbery
The Elegance of the Hedgehog • 978-1-933372-60-0 • Ebook • Territories: World (excl. UK & EU)
Gourmet Rhapsody • 978-1-933372-95-2 • Ebook • Territories: World (excl. UK & EU)

Stefano Benni
Margherita Dolce Vita • 978-1-933372-20-4 • Territories: World
Timeskipper • 978-1-933372-44-0 • Territories: World

Romano Bilenchi
The Chill • 978-1-933372-90-7 • Territories: World

Kazimierz Brandys
Rondo • 978-1-60945-004-5 • Territories: World

Alina Bronsky
Broken Glass Park • 978-1-933372-96-9 • Ebook • Territories: World
The Hottest Dishes of the Tartar Cuisine • 978-1-60945-006-9 • Ebook •
Territories: World

Jesse Browner
Everything Happens Today • 978-1-60945-051-9 • Ebook • Territories:
World (excl. UK & EU)

Francisco Coloane
Tierra del Fuego • 978-1-933372-63-1 • Ebook • Territories: World

Rebecca Connell
The Art of Losing • 978-1-933372-78-5 • Territories: US

Laurence Cossé
A Novel Bookstore • 978-1-933372-82-2 • Ebook • Territories: World
An Accident in August • 978-1-60945-049-6 • Territories: World (excl. UK)

Diego De Silva
I Hadn't Understood • 978-1-60945-065-6 • Territories: World

Shashi Deshpande
The Dark Holds No Terrors • 978-1-933372-67-9 • Territories: US

www.europaeditions.com

Steve Erickson
Zeroville • 978-1-933372-39-6 • Territories: US & Can
These Dreams of You • 978-1-60945-063-2 • Territories: US & Can

Elena Ferrante
The Days of Abandonment • 978-1-933372-00-6 • Ebook • Territories: World
Troubling Love • 978-1-933372-16-7 • Territories: World
The Lost Daughter • 978-1-933372-42-6 • Territories: World

Linda Ferri
Cecilia • 978-1-933372-87-7 • Territories: World

Damon Galgut
In a Strange Room • 978-1-60945-011-3 • Ebook • Territories: USA

Santiago Gamboa
Necropolis • 978-1-60945-073-1 • Ebook • Territories: World

Jane Gardam
Old Filth • 978-1-933372-13-6 • Ebook • Territories: US
The Queen of the Tambourine • 978-1-933372-36-5 • Ebook • Territories: US
The People on Privilege Hill • 978-1-933372-56-3 • Ebook • Territories: US
The Man in the Wooden Hat • 978-1-933372-89-1 • Ebook • Territories: US
God on the Rocks • 978-1-933372-76-1 • Ebook • Territories: US
Crusoe's Daughter • 978-1-60945-069-4 • Ebook • Territories: US

Anna Gavalda
French Leave • 978-1-60945-005-2 • Ebook • Territories: US & Can

Seth Greenland
The Angry Buddhist • 978-1-60945-068-7 • Ebook • Territories: World

Katharina Hacker
The Have-Nots • 978-1-933372-41-9 • Territories: World (excl. India)

Patrick Hamilton
Hangover Square • 978-1-933372-06-8 • Territories: US & Can

James Hamilton-Paterson
Cooking with Fernet Branca • 978-1-933372-01-3 • Territories: US
Amazing Disgrace • 978-1-933372-19-8 • Territories: US
Rancid Pansies • 978-1-933372-62-4 • Territories: USA

Alfred Hayes
The Girl on the Via Flaminia • 978-1-933372-24-2 • Ebook •
Territories: World

Jean-Claude Izzo
The Lost Sailors • 978-1-933372-35-8 • Territories: World
A Sun for the Dying • 978-1-933372-59-4 • Territories: World

Gail Jones
Sorry • 978-1-933372-55-6 • Territories: US & Can

Ioanna Karystiani
The Jasmine Isle • 978-1-933372-10-5 • Territories: World
Swell • 978-1-933372-98-3 • Territories: World

Peter Kocan
Fresh Fields • 978-1-933372-29-7 • Territories: US, EU & Can
The Treatment and the Cure • 978-1-933372-45-7 • Territories: US, EU & Can

Helmut Krausser
Eros • 978-1-933372-58-7 • Territories: World

Amara Lakhous
Clash of Civilizations Over an Elevator in Piazza Vittorio •
978-1-933372-61-7 • Ebook • Territories: World
Divorce Islamic Style • 978-1-60945-066-3 • Ebook • Territories: World

Lia Levi
The Jewish Husband • 978-1-933372-93-8 • Territories: World

Valerio Massimo Manfredi
The Ides of March • 978-1-933372-99-0 • Territories: US

Leïla Marouane
The Sexual Life of an Islamist in Paris • 978-1-933372-85-3 •
Territories: World

Lorenzo Mediano
The Frost on His Shoulders • 978-1-60945-072-4 • Ebook •
Territories: World

Sélim Nassib
I Loved You for Your Voice • 978-1-933372-07-5 • Territories: World
The Palestinian Lover • 978-1-933372-23-5 • Territories: World

Amélie Nothomb
Tokyo Fiancée • 978-1-933372-64-8 • Territories: US & Can
Hygiene and the Assassin • 978-1-933372-77-8 • Ebook • Territories: US & Can

Valeria Parrella
For Grace Received • 978-1-933372-94-5 • Territories: World

Alessandro Piperno
The Worst Intentions • 978-1-933372-33-4 • Territories: World
Persecution • 978-1-60945-074-8 • Ebook • Territories: World

Lorcan Roche
The Companion • 978-1-933372-84-6 • Territories: World

Boualem Sansal
The German Mujahid • 978-1-933372-92-1 • Ebook • Territories: US & Can

Eric-Emmanuel Schmitt
The Most Beautiful Book in the World • 978-1-933372-74-7 • Ebook •
Territories: World
The Woman with the Bouquet • 978-1-933372-81-5 • Ebook • Territories:
US & Can

Angelika Schrobsdorff
You Are Not Like Other Mothers • 978-1-60945-075-5 • Ebook •
Territories: World

Audrey Schulman
Three Weeks in December • 978-1-60945-064-9 • Ebook • Territories: US
& Can

James Scudamore
Heliopolis • 978-1-933372-73-0 • Ebook • Territories: US

Luis Sepúlveda
The Shadow of What We Were • 978-1-60945-002-1 • Ebook • Territories:
World

Paolo Sorrentino
Everybody's Right • 978-1-60945-052-6 • Ebook • Territories: US & Can

Domenico Starnone
First Execution • 978-1-933372-66-2 • Territories: World

Henry Sutton
Get Me out of Here • 978-1-60945-007-6 • Ebook • Territories: US & Can

Chad Taylor
Departure Lounge • 978-1-933372-09-9 • Territories: US, EU & Can

Roma Tearne
Mosquito • 978-1-933372-57-0 • Territories: US & Can
Bone China • 978-1-933372-75-4 • Territories: US

André Carl van der Merwe
Moffie • 978-1-60945-050-2 • Ebook • Territories: World
(excl. S. Africa)

Fay Weldon
Chalcot Crescent • 978-1-933372-79-2 • Territories: US

Anne Wiazemsky
My Berlin Child • 978-1-60945-003-8 • Territories: US & Can

Jonathan Yardley
Second Reading • 978-1-60945-008-3 • Ebook • Territories: US & Can

Edwin M. Yoder Jr.
Lions at Lamb House • 978-1-933372-34-1 • Territories: World

Michele Zackheim
Broken Colors • 978-1-933372-37-2 • Territories: World

Alice Zeniter
Take This Man • 978-1-60945-053-3 • Territories: World

Tonga Books

Ian Holding
Of Beasts and Beings • 978-1-60945-054-0 • Ebook • Territories: US & Can

Sara Levine
Treasure Island!!! • 978-0-14043-768-3 • Ebook • Territories: World

Alexander Maksik
You Deserve Nothing • 978-1-60945-048-9 • Ebook • Territories: US, Can & EU (excl. UK)

Thad Ziolkowski
Wichita • 978-1-60945-070-0 • Ebook • Territories: World

Crime/Noir

Massimo Carlotto
The Goodbye Kiss • 978-1-933372-05-1 • Ebook • Territories: World
Death's Dark Abyss • 978-1-933372-18-1 • Ebook • Territories: World
The Fugitive • 978-1-933372-25-9 • Ebook • Territories: World
Bandit Love • 978-1-933372-80-8 • Ebook • Territories: World
Poisonville • 978-1-933372-91-4 • Ebook • Territories: World

Giancarlo De Cataldo
The Father and the Foreigner • 978-1-933372-72-3 • Territories: World

Caryl Férey
Zulu • 978-1-933372-88-4 • Ebook • Territories: World (excl. UK & EU)
Utu • 978-1-60945-055-7 • Ebook • Territories: World (excl. UK & EU)

Alicia Giménez-Bartlett
Dog Day • 978-1-933372-14-3 • Territories: US & Can
Prime Time Suspect • 978-1-933372-31-0 • Territories: US & Can
Death Rites • 978-1-933372-54-9 • Territories: US & Can

Jean-Claude Izzo
Total Chaos • 978-1-933372-04-4 • Territories: US & Can
Chourmo • 978-1-933372-17-4 • Territories: US & Can
Solea • 978-1-933372-30-3 • Territories: US & Can

Matthew F. Jones
Boot Tracks • 978-1-933372-11-2 • Territories: US & Can

Gene Kerrigan
The Midnight Choir • 978-1-933372-26-6 • Territories: US & Can
Little Criminals • 978-1-933372-43-3 • Territories: US & Can

Carlo Lucarelli
Carte Blanche • 978-1-933372-15-0 • Territories: World
The Damned Season • 978-1-933372-27-3 • Territories: World
Via delle Oche • 978-1-933372-53-2 • Territories: World

Edna Mazya
Love Burns • 978-1-933372-08-2 • Territories: World (excl. ANZ)

Yishai Sarid
Limassol • 978-1-60945-000-7 • Ebook • Territories: World (excl. UK,
AUS & India)

Joel Stone
The Jerusalem File • 978-1-933372-65-5 • Ebook • Territories: World

Benjamin Tammuz
Minotaur • 978-1-933372-02-0 • Ebook • Territories: World

Non-fiction

Alberto Angela
A Day in the Life of Ancient Rome • 978-1-933372-71-6 • Territories:
World • History

Helmut Dubiel
Deep In the Brain: Living with Parkinson's Disease • 978-1-933372-70-9 •
Ebook • Territories: World • Medicine/Memoir

James Hamilton-Paterson
Seven-Tenths: The Sea and Its Thresholds • 978-1-933372-69-3 • Territories:
USA • Nature/Essays

Daniele Mastrogiacomo
Days of Fear • 978-1-933372-97-6 • Ebook • Territories: World • Current
affairs/Memoir/Afghanistan/Journalism

Valery Panyushkin
Twelve Who Don't Agree • 978-1-60945-010-6 • Ebook • Territories:
World • Current affairs/Memoir/Russia/Journalism

Christa Wolf
One Day a Year: 1960-2000 • 978-1-933372-22-8 • Territories: World •
Memoir/History/20th Century

Children's Illustrated Fiction

Altan
Here Comes Timpa • 978-1-933372-28-0 • Territories: World (excl. Italy)
Timpa Goes to the Sea • 978-1-933372-32-7 • Territories: World (excl. Italy)
Fairy Tale Timpa • 978-1-933372-38-9 • Territories: World (excl. Italy)

Wolf Erlbruch
The Big Question • 978-1-933372-03-7 • Territories: US & Can
The Miracle of the Bears • 978-1-933372-21-1 • Territories: US & Can
(with **Gioconda Belli**) *The Butterfly Workshop* • 978-1-933372-12-9 •
Territories: US & Can